REBEL

TIMBER-GHOST, MONTANA CHAPTER

DEVIL'S HANDMAIDENS MC
BOOK 8

D.M. EARL

© Copyright 2025 D.M. Earl
All rights reserved.
Cover by Drue Hoffman, Buoni Amici Press
Editing by Karen Hrdlicka
Proofread by Joanne Thompson

All rights reserved. No part of this book may be reproduced in any form or by any electronic or mechanical means, including information storage and retrieval systems—except in the case of brief quotations embodied in critical articles or reviews—without permission in writing from the author.

This book is a work of fiction. The names, characters, and places portrayed in this book are entirely products of the author's imagination or used fictitiously. Any resemblance to actual events, locales, or persons, living or dead, is entirely coincidental and not intended by the author.

The unauthorized reproduction or distribution of this copyrighted work is illegal. Criminal copyright infringement, including infringement without monetary gain, is investigated by the FBI and is punishable by up to five years in federal prison and a fine of $250,000.

If you find any eBooks being sold or shared illegally, please contact the author at dm@dmearl.com.

ACKNOWLEDGMENTS

Karen Hrdlicka and **Joanne Thompson** my editing and proofreading team. I'm totally blessed to be working with these two ladies. Between them Karen and Joanne polish my stories so they shine. With their eyes on my stories I feel y'all are getting the best book possible due to their experience and knowledge of how I write.

Debra Presley and **Drue Hoffman** @ **Buoni Amici Press**. These two women are the BOMB. My two publicists work endlessly to handle the social media aspect, formatting, publishing and so much more which then allows me to concentrate on my writing. With them as part of the team I know everything is getting done and correctly and timely.

Enticing Journey Promotions. Ena helps me with every new release and are very professional and always on top of everything.

Bloggers. To every single one of you. What you do for each and every one of my releases and stories is something that I can never repay. Please know how much I appreciate each share, mention, post, and video.

My **DM's Babes** (ARC Team) and **DM's Horde** (Reader's group). These women in these two groups have become part of my chosen family. I'm thrilled to spend time and engage with each and every one of them.

READERS without each of Y'all I'd not be able to live out my life's dream of writing books that make people tingle and just feel deep in their souls. Your support fills my heart and feeds my soul.

Chuck. Without you and your support not sure I'd have written as much as I have. Thank you for always having my back and supporting me. Means the world babe. Luv ya.

ONE
'REBEL'

MYA

Damn, these women are driving me bat-ass crazy. Yeah, I'm part owner of the Handmaidens Fitness & Holistic Center. My club sister and partner, Raven, reached out to me for help to see if I wanted to maybe get involved in the gym. Or should I say since Raven's kidnapping and being shot, she's reached out. We've been going over the logistics of her bringing me on as a partner, but she already has a silent partner in the center, our prez, Tink. She was all for Raven starting this club. Our prez likes, as she puts it, "the Handmaidens to have their hands in everything in Timber-Ghost." So now I'm going to be a business owner along with Raven and, I guess, Tink too. Good thing is I don't have to provide a huge amount of cash to buy in. Our prez handles all the financials in every business the club is involved with. Helps our prospects, sisters, and the survivors who end up at her ranch find work while she makes sure to support our town with businesses and jobs also.

Last year, when Taz came to Raven after talking to me, her bestie, after all the shit that went down with Raven, they talked it out and added the holistic section to the center. There isn't much I wouldn't do for Taz. Fuck, when all her drama hit, I lost my fucking mind. She's not my sister by blood, but she means more than both of those bitches I call my sisters, though in reality they are my stepsisters. Then she shocked the ever-lovin' fuck out of me when she decided to hook her star to Enforcer. That decision took me by surprise, though it works for them and that's all that truly matters. That Taz and little Teddy are happy.

Recently, Taz and Enforcer's family has been going through a rough time. I'm trying to be as supportive as they'll let me. After a battle with cancer, they lost their pit bull, Pituynia, or as we all called her Tuna. Little Teddy is devastated, but I'm more worried about Taz. She's pregnant, ready to drop any day, and she doesn't need the added stress. Since Tuna passed, she's not been in here and is hanging out by herself in their new home. Enforcer texted me yesterday to tell me that his Que, which is his nickname for my sister Taz, kicked him out of their house. He's also beside himself. Right now, I have to deal with these self-centered members, who think I owe them every damn minute of my time. The one giving me the hardest time is a young woman named Cleo. She had a baby almost a year ago, and she's pissed her two days a week gossip session hasn't given her the body she wants. I don't fucking know, but the actress photo she showed me when she joined is never gonna happen. I honestly told her that. I just had a fifteen-minute conversation with her, trying once again to explain that two thirty-minute sessions of treadmill exercise is not going to remove extra weight if she's not controlling her food intake. I didn't mention out of those thirty minutes, she's probably only exercising maybe half the time because the speed on the treadmill is slower than a turtle, and she doesn't even break a sweat. She got really pissed at me, telling me she lives on salads, fruit, and protein. Personally, I know she's lying, because Peanut, who works at our bar and grill in town, told me she's there a few times a week either stuffing her face or guzzling wine like there's no tomorrow. Not my business, but one thing I can't stand is someone who lies. So, in a roundabout way, I brought it up and she immediately told me she was quitting, and I'm just a queer-ass bitch who's probably on steroids and can't catch a man. Oh, her parting sneer was she planned to leave a one-star review on not only our website but also on Google. Okay, well, good morning to me.

Hearing the door's bells chiming, I walk to the front of the building to see Taz waddling in. She's got a bag in one hand and her oversized purse in the other, while her pregnant tummy is sticking out way in front of her. With her rainbow hair and all her crystals, she's such a sight to see. She is so truly unique that you have to love her and her free spirit.

'What the hell are you doing here, Taz? Thought the doc said you were to take it easy, feet up? Please tell me you didn't drive yourself."

"Well, hello to you too, Rebel. Nice way to greet your best friend and godchild, who's not here yet. Crap, thought I'd catch a break here, at least. Want to use the meditation room to manifest my baby being born, maybe then the little one will come finally. Not sure how much more of this I can take."

Smiling as I walk toward her and grabbing the bag, her words alarm me. Taz is always the positive sister in the Devil's Handmaidens club. Damn, this bag is pretty heavy, and before I look in it, I know it's filled with her crystals and other shit. I don't understand any of the crystal stuff or the meanings, but I love her so much, I try to respect her ways. I noticed her face is flushed so when she tries to grab her belly in a sneaky way and I catch her body language, my gut tightens as my heart rate increases with sudden concern and not a little bit of anger.

"Fuck, Taz! Sister, are you in labor? Where the hell is Enforcer?"

Her head flings up and, by the look in those big, beautiful eyes, I don't need a verbal answer from her. Reaching for my phone, I go to text Enforcer when suddenly my phone goes flying from her hitting it out of my hand.

"What in the ever-lovin' fuck, Taz? We need to let people know so you can go to the hospital."

"No, Rebel, you are going to help me set up the meditation room so I can have my baby here in serenity and peace. I don't want the sterile environment of a hospital welcoming my baby. It starts the baby's entrance into the world with bad vibes, and you know that will stress me out, which in turn will affect the birthing process. Our baby needs to come into the world naturally, without strangers all around ogling its journey into the Universe."

Is she goddamn nuts? For Pete's sake, she's been ranting about having the baby in a bathtub for Christ's sake. Enforcer is totally against it. Thought he was gonna stroke out when she mentioned it again last week. Oh shit, what the fuck? Did she come here to try and drag that steel tub we use for cryotherapy from the back to have her baby in? And then what... after she kills herself dragging it into her meditation room, then is she gonna try to fill it between her contractions? And if she doesn't drop dead of a heart attack, then what? I guess, she'll soak for a bit, and I don't know, push out her goddamn baby with no pain meds by herself. HERE. In my gym, while it's open and folks are working out or taking classes. Holy shit, no way in God's name is that happening here. I'm no doula, which is what Taz looked for but couldn't find in Bumfuck, Montana. I can't handle this, no way. What if something goes wrong? Oh God, that would kill me if something happened to Taz or our lil' peanut. Yeah, ours.

"Taz, no way in hell am I letting you do this. It's not safe or even sterile here. That baby needs to be given the best chance when it's born. Think, sister, we can take some of your crystal shit to the hospital."

Before she can reply, she leans forward then doubles over, letting out a loud groan of pain. I mean, it sounds like she's in intense pain. Shit, she's not just going into labor; she's having full-blown contractions. Since I've been her second coach in the Lamaze classes, I know we need to get her to try and relax so she can breathe through each contraction. We have to time how far apart they are too. First, I need to know how she got here.

"How the hell did you get here, Taz? If you tell me you drove yourself, when you're done giving birth to my godchild I'm gonna kick your ass before I kill you. Son of a bitch, what are you thinking?"

She starts to giggle then, holy shit, lets out a loud as fuck fart and doubles over again. The stench hits me instantly and, to say the least, is slowly killing me every time I breathe in. I'm really trying to be a good best friend and not say anything as my eyes water, but I can't hold it in—my Christ—what did she eat last?

"Damn, Travis is right, those pregnancy farts

really stink. Shit, Rebel, it hurts so frigging bad. Damn, how did I do this with Teddy? I can't remember everything but I don't think it was this bad, though I had drugs back then."

I know we're in trouble because she doesn't swear all that often. I grab her arm and walk her to the room in question. Off to the one side is a smaller room for massage. I turn the light on, pull the weighted blanket off the table, grab a sheet, flip it open and on the bed, then lower it as far as it will go. I grab her purse, throwing it on the floor next to her bag of crystals. She waddles to me, trying to bend for that bag.

"What do you want, Taz? I'll get it, need you to get on that bed immediately, lie down and breathe."

"No, I want a water birth, you know that. It's better and more relaxing for me and the baby. Travis is against it, but that's what I want. Oh crap, forgot to tell you I didn't drive here, I called an Uber."

I knew bringing that modern-ass shit to our town was gonna cause trouble, though it helps folks make a living, sort of, I guess, and helps our seniors get around since nothing is within walking distance. I feel horrible because whoever picked up Taz doesn't have a clue how much trouble they are going to be in. Enforcer is gonna lose his fucking mind. And whoever was supposed to be on Taz duty will be getting an ass kicking from me. Told Tink that shit wouldn't work. We should have put both pregnant sisters together in one of the safe rooms at the ranch.

Don't care how crazy that sounds, at least we'd have eyes on them twenty-four seven.

Looking up, I see my bestie watching me with sweat on her forehead. She's pulling her rainbow hair up with a scrunchy. Damn, why can't I tell her no? It hits me why... she's my sister of my heart. That makes me literally snarl at her.

"Swear to Christ, Taz, you're lucky I love your rainbow ass. I'll go grab that big metal pool thing we use out in the back room. Gonna take me a minute or ten, so just breathe and try to relax. Oh yeah, text your ol' man and tell him what's going on right now."

With that I walk out, leaving the door open. When out of sight, I start to jog while pulling my phone out. I text Tink, Shadow, and Glory with a SOS then the words "Taz is in heavy labor at our gym. Need fucking HELP."

Not paying attention, I plow into something hard and extremely huge. I drop my phone and when I go to reach down for it, my head hits something that feels like either a large boulder or maybe a bowling ball. It literally knocks me to my knees as I hear a deep, gravelly, husky male voice saying, "What in the motherfucking shit? Damn, woman, watch where you're going. Oh shit, are you okay? Hey, can you hear me?"

Trying to open my eyes, I feel like I was hit by a frigging freight train. Slowly, I pry my eyelids up and see the most beautiful eyes I've ever seen set in a scowl that makes Enforcer's and Shadow's look like a grin. Dark-brown hair with just a slight scattering of gray at the sides. Those eyes are like a sapphire gem with a dark blue around the pupils. He's leaning over me, literally shaking me by the shoulders.

"Hey, you trying to finish the job, you asshole? You ever hear of Shaken Adult Syndrome? Let go of me before I seriously hurt you. I said, get your damn hands off me, mister."

He leans his ass onto his calves, never taking his eyes off me, though with my words a sexy as hell grin appears on his face as his eyes sparkle even more. *Oh, one of those types* I think to myself as I rub my head. Just what I need, a confident, built, hot motherfucker full of himself in my gym. I don't recognize him, but kind of remember one of the part-timers telling me we had a hottie join the club. This must be him. Great way to meet, though he's excellent on the eyes, that's for sure. Need to let the single sisters at the club know to come take a peek. On second thought, I'll keep him my little secret for now.

"Just checking to make sure you're okay. Took a pretty hard hit when we knocked heads."

"No, you mean when not only did you plow into me, but instead of stepping back, you rammed me with that enormous ninepin you call a noggin."

His face tightens as his eyes narrow at me. *Whatever*, I think to myself as it hits me; I'm on a mission. That's when I remember my sister, Taz, and where I was headed when I hear tiny footsteps rushing our way. Before I can turn my head, I hear the Mickey Mouse voices of young children.

"Daddy, hurry, a lady is in pain. You got to get your bag out of the car and come with us."

"Yeah, Dad, she's in labor, I think. Looks like she peed herself, I told these two to find you so I could stay with her, but they were fascinated with her hair, which looks like a rainbow."

Before any of them can move, I'm running back to the meditation room to find Taz on the floor, curled up on herself. Oh, fucking shit.

"Taz, hey, I'm here. Taz, look at me. RAQUEL, look at me now. Please, sister."

"As usual, you can never handle a delicate situation. Rebel, my water broke, and my contractions are like three to four minutes apart. I think the baby is coming now."

Hearing noise behind me, I see first the three kids: one older, one in the middle, and then the youngest one, all boys. Then Mr. Sexy Macho gently moves them to the side and walks in, kneeling next to Taz.

"Oh no, get the hell outta here, mister. We don't need you here. You want to be useful call nine-one-one for an ambulance. Otherwise, get gone now, mister."

His head lifts and, believe it or not, he winks at me. Then I hear the older boy start talking as he moves closer to us after he motions for the little ones to stay by the door.

"Lady, you should be glad my dad's here. He's a doctor, no, he's an obstetrician, which is a doctor for women and babies. Let him help your friend, he knows what he's doing. Dad, I'll go grab your bag from the car after I take these two out front, maybe put them in the kids' room and let them play. I'll call nine-one-one too."

Just as he walks out, Taz lets out a wail like nothing I've ever heard before. I look down to see she's biting her lip, which is starting to bleed pretty bad. Fuck. Then Mr. Macho stands and leans down and picks—yeah, gently picks Taz up—and is getting ready to place her on the massage table as we both hear a herd of cattle running down the hall. First in is Enforcer, and when he sees his wife not only in pain but also in the arms of a stranger, his face instantly goes blank, which is not a good thing for anyone especially Mr. Sexy Mister. I'm sure he's thinking about when Raven had her shit that started right here in this gym.

"Hey, brother, he's a doctor or something. She's close, Enforcer, so please don't be a total dick. Go to her, she needs you."

I watch as the dude gently lays Taz down and Enforcer goes to the other side, grabbing her hand and using his other hand to push her sweaty hair back. Half my club sisters are trying to squeeze into this average-size room, so I start shouting orders.

"Need someone to get some water. Another, some sheets and towels from the storage room. Shadow, you can stand the sight of blood, go help him. I doubt Enforcer is going to be any help. Peanut and Kitty, go check on this man's kids, think they're in the front room. Give them some juice boxes and snacks."

The older kid dropped the bag off and went back to his brothers right before the crowd burst in. So when the doctor-guy turns around to look at us, I stop and listen to him.

"No juice for my older boy, Konstantin. He's diabetic, type 1, so nothing with sugar if possible. Maybe some water or even a sports water with electrolytes. I'd appreciate it. No candy either, no matter what he says."

The smile that appears on his face has every one of my sisters, and if I admit it, even me, taking a breath then letting out a sigh. His eyes twinkle like he knows the effect he has on women, but those eyes are locked on me.

Again, Taz begins wailing and, shit, I don't know his name, so I ask.

"Hey, Doc, what's your name?"

Turning, he looks at me and grins.

"If you promise not to laugh, badass, I'll tell you."

As I nod, he's checking Taz's pulse and asking Enforcer some questions quietly.

"My name is Atlas Giannopoulos. And you are?"

"Motherfucker, we ain't on some goddamn dating game show or one of those computer fuckin' apps. Take care of my wife if you want to continue breathing. Rebel, where the hell is that ambulance?"

Taz reaches up and gently caresses Enforcer's face.

"Travis, honey, it'll be all right. Can you grab my bag and place my crystals around the room? Give my sage to one of my sisters so she can smudge this room. Hurry, this little one is going to make their appearance soon."

"I'm not leaving your side, Que. Tink, Glory, you heard her, grab that bag and place her rocks around the room. Heartbreaker, can you get the dried weeds and blow smoke around the room, please?"

Taz giggles at his attempt to do what she wants. I hear Atlas tell Enforcer they need to get her undressed and Enforcer loses his mind. The doc never flinches, just calmly explains that for him to help deliver the baby, she can't be wearing yoga pants and drawers. Taz is giggling so hard she passes wind again. The room immediately empties pretty quickly. Well, except for Doc Atlas, Enforcer, Shadow, Tink, Glory, and me. Taz's face is as red as an apple, but Atlas just keeps explaining the ABCs of labor and delivery to Enforcer. Finally, he agrees and very carefully the two men slowly start to remove Taz's clothes. I just saw her the other day when I helped her take a shower but, man, her belly seems even bigger than that day, though now it's really dropped down low. It's huge when they get her to shift to remove her yoga pants, undies, and socks. Once she's naked from the waist down, Atlas puts her feet flat on the table and he flips the blanket on top of her tummy for privacy and so he can see underneath to examine her.

"Well, Miss Taz, you're right, this little one is on their way. Don't push until I tell you to. Can someone get me a clean sheet, preferably white? Also, that tray in the corner, push it next to the bed. Enforcer, before we get too involved, pull that T-shirt off of her. Bra too. Once the baby comes, we will need to put the child on her belly and chest. On second thought, take your shirt off too. No, don't argue, man, just do it. You'll thank me later."

Watching Atlas, you can tell the man knows exactly what he's doing. The confidence he has in himself is pretty damn sexy. So is every movement as he whispers words to Taz, trying to keep her calm and in the moment. The room now has crystals all over on the counters, floor, and even on the table she's lying on. Enforcer will do whatever she wants.

"Doctor, do we have time before the baby arrives for my sisters to set up the water bath so I can deliver my little one in there? I've researched it, and they say it's a better experience for the baby."

Before Atlas can even respond, Enforcer loses it.

"Que, goddamn it, woman, told you that shit ain't gonna happen. Not having my kid drown before it takes its first breath. Let that shit go, please. I let you have the rocks and that smelly shit blown all over, let's be happy with that, woman."

I know it's coming, but damn, when it does, we all watch with our mouths open wide. With tears running down her face, Taz looks at her ol' man and lets loose. Probably all of her stress and worrying about this pregnancy. I'm totally shocked, as are all of our club sisters 'cause Taz is the calm one of the bunch.

"Travis, get the hell out of here. I don't want your negative energy around me or my baby. Yeah, you donated the sperm, but that's it. I've been growing and nurturing this child for nine months, so I should be able to decide how it makes its journey out into this fucked-up world we live in. My job as this baby's mother is to protect it, even from you if I have too. I said get out, until you can keep your bad energy down. Right now, I don't want to see or have you in here. Please go."

Enforcer's mouth is open, eyes huge. Taz is now sobbing, trying to hide her face. He leans down, grabbing her hands and again shocks the shit outta all of us in the room.

"Que, shit, I'm so sorry. Please, Raquel, don't cry. You don't want our baby being born with you having what do you call that shit… yeah, sad energy. I'll personally go get that tub. Doc, what type of water should be in it?"

"Enforcer, usually lukewarm, not too cold or hot. If that's the plan, I suggest you move your ass. This baby isn't going to wait too long. Taz is dilated to just about eight centimeters, so I'd get moving."

At this moment more boots are hitting the floor as the rest of the Intruders make their presence known. Tank is the first in, followed by Yoggie with a huge black bag. Yeah, always a medic.

In no time at all, between the Intruders and Devil's Handmaidens, the tub is cleaned and almost filled by the assembly line Duchess started. The room is now almost empty. Atlas said he wanted it to be calm for Taz, so it's just Enforcer, Tink, Shadow, and me. Glory stepped out when she got a call from Momma Diane.

Shadow and I help Taz off the bed after we lowered it as far down as we could. Next, between all of us, we get her into the tub. She smiles when she's sitting in there looking at Enforcer.

"Come on, Travis, you know what I want."

He looks around at us with a scowl.

"If any of you say a word, I'll kill you with my own two hands, swear to Christ.

Then he takes his kutte off, placing it on one of the robe hooks, and then empties his pockets. Boots and socks are next. With his T-shirt already off, by the time his jeans hit the table Taz is panting through another contraction. Atlas is reaching in, trying to gauge how far along she is.

"Is there someone here who has some medical

background? How about that man who brought in the bag? I could use a hand, no, actually two."

Tink walks to the door and yells for Yoggie. When he walks to the door, she tells him he's needed.

Time seems to go by quickly, as each contraction gets closer and closer. Enforcer is now behind Taz in the tub, holding her up. Atlas is scrunched down at the other end of the tub, doing what baby doctors do, I guess. He took his socks and gym shoes off. He was already in workout shorts, showing off his muscular calves. No, I didn't just think that. Yoggie is on the outside of the pool, right across from the doctor.

"Rebel, come here, I need you close."

Shit, just what I don't need, never done anything like this before. When I walk toward the tub, Enforcer smirks, so I flip him off.

"Keep it up, Dad, and you'll be sorry. Shadow, snap a picture of the Intruder's Enforcer in his boxers."

Just as Shadow snaps the pic, Taz screams and squeezes my hand so tight I think she might break it.

"That's it, Taz, doing great. Breathe, in and out. Come on, follow me. Take a deep breath, hold it for five, four, three, two, and one, release. Again, take your time and hold. Okay, we are there, so on the next contraction I need you to bear down and push as hard as you can."

We all wait for maybe thirty seconds when she lifts up a bit and bears down, moaning the whole time, sweat running down her cheeks. Travis is holding her up and I'm letting her break one hand as the other is pushing her hair out of her face. When she leans back, I see Atlas and Yoggie looking at each other.

"What? Is there a problem? Come on, tell us so we can fix it, and let this little one celebrate their birthday."

"I think the cord is around the baby's neck, so just want Yoggie to be ready when the baby arrives. That's it, Auntie Rebel, so calm down. Shit, I mean, here we go. This time when she starts to push, Enforcer, lean down, push her forward so she bends more, which will help with pressure so the baby comes out. Everyone, get ready, it's go time."

In my entire life I've never experienced anything like this. Taz breathing hard, face red, body tight, muscles all popping. Enforcer sweating as he helps Taz push their child out. Shadow is on the other side of Atlas, helping Yoggie out. Tink is the only one standing back and I know why. This has to hurt because she and Noodles have been trying to have their own baby. *And damn it, after all she's been through, she deserves it*, I think right before hell breaks loose.

I hear Atlas yelling so I look down and can't believe it. The baby is half in and half out. Yoggie is pulling the cord off its neck, and Shadow is holding one shoulder. Meanwhile, Atlas rotates the baby one way, then the other, until the other shoulder literally pops out. In less than a second, Atlas has the baby out, and instead of a crack on its tiny wrinkly ass, he's rubbing up and down its back. Then he looks to the parents and smiles.

"Congratulations. It's a baby girl. Dad, want to cut the cord?"

Enforcer looks at Atlas then me and shakes his head.

"Let Rebel do it. I'm good where I'm at."

Atlas gives me what looks to be some sort of scissors and shows me where to cut between some clamps. When I do, I feel wet rolling down my face. Shit. When I look up, Shadow and Tink are wiping their faces.

"What's her name, Mom and Dad?"

Taz and Enforcer both look to Atlas for a second then she leans back, whispering in his ear. They look at each other and kiss first, then look back to Atlas.

"Doc, her name is Michelle, but we're going to call her Mickie."

My mouth falls open as my eyes fill even more. No way, they're naming their baby girl after me.

"Rebel, didn't think taking your club name was right, so Travis and I talked and this is what we came up with. Hope you don't mind?"

I shake my head as I have no words. When Atlas grabs Mickie from Taz's tummy and gets done cleaning the baby best he can and fumbles with whatever he does, he then shows Enforcer why he wanted him to take his shirt off. This is after Taz has gotten out of the water and so did her ol' man. Atlas gives Mickie to her daddy, who then places her on his bare chest. The look on his face is beyond priceless and when I look, Shadow is snapping pics. She looks my way and grins. Yeah, this is truly a once in a lifetime moment that we are so totally blessed to be a part of.

Finally, we hear the sirens and not too long after paramedics come running down the hall apologizing, saying they were stuck in traffic due to an accident shutting down the highway. Everyone in the hallway is waiting on news. No one says a word until Enforcer in his boxers leans out into the hallway and screams loudly for all to hear.

"It's a fuckin' baby girl. Our princess, Mickie, has arrived."

Seems like the paramedics know Atlas, well, at least the female one does. Once Taz and Mickie are all bundled up on the gurney, they wheel her out as everyone cheers. I look at the bloody water and the shit on the outside on the floor. Damn, I feel dizzy for some reason. What the fuck?

"Sit down, Rebel. Adrenaline can drop pretty fast. Hey, can someone grab me a bottle of water?"

I hear the little feet running down the hall. Atlas moves quickly to the doorway.

"Hey, guys, give me a few minutes then we can

go. I'll take you for ice cream if you wait and be good. We got a deal?"

They nod and the little ones run back to the kids' room while the older one looks at his dad.

"All good, Dad?"

"Yeah, Son, she had a baby girl."

The kid smiles then turns and leaves. Atlas turns back to me with a bottle of water in his hands.

"Drink all of this. Now to even up. I did you a favor helping your friend out, so when do you want to go to dinner?"

I look at him like he has two heads. What the fuck is he talking about? So I ask. He smiles that sexy as shit smirk my way. Bet he's gotten a lot of women to spread their legs just with that. Sorry to disappoint, but it takes a whole hell of a lot more than a smile for me to open my legs.

"Don't remember our deal? I help and you go to dinner with me. Can't back out now. I'll give you a day or two, but we are going to dinner, Rebel, or should I call you, Michelle?"

I feel nauseated when he says that name. No one, and I mean not a single soul, calls me that anymore. If anything, I go by Mya. I've even changed it legally.

"Atlas, don't ever call me that name again. And as grateful as I am for what you did for Taz, ain't no way in hell I'm going to dinner with someone who's head won't fit through any of the restaurants' doors in town. It's just too damn big and cocky."

He throws his head back and laughs. Then his eyes get serious when he leans close.

"We'll see, Rebel. Something you should know about me is, sweetheart, I always get what I want. See ya around, Feisty Rebel."

I watch him leave as a weird feeling takes shape in my stomach. I've come too far to fall for a good-looking, sexy guy who's full of himself. That ain't ever happening. Though I did feel my nipples harden and my girlie garden start to tingle. Fuck it, not happening, no matter how gorgeous his eyes are. He's a dad of three boys and, shit, he could be married or have a partner. Besides, I'm good by myself. I've got my business, club, and sisters, which is all I need right now, or I try to convince myself as I get busy with cleaning up everything so I can go see my goddaughter. *Mickie is probably the closest thing I'll ever come to having my own child* is my thought as I pick up all the soiled towels and sheets.

TWO
'REBEL'

MYA

I'm in total awe of my bestie, Taz. Just two weeks ago she gave birth to my goddaughter, Mickie. Right now, as I hold the most beautiful baby against my chest, Taz is trying to console her son, Teddy, who has had his first fight with his girlfriend—nope his fiancée—Olivia, who is the adopted daughter of our club sister, Glory. The kids have been inseparable since Olivia arrived, but it seems there's a boy in their class who has been showing interest. Today we come to find out the boy causing all the trouble has a similar last name we all know, Giannopoulos. Yeah, the kid's father is the one who saved the day when Taz went into labor at Handmaidens Fitness & Holistic Center. Personally, I don't need anything that will put me in the same room as Atlas Giannopoulos. The man is constantly on my mind and, worse, in my dreams too. Son of a bitch, wish I never met him. Between flowers, candy, and even a new motorcycle cover, Atlas doesn't seem to comprehend what the word "NO" means. And now his kid is fucking around with little Teddy and Olivia. Well, not on my watch, that's for damn sure.

I stand up with Mickie in my arms and move to where Taz and Teddy are sitting. I try to lean down, hanging on for dear life to the baby. Well, until Taz stands and reaches for her daughter. I grab Teddy and hold on to him tightly. It's taken years for him to be comfortable with all of us in the club. Teddy is autistic and has adjusted to the Devil's Handmaidens Motorcycle Club sisters or, as he calls all of us, his aunties. When he lifts his head and tears are all over his face, for once I want to kick a kid's ass. Taking in a deep breath, I think before I speak.

"Teddy, I need you to listen to me for a second. Come on, here, dry your eyes. Since you two met, Olivia has been at your side. For Christ's sake, I mean, dang, you two are planning your wedding, right, so why are you so concerned my man? You got this; they could just be friends."

"Auntie Rebel, I thought that too. Today that kid came up to me and said he was interested in Olivia and if I cared for her, I'd let her go. If she wanted to be with me she'd come back, otherwise it wasn't meant to be."

"Teddy, have you spoken to your girl or are you taking the word of a boy who is after her? Think for a second, he was trying to take away your power and, buddy, looks like you might have handed it to him. Do me a favor. Call Olivia and talk to her. Don't panic until there is something to worry about. Now go, I'll wait with your momma. We got your back, Teddy. And if he truly wants your girl, we'll get all the Devil's Handmaidens to pay him a visit. You know, scare the sh...crap out of him."

He gives me a small sad smile then I watch him run to Taz, asking to use her phone. With Mickie on her boob eating, Taz manages to grab her cell and find the number, pushing it before handing it to Teddy. He immediately walks away and heads toward the office, I guess for some privacy. Feeling eyes on me, I turn to see Taz staring at me, surprise and wonder across her face.

"What are you staring at?"

"You. Where is my best friend and sister, Rebel? Bring her back, even though she's a pain in my ass most times, I understand her you, woman, not so much."

She's laughing by the end of her rant and so am I. Sometimes I can shock even myself. I've been a part of Taz and Teddy's life since they came to Timber-Ghost, Montana. And when Taz and Enforcer got together, I was their biggest supporter. Well, as long as he didn't hurt her, which I told him up close and personal. Enforcer and I have found our way to share Taz. And I'll never tell him this, but I'm so proud of how he accepted me into her, no, their lives with hardly any lip.

"When did you get so smart about relationships, Rebel? You don't even date, so where is this knowledge coming from? Are you holding out on me? Because what you told Teddy is so right it's scary. You directed him to face his problem head-on, when you've never done that since I met you. Now, let's get to the good stuff. What are your thoughts about Dr. Atlas's son trying to poach Olivia from Teddy? Kind of too close for comfort, don't you think?"

Taking a second to think about it, I pray I'm wrong, but he's tried everything else.

"Do you think he'd use his own kid to try and engage with me? Taz, he's tried everything, including planting his and his boys' asses at the Wooden Spirits almost every single day. I'm going nuts with his constant presence and pressure on me. Why won't he let this fucked-up shit go already?"

"Auntie Rebel, swear jar."

Teddy's eyes are red-rimmed, which tells me he was crying again. I wait to give him a moment to collect himself. He plops down beside me, leaning into my side. I ruffle his hair and wait.

"Olivia said hi and thanks to you, Auntie Rebel. She said she's glad someone trusts her and didn't jump to conclusions. Olivia told me I have nothing to worry about. Auntie Glory had a conversation with her and explained that relationships are work and you must both be on the same page. Olivia told me Thanos was only talking to her to ask about you, Auntie Rebel. Seems like he found out from some of the other kids that you and Momma are close. What he said to me is because he wanted to, as he told Olivia, 'rock the boat' but didn't know how. He heard his dad telling someone how he can't reach you because he doesn't have your phone number and he's feeling sad. Thanos wanted to help his dad, but Olivia said he doesn't like her like that and came out and told her that, though seemed to be very careful about it. He eventually shared with her he's a loner or his dad calls him an introvert, who likes to stay home and play video games. He told her he doesn't have very good, as he said his dad calls it, communication skills. Olivia said she felt sorry for him because he's always getting picked on for being different, which I know that feeling. Then she told me we should invite Thanos when a bunch of us club kids get together. Seems like he's more of a loner. I told her sure, once I knew he wasn't trying to poach my girl. I feel better, so glad I did what you told me to, Auntie Rebel. Momma, can I go play my game now?"

Taz looks between her son and me while she has Mickie on her shoulder, trying to get the little princess to belch after eating. All of a sudden a huge burp is heard and both Teddy and I start to laugh loudly, while Taz whispers to Mickie what a good girl she is. Then she walks to the bassinet set up in the family room next to their enormous sectional. Little Mickie falls asleep immediately with her full tummy. Teddy is off to play his game, so Taz and I are alone and my sister doesn't waste a second.

"So explain to me why you haven't returned any of the sexy Dr. Atlas Giannopoulos's attempts? I know he's sent flowers, chocolates, and even a new motorcycle cover. What's the holdup? Even if you don't want a lifetime commitment, he might just be the one to scratch that itch you've been ignoring forever. I mean, even the BOB you bought with the rechargeable USB port can't keep up with your needs and drive."

She's smiling widely at me, which makes it extremely hard to punch her in the face. Well, that grin and the little girl next to the sectional making the cutest noises as she sleeps. How do I explain to my best friend that Atlas scares the ever-lovin' fuck out of me? He's gorgeous, educated, a family man of three boys, and single—if what Raven found out is right—which if she researched him, it's true. I trust whatever she finds when she does her searches. His wife and mother of his kids just up and disappeared about two in a half years ago. Eventually, she resurfaced with her boyfriend, who is a convict and drug dealer. Atlas has full custody as she wants nothing to do with the three brats. That was said in the last court date when she signed away her rights to the boys. When I read that I wanted to strangle her. I don't know Atlas or the boys, but all of them stepped up for Taz and that, in my book, is beyond good. Atlas divorced her and according to Raven hasn't been involved with anyone since. Well, except his occasional weekends away to Billings. His parents watch the boys as he lets his hair down and fucks as many women as he can in two or three days. Raven said he's very upfront and honest and there isn't a woman he's been with that has any hard feelings from what she could find out, however she does that shit. And that right there is what has me hiding like a teenage girl with her first crush. Taz is tapping her fingers on the side of her travel mug filled with water.

"Give me a minute, not sure how to explain this to you."

"What, that you're afraid to let him past the walls you've built? Rebel, that's obvious. Remember who you're talking to. I get it, but at some point, you have to take a chance, and I mean a doctor. Really? Who'd have thought that you would be fantasizing about a hot Greek doctor?"

We both giggle, then I get serious.

"Come on, Taz, he looks at women's 'girlie gardens' all day long."

I stop because she's choking on a mouthful of water, which she spits out all over their table. I jump up to grab some paper towels as Taz tries to stop coughing. Her face is pink and eyes are running while she tries to talk.

"Girlie garden. Jesus Christ, Rebel, how do you come up with this shit?"

"What? You never heard that before? Don't you have a personal name for your love shack?"

That sends Taz into a hysterical laugh, which I join in. Maybe I am strange, but I am who I am. Once she's gotten control back, my sister looks me in the eye and shocks the shit out of me.

"Give him a chance, Mya. What do you have to lose besides some time, which you have plenty of. I mean he's responsible, as he has a very important job which, apparently, he's good at. He has a home, which he is raising those three boys in. I know you're scared, but have I ever steered you wrong? You know I love you and would take a bullet if needed. Please, for me, just give it a go and if it doesn't work, or you don't like him, then I'll let it go, promise."

Listening to her, it hits me how much she actually cares about me. That's why she's pushing so hard; she doesn't want me to be alone. Ever since she hooked her star to Enforcer, she's been trying her matchmaking skills out on me. Not that there are many eligible, available men in Timber-Ghost and those who are, are either bums or men I know and aren't interested in. Both the Blue Sky Sanctuary and Panther's ranch have available men working there. No one interests me. Well, one does, but he's not interested and I think that's what drew my eye. Avalanche is a tall lick of deliciousness, but he's also more like a brother than a lover. Seeing Taz watching me, I know she knows where my mind went. She's shaking her head. Great, now she can read my mind.

"Fine, Raquel, I'll give him a chance. But when I tell you I've had enough, will you leave it alone?"

"Mya, we only use each other's given names when we are fighting. And, yeah, give Atlas a chance and if it don't work, I'll work on Avalanche for you, though you know he's got his eye on someone else."

Yeah, I know that little fact. Story of my life.

* * *

After playing with both Teddy and Mickie, I leave Taz's place, not sure where to go. I could go back to the ranch but don't feel like peopling, had my share. Instead, I head into town to hit up the Wooden Spirits Bar & Grill for some home cooking for dinner. Otherwise, it's go home and wing it. Which generally means either breakfast for dinner, which is cool, though my other choices like cereal or ice cream are lame as shit, and far from healthy, but I don't give a fuck. Kind of explains the curves I'm sporting, even with all the working out I do. When I turn the corner to the bar and grill, I almost keep going. It looks to be packed and all I can hope for is the bar side is not hopping. Or as I planned, I can sit in the kitchen at the small table, scarf down my food, then leave quietly. Or have Cook put together a take-out order and go home where it's quiet and then I can eat in peace.

Since I know tonight is one of Cook's highlight nights, I generally don't miss when she's in and cooking. Wildcat and Heartbreaker are also on the schedule, so maybe I can grab a bite to eat and catch up with one or both of them. I don't mind spending time with my sisters, don't consider that peopling. Working at the center, dealing with those kinds of folks, is what wears me down. The weather is shit so I'm in my cage, which is decent enough but not my bike. Being the club's S-a-A, it's kind of weird to be riding around in a cage but, shit, don't want to face-plant when going seventy plus miles an hour. I've seen the results of that on other bikers, who not only were driving like maniacs from hell but drunk off of their asses. The only reason they made it at all was from the amount of alcohol in their systems, which kept them loose so they didn't tense up when they hit the pavement. They were either close to passing out or already gone.

I pull around the back where there's always parking for the club sisters. After I find a spot and shut my SUV off, I grab my crossbody purse and get out. Damn, the wind has picked up and all I have on is a Devil's Handmaidens Henley and my kutte. At the back door I noticed its propped open, which is a definite fucking no-no. So as I swing it wide, Peanut appears out of nowhere, arms filled so high I can't see her head. She walks right into me, dropping her tower of garbage bags.

"God dang it, why can't anyone watch were they're going? Now I have to try to get them all stacked so I can carry them to the garbage can. Or make a bunch of trips, which I have no time for."

I know she's talking to herself, one of her unique habits, so I stand and wait. When she lifts her head and those silver-gray eyes of hers see it's me, I watch as her mouth forms the perfect 'O' right before terror crosses her face. Well, what in the ever-lovin' fuck, I'm not Shadow. I'm one of the good sisters, for crying out loud, or so I think. I try to smile but she actually steps back.

"Holy shit, Rebel, damn, I'm so sorry. I didn't see you there. I was ranting because it's busy as all hell in there and not only am I starving but got to pee too. My one new employee quit over the phone so our bussers are working hard as they can, but are barely keeping up. So here I am, trying to give them a hand, so I disrespected you, so sorry, sister. And I'm ranting too because I'm nervous as hell on top of it all. I'm just thankful I didn't pee myself, don't have any spare jeans."

I watch as she lowers her head and eyes from me. Not sure why since we are both members of the Devil's Handmaidens MC. She's been this way from the minute she was patched in. I get it, she feels inferior because, my God, a good wind would blow her tiny bony ass across town, but she does her duty as a sister and never complains, so this surprises and concerns me.

"Hey, Peanut, quit apologizing. We're equals in the club, both active members. So what can I do to help you with your load tonight?"

Her head snaps up, while her eyes seem to grow right before my eyes. I can almost see her brain going through the gears, so again I wait. Peanut is not only a planner but also a lot OCD, so I know not to rush her. Together we walk the garbage out then go back in, making sure the back door is locked before she leads me to the employee lounge and plops down into a chair. I go to the refrigerator and grab two vitamin waters, placing her favorite flavor, grape, in front of her. She looks at it then at me with a silent thanks and small grin.

"Rebel, we could use some help on the floor or maybe running the front counter, ringing up customers. I'll take care of the grunt stuff if you could maybe give a hand where it pertains to mingling with customers, if you're not too busy."

Reaching over, I grab her by her tiny shoulders, pulling her across the table so our eyes are even before I reply.

"Sister, is this bar and grill one of our club's businesses? Then I will definitely help out, no problem. Let me grab a quick bite and then you can tell me what ya need. Give me like ten minutes to scarf down some chow."

She nods then moves quickly toward the employee bathroom, then I'm sure she heads back to the dining room while I go into the kitchen. Cook sees me, grabs a plate, and starts to fill it up with her usual deliciousness. My stomach growls loudly and Heartbreaker laughs when she walks in. Taking the small table, I quickly inhale my food, then tell Cook thanks and that the food was awesome. Washing my hands, I grab a clean apron and put it on. Walking out the swinging door, I look around for Peanut.

Suddenly I hear someone screaming for a doctor, "Is there a doctor in the room?" Starting to jog around the corner, I see an older man choking on something he'd just eaten. Son of a bitch, not again. Last time this happened we got sued because some chick was too busy flirting with some dude and choked on her salad. Yeah, a frigging salad. I move quickly to the man but am roughly pushed out of the way by someone going in the same direction. When that someone, who I can now see is a guy, is reaching for the older man, I gasp. When those dark, sapphire-blue eyes look in my direction for a split second, I feel almost woozy. Atlas pulls the man to his knees, then gets behind him doing the Heimlich maneuver while everyone, including his three sons, watch. By the fourth abdominal thrust, a pretty good-sized piece of steak flies out of the man's mouth. Once his mouth is empty, he takes in a deep breath as everyone claps for Atlas, who makes sure the older man is able to stand on his own. The man's wife is thanking Atlas as the older man takes a seat to try and catch his breath. The couple offers to buy Atlas's dinner but he politely refuses, saying he's here with his three boys. The couple again asks to pay his tab, telling him they'll pick up his entire bill because he saved the gentleman's life, but Atlas softly refuses and quietly tells the man to try smaller pieces of meat. Once everyone is calmed down and okay, Atlas makes his way to his boys, who are giving him high fives and hugs. He manages to maneuver them toward me so when I go to move, I'm surrounded by four Giannopouloses—one man and three boys. I don't know Atlas's kids' names but *the older one is at that cocky teenage stage;* I think to myself as he smirks my way.

"Konstantin, don't start, you just got your electronics back yesterday. Be a gentleman like I've taught you. Knock that cocky grin off your face."

I watch as the boy looks at me then winks before he turns to his dad, face blank. Atlas moves past his sons and gets in my space.

"Well, if it's not, my feisty Rebel, finally making time to come out of hiding and luckily finding me here. Since we both have the same idea, why don't we share a meal, if you don't mind my three boys eating with us? I can guarantee they will be on their best behavior, as I'll bribe them if I have to."

The boys and I start to chuckle at the same time, while Atlas never takes his eyes off of me. Thank God Heartbreaker makes her way to me, her eyes shooting fire.

"Rebel, we need you in the bar side. A few twenty-something-year-old tourists are giving Kiwi a hard-ass time. Oh sorry, kids, my bad. They are pushing her buttons about stuff. Even though they think she's hot, their words not mine, want to know what she's going to do about them being dic—well, you know, jerks. She's refusing to serve them anymore, that's what started it."

Turning back to Atlas, I shrug my shoulders but ask for his phone. With his eyebrows up, he hands it to me and I enter my phone number then hit dial. When my phone starts to ring, I disconnect and hand it back.

"Atlas, sorry, gotta take care of this. If y'all are still here when I'm done, I'll join the Giannopoulos table for dessert, on the Wooden Spirits Bar and Grill, for what you did for that man. Now please, excuse me and enjoy your meals."

As I'm walking away, I hear his boys giving him tons of shit because, without asking, I gave him my "digits." Their laughter causes my heart to miss a beat because it sounds so normal. That's my last thought as I get into my mode as a Devil's Handmaidens sister and turn the corner, moving quickly toward the bar to back up my club sister.

THREE
'ATLAS'

Watching Rebel walk away, I can feel my blood turning to molten lava as it tries to move through my veins. Great, not only am I as horny as my own teenage boy, but my cock is about to burst through my trousers. Jesus Christ, what is it about this woman that has me acting inappropriately every time I see her? Feeling a shoulder hit my side, I look down to see the laughter in Konstantin's eyes, even before he opens that young sarcastic mouth of his.

"So what's up with the hot chick giving you her digits without you asking? Isn't that the same one who wiped the floor with ya when you helped deliver her friend's baby? Piece of advice, Dad, stay clear, she might not be all there. I mean, look at all you have to offer and she's been giving you the cold shoulder. Yeah, anyone can see she's smokin' hot, Dad, but she needs to learn there's a limit to playing hard to get. She has to give a good guy a chance and you're a good one, Dad."

It's pretty sad that I'm getting relationship advice from my teenage kid. Though he has some good points I should pay attention to and listen, but my mind isn't going to because my small head is who's leading this show. Looking around, I see both Stefanos and Athanasios together, waiting to see what I do next. Time to feed my boys. Walking toward them, they both envelop me into hugs before letting me go. All three kids are good boys, just way different personalities. Konstantin or, as I call him, Kon is a teenager with a chip on his shoulder, and there is nothing I can do about. He was diagnosed very young with type 1 diabetes, so he's growing up with so many limitations. Stefanos or Stephen, my preteen, is my quiet thinker, who at times seems to be on the spectrum, though I've never had him tested. Finally, Athanasios or Thanos is my baby, who knows how to play me to the fullest. I have my hands full but wouldn't change it for the world. Between the boys and my position at the hospital, along with my volunteer time at the clinic, I try to tell myself repeatedly that my life is really good and full. Though it's lonely at times, especially when a woman in my life would take it from good to phenomenal.

The hostess makes her way to us, telling me she

has a table ready. No one argues because there are folks who have been waiting longer but not going to complain. I just want to feed the crew and get home so we can do our nightly routine of gathering our dirty clothes and shoving them into the laundry room, then showers, and of course their nighttime snacks before they make their way to their bedrooms to watch television, play games for forty-five minutes —or here's a concept—read a damn book.

Once we are seated and have given our drink orders, the waitress starts to go over the specials of the day. This is when Kon starts to push my buttons. He asks her if he can substitute something for fries because he's diabetic. This has the younger woman start to fawn over him, which is exactly what he wanted her to do. I can tell Thanos and Stefanos are starving, so I push his games along.

"Kon, if you are so worried about your sugars get a plain salad with extra protein and a hot tea. Maybe add that vegetable soup too."

My oldest son glares at me, though he finally puts in his order. His two younger brothers follow and then the waitress looks at me.

"Give me the special, extra biscuits and gravy on the side. Oh, can I get a house salad with garlic dressing also?"

She nods then gathers our menus and moves to place our order at the kiosk off to the side. All three boys are getting soup and I'm getting a salad. I'm curious to see how fast our food is served. Never been to the grill part of this place, only the bar side with some coworkers when one of the doctors was leaving.

"Daddy, is that man going to be okay? You saved him, right?"

Looking at Thanos, I smile. He looks more like his mother than me, lighter-brown hair and the hazel eyes, but he has my heart.

"Yeah, Son, he should be fine. Just needs to slow down and pay attention when eating, just like I tell all of you. Time and place for everything."

Before I can get another word out, the woman with long deep-red hair approaches our table with a tray filled with soups and a nice-looking salad. She puts the tray on the holder another woman pops open for her. As she passes soups out to the boys, I can feel her eyes on me but she does nothing to catch my attention. Finally, when she has my salad in her hands, she glances up and whispers quietly to me.

"Hey, stud, Rebel doesn't like garlic so I brought out an Italian and Thousand Island. Trying to help out, if you know what I mean. Oh, wow, speak of the she-devil, here she comes. Enjoy."

She turns and walks away as Rebel slowly approaches our table. I'm shocked to see her knuckles are ripped up and slightly bleeding and, holy shit, she's got some blood on the corner of her lips like someone cracked her in the face. When she sees my face, she barely shakes her head but looks to the boys, and I get it. I'm not ignoring it, just pushing aside for now.

"Hey, guys, mind if I join you? I could use a coffee and maybe a piece of Cook's sugar-free apple pie. Hey, don't be making faces unless you try it."

The boys shift over so Rebel is right next to me. Suddenly, my throat tightens and I feel like I'm about to choke, so I take a deep breath and a sip of my tea. Our waitress stops by with a coffee mug and a carafe, I'm guessing of coffee, and a huge number of creamers in a bowl. Rebel reaches for a handful of cream and starts opening and pouring them into her mug. Kon is watching her, along with Thanos. Stefanos is starving so unless someone starts to choke again his head isn't coming up at all, he's enjoying his food too much.

"Why do you use so much cream? Maybe ask for a cup of cream with a drip of coffee."

Shocked, I look over to Stefanos, as he's shoving chicken nuggets in his mouth after dipping them in honey mustard sauce. Rebel looks at him as the wheels in her head are moving, so I lean back and watch the interaction between the two of them. Glancing at Kon, he's mimicking me. My little stud in training.

"First, I'm Rebel, nice to meet you all. Second, I'm

not a fan of the taste of coffee but love the bump of energy I get from it. Hope that answers your question. Now give it to me, what are all of you guys' names."

Each boy introduces themselves, well, Thanos does when I give him an elbow. He puts his triple cheeseburger down with the "what" look. I look at him then Rebel. He grins and then introduces himself. She's looking at us and then shocks the shit out of me.

"Well, that's a lot of Giannopoulos testosterone to be in the company of. So we have a doctor, teenager, preteen, and a cute kid. Good to know."

I can see the boys are taken aback but I don't know what to say. Leave it to Kon to jump right in.

"So we have a Rebel biker chick. Good to know."

My mouth drops as both younger boys' forks land on their plates loudly. There are eight eyes looking at Rebel. Those gorgeous warm caramel eyes of hers are looking intently at Kon. He's squirming under her glare and I kind of like that she's not afraid to hold her own ground. With these three boys, any woman would have to because I'm not around all the time. If I hook my star to a woman who is weaker and not sure of herself, that could be disastrous. I literally shake my head to shut my fucking thoughts off. Just when I think I should say something, Rebel beats me to it.

"Konstantin, right? Or do you prefer Kon? I like the full name, just sayin'. Well, let me explain something to you, stud. First, don't be a dick to any woman because it just ain't cool. Second, I wasn't being a smart-ass, that's just me being me, but I'll cut you some slack because obviously you don't know me. Third, if you don't have any experience with someone, don't jump to conclusions. Fourth and finally, I get you're finding yourself but remember, kid, we all are, no matter our age. Knock the chip off your shoulder and you might see life really isn't that bad."

Not only is my mouth open, but my hand is also gripping my seat for dear life. It's like this woman was in my head reading my thoughts to my son. Holy Mother of God, how did she do that? I glance from Rebel to Kon to see his face is white and no—please no—his eyes are filling up. Damn it. I go to stand up but Rebel puts her warm hand on my thigh and I'm a goner. She stands and walks to where Kon is sitting. She crouches down next to him and starts to whisper in his ear. His face goes from white to normal to slightly blushing. He wipes his eyes but never pulls away from the woman whispering in his ear. All three of the remaining Giannopoulos men are watching intently. When Rebel stands and pulls Kon to his feet, I'm impressed. All of my boys are big, like me, and my oldest has been trying to work out to build muscles and bulk. Rebel pulled him up like he was a kid. What amazes me more than anything is when she put her arms around him and hugs him close to her. Kon instantly put his hands around her and hangs on for dear life. In that moment, I realize what all my boys are missing out on without a woman around and in their lives. No matter how much I try to be their "everything," it just isn't working. Blinking to clear the wet from my eyes, I'm shocked to see Kon whispering in Rebel's ear. Her head is nodding and she's speaking to him softly. When she pulls back, I can see Kon is reluctant to let her go. Rebel must feel it because she stops and grabs his shoulders, squeezing tightly. Something she says brings a huge smile to his face and both sets of eyes look my way. I throw my arms up in the air.

"What now? I didn't say a word."

That brings chuckles from Rebel and Kon. Eventually, Stefanos and Thanos join in. The two break apart with Rebel ruffling Kon's hair, which brings a smile to his face. When he sits, his eyes never leave Rebel's form as she walks to her own chair. She sits and leans over, hitting my shoulder with hers. Looking down, holy fuck, those eyes seem to drag my soul out of my body, dusting it off and then throwing it back in. I feel lighter and, more importantly, happier. Who the fuck am I and what's going on? I don't do relationships because of the three kids sitting around this table. I won't because don't ever want them to get connected to someone and that person will then have the opportunity to hurt them. Even with my Hippocratic oath to save lives—along with all the other shit like respect, care, being professional, and being selfless—anyone hurts my boys and I'll kill them with my bare hands, not feeling an ounce of guilt at all.

"Hey, Doc, you still with us? Do we need to call a doctor?"

I jump back as two fingers snap in front of my face. Rebel is grinning and I can hear the boys cackling. I shake my head and grab her fingers, pulling them down onto my thigh. Her eyes pop and I can see the shock and fear on her face for a brief second before she relaxes and squeezes said thigh, which has my body reacting in a way not meant for being in public.

"Sorry about that, somehow, even with this table full of characters I drifted. What did I miss?"

Immediately everyone starts talking at the same time, but the tense moment is gone. I go to release Rebel's hand. She gives me a brief squeeze before she pulls her hand off of my thigh. Her touch has every nerve in my body at full alert. If I'm this "energized" by her simple touch, she'll probably kill me if we ever make it to the point of sharing a bed. Hearing her giggle, I look to see her watching me.

"Atlas, don't go jumping the gun. We haven't even gone on a first date. Patience, grasshopper."

My eyes get wide. Fuck, did I say that out loud? Looking at the boys, they are eating and talking to each other, so no, thank God I didn't. How the hell does she do that? If she can get in my head that gives her the advantage I usually want and need. With her continuing to giggle, I shoot her a grin, but deep down inside I know this moment is one you remember the rest of your life. So, I take a chance, with my fingers crossed, I lean down and place a gentle, innocent kiss on Rebel's lips. That's when my life changes immediately.

FOUR
'REBEL'
MYA

I'm so not prepared for Atlas's sneaky approach, so when his lips touch mine, I feel my body hold in all of my air. Feeling a bit loopy and forgetting where we are at, I shift toward him and my arms tentatively go around his neck. With that little encouragement, his hands grab my cheeks and move my head a bit to the left. When his tongue rolls over my lips, I open and, holy-moly, shit, what they say in those books the prospects read is totally true, who knew? Not only do I see fireworks, the feeling of safety I get in his arms almost knocks me off the chair and right on my ass.

We are so involved in each other, that is until I hear a throat clear and it somehow penetrates, as we are going at it like teenagers. Oh no, shit, we are in front of his boys. I quickly pull back and my eyes hit Konstantin's first. His expression is blank at first, but a slow cocky smile hits his handsome face. When he stares back at me, I feel horrible, until he winks at me and starts to chuckle. Stefanos and Thanos are also staring but with younger eyes. It's the throat behind Atlas and me that startles me. I look up to see Heartbreaker with a shit-eating grin on her face.

"Sorry to interrupt, but the customers were watching the show and staring. Dude, bet you're happy I didn't bring the garlic dressing. Anyway, just throwing it out there, you two might want to plan a dinner without the children so if the urge to do what you two were just doing, you can, without young eyes on you. Rebel, you know any one of the sisters would offer to babysit these three handsome men."

Atlas grins at Heartbreaker as I hear Konstantin readily agree to Heartbreaker "babysitting" them.

"Definitely, thanks so much for the tidbit with the garlic. And you are right so, Rebel, pull that phone out, let's get something on the calendar right now. And sorry, I know you two are in that girl club together. I'm Atlas, you are?"

Snarling at his comment, I hold my tongue as the two of them share names and shift out of their way. What the hell was I thinking? Yeah, so I told Taz I'd give him a chance, but shit, we almost were ready to start fucking on the dinner table in the Wooden Spirits. I'll never live this one down. My sisters in the club are going to have a heyday with this. Damn, I'm sure Raven is already making copies and sending the video of Atlas's tongue down my throat to everyone. I'll kill her if she did that, swear to Christ. Hearing my name, I look to see Heartbreaker smiling hugely. Damn, why didn't I ever notice how simply gorgeous she is? Yeah, I'm under Atlas's spell. Why would I be acting like I've never noticed her before?

"Yeah, what's up, sister?"

"Asking if anyone wants dessert? Though looked like you were enjoying yours already with this one here."

I glance at Atlas, who's already asking the boys. I'm shocked when each and every one tells Heartbreaker they want to try the sugar-free apple pie because I said it was so good. Atlas stares at his boys for a second then looks at me. Something in his eyes warms my heart. Before I can say anything, he also asks for the sugar-free apple pie. I nod, telling Heartbreaker to bring me one then she turns, going to put the order in. Thank God for Thanos, who starts to ask if when they get home if he could skip his shower. He wants to catch up on the series *Will Trent*. That catches my attention because I'm hooked on that show, but looking at Thanos, I mean, he's like what, nine-ish or so.

"Rebel, we all love that show. Yeah, he might be a tad young for it but not as bad as some he's watched."

Looking around the table again, I have all their eyes. I think for a minute and remember my promise to Taz.

"Yeah, I love *Will Trent* too. In fact, we record it at the conference building so if y'all ever want to come and watch, just let me know."

The boys are all smiling but it's the man next to me who gets me the most. He leans toward me, his thigh touching mine. When he speaks, I can feel his breath on my cheek, that's how close he is. If I turned to look at him, I bet our lips would be not even an inch or two apart.

"We accept your invitation, Rebel, if you would join us at our house for a night of watching movies with some of my famous popcorn."

The boys are snickering and Atlas's green eyes are sparkling. I know this is his way to get me to his home and, in fact, I'd like to see it. Want to know how a single dad would set his home up.

"Sure, Atlas, just let me know when."

The conversation starts to get loud and that's when Heartbreaker comes back too. As she's placing a piece of pie in front of Thanos, he just has to tell her our arrangement.

"Heartbreaker, we're going to be coming to the conference hall to watch *Will Trent.* You want to watch with us?"

Feeling my sister's eyes, I shift my head. She gives me raised eyebrows and big eyes. I shrug, not knowing what to say. Heartbreaker puts all the pieces of pie down then moves to Thanos's side.

"Honey, I'd love to. Maybe we do it on the

weekend and the entire club and their families can watch it too. You've got to promise me that you'll save me a seat, cutie."

Thanos blushes bright red. He looks to Konstantin, who gives him a small chin lift. Thanos looks up to Heartbreaker with his own cocky grin.

"It's a date, Heartbreaker. Tell me your favorite candy and I'll make sure Dad takes me to get it before we come out."

Hearing Heartbreaker laugh out loud brings a smile to my face. That sister has been through hell and back a few times. She walks back to me, leaning between Atlas and me.

"Sister, you got your hands full with this crowd. I can feel the hot guy testosterone all around this table. This is going to get interesting fast. Good luck and remember what I tell ya. Don't do anything I wouldn't. Though, Atlas, just so you know, there's nothing I won't try once."

Her laughter lingers as she turns and walks away. My eyes are trapped by the emerald gems of Atlas's as his eyes move all over my face. I'm shocked he doesn't look farther down, but gotta give him credit, he doesn't. He turns and grabs his fork, digging into the pie. I watch as all four males put pie in their mouths. I wait for it and when it comes, it shocks me.

"Holy fuck, this is beyond good. I can't remember when I ate anything so good. How does the cook make this, Rebel?"

Konstantin is staring at me. It hits me that this poor kid is diabetic. I know for a fact Cook doesn't use sugar because her momma has the same condition. I don't know what or how she does it, but it's the best pie I've ever had.

"Konstantin, I'm not sure but I'll ask Cook. Figure it out with your dad, and we'll schedule a day of lessons for you from Cook. Her momma has diabetes and she makes all kinds of food that tastes better than anything I've ever eaten. You good with that?"

He's nodding and grinning, so guess I did the right thing. When Atlas leans into me that tells me I'm right. By the time we finish our pieces of pie, I give a look to Heartbreaker to hand me the check as I'll take care of it. Especially since Atlas probably saved that man's life and the club another lawsuit. When I make the check mark action, she shakes her head then chuckles before she smiles and walks our way. So, when Atlas asks her for the check, she smiles at him then shifts her head my way. The look in his eyes immediately heats up my girlie garden. I can feel my nipples hard against my bra. Somehow, he knows because the grin he gives me actually has my entire body trembling. With a look. I'm so screwed it isn't funny.

"Rebel, when I have dinner with a woman, I pay the bill. That's my dominant side. So how much is it?"

I grin as my panties get wetter. Two can play that game.

"Well, Atlas, when someone saves a person's life in my restaurant, I pay the bill. So we can argue all night, but your boys need to get home. Let's agree that instead of fighting about a dinner check, we just make sure we have another one and you can pay that bill. Deal?"

I put my hand out, thinking he'd take it and shake. No, not him. Instead, he gently takes my hand and brings it to his mouth, placing a kiss on the top of it. When I feel the heat of his tongue, I flood my panties. Damn him. And he knows it because he lets go and tells the boys to get ready to go. Then he looks at me and with a deep gruff in his voice he tells me the two of us are going to dinner, I just need to pick a date. He tells me he'll text his schedule over so I know when he's available. Then he stands and starts to put his coat on. When I get up, he looks for my coat, I guess.

"I didn't bring one, Atlas. Just this." And I point to my kutte.

He takes his coat off and starts to fuss with it. When I see what he's doing, I take a small step back. He's separating his coat and when he's done, he holds the fleece part. He puts the windbreaker on his chair. Then he motions for me to turn around. I do and he helps me into his coat. His smell and heat is surrounding me and, for some reason, I feel safe again. The boys come to me one by one, saying goodbye. Thanos gives me a young boy hug and tells me he's definitely coming for movie night. Then he surprises me by asking what kind of flower Heartbreaker likes. *Well, we have a crush*, I think to myself. I think for a second then tell him not sure on her favorite flower but when I've seen her with flowers, they are always colorful. Stefanos stands a bit away and says goodbye, which makes me think he may be on the spectrum. I mean, we have Teddy in our lives and after all these years can recognize the signs. I've come to kind of understand the condition. Finally Konstantin is in front of me. For some reason he looks so innocent, I just have to pull him in for a hug. He returns it then pulls back. Not sure why, but I ask him for his phone, which he immediately gives me.

"Konstantin, if you ever need something or someone, here's my number. I know your grown but with your dad and his schedule, don't want you three to feel like you have no one. I enjoyed spending the night with y'all."

I've never seen a teenage boy look so lost for a quick second before that wall comes up. Yeah, this kid has some issues. He looks me straight in the eye and softly tells me thanks. When he reaches down and squeezes my hand, I know it was the right thing to do. The boys start toward the front of the restaurant side. Atlas puts his hands on my shoulders and squeezes.

"Damn it, Rebel, with one meal you've captured three of the four Giannopoulos men's hearts. And the only reason you didn't get Stefanos is because my boy might not understand his emotions. Thanks for tonight, it was very interesting. Now I'm gonna kiss you, Rebel, so tell me no before I do."

I hold my tongue and, man, Atlas does kiss me. When he turns to catch up to his boys, I have to grab on to the chair to stay standing. Feeling someone behind me, I turn and almost scream when I see Shadow's face right there. When she grins, it's actually even scarier. Knowing it is coming, I just impatiently wait. She doesn't disappoint.

"So what did I just walk in on? Rebel, you of all the sisters, I'm pleasantly surprised. From what I hear, a doctor and not just anyone, but the one who delivered our little Mickie. Not bad, sister, not bad at all. Even so, just so you know, I'll make some time to have a conversation with the Greek stud muffin. That's when I can get to know him. Sister, I will always have your back, never doubt that. If you two start this, don't forget those three kids. You won't just be dating the stud muffin, you'll be taking on that entire family, and my gut is telling me there's a story and it ain't a pretty one. Oh, loved the video, though, sister, in front of the kiddos? Not cool. Gotta say, and don't ever tell Panther I said this, but you did good. Real good."

I can't help it, before I know it, I'm laughing so hard I'm bent over. Shadow's also sniggering but, by the look on her face I see this woman will protect me, no matter what. To her utter surprise and mine, I hug her, saying thanks softly in her ear. She then shocks me when her arms go around me and she tells me you're welcome. My God, I think Shadow and I just had a moment. One for the books.

FIVE
'REBEL'
MYA

My head is killing me but my responsibilities as S-a-A are knocking on my door, so to speak. So, after putting in a couple of hours at the Handmaidens Fitness & Holistic Center, instead of doing what I want, which is taking some Advil or Tylenol and lying down in bed with ice on my neck and head 'til the pounding stops, I'm at the clubhouse, at my desk, struggling to even look at emails, let alone the mail sitting on the edge of my desk. When I hear my cell phone ringing, I reach into my back pocket and pull it out.

"Hello."

"Rebel, is that you?"

"Yeah, it's me. Who is this?"

As I wait for the person to identify themselves, I fight through my head pain and the light bulb goes off.

"Konstantin, what's wrong?"

I hear what sounds like sniffling then a cough.

"I'm in the principal's office and can't get ahold of Dad. He might be in surgery or something, but his phone keeps going to voicemail. Can you come to the high school? Please?"

Hearing the desperation in his voice, I'm out of my chair before my brain neurons can even heat up. I grab my kutte and am moving quickly down the hall, not paying attention and plowing into someone big and hard. Looking way up, I see I've connected with Avalanche and Panther is behind him. It's the man in front of me who keeps my attention, though gotta say Shadow's man is definitely hawt. And not something I'll ever be mentioning to her. Feeling big hands on my arms, my mind goes back to Avalanche.

"Rebel, you okay, little sister?"

That right there is why I finally accepted that no matter what kind of feelings I had for Avalanche, he would only see me as his kid sister. Trying to remember his question, it dawns on me that they are both staring at me, worry on each of their faces.

"Everything is fine, as far as I know. Got to run, a friend might be in trouble."

Panther's look gets intense.

"What did Zoey do now? I'll go with you because, as you know, I'm one of the few who can calm my woman down."

Shaking my head, which makes it hurt more, I peek around Avalanche to look at Panther's face.

"No, Panther, believe it or not, this time it's not Shadow. It's a friend of mine's teenage son. He called me asking for some help, so that's what I'm going to do. Thanks though for the offer."

Avalanche is watching me carefully with something similar to surprise on his face.

"Which friend, Rebel, has a teenage son? Do I know them?"

"No, don't think so or maybe you might have met him when Mickie was born. It's Atlas, or as everyone calls him, Dr. Atlas. His son, Konstantin, is in trouble. Sorry, Avalanche, but he sounded scared on the phone. I have to go now."

As I go to walk around him, his hand holds on to my arm and he starts walking with me. I literally put my brakes on and since Avalanche keeps going, I lock my leg muscles, which finally gets his attention.

"Come on, Rebel, you said the boy is in trouble, we need to go. Why are you stopping?"

I'm suddenly so furious with this man and for some reason figure this is the best time to let it out, loudly.

"Seriously, Avalanche? Since when did you become part of Konstantin's issue? You don't even know the 'boy,' who is actually a teenager. And you might not think it's strange for you to show up to help someone who doesn't even know you but damn, dude, did you not hear me tell you that his dad is Atlas? Or did you just jump over that comment. For fuck's sake, are you truly this blind and dumb? Don't tell me you haven't figured it out that I've been crushing on your big ass forever. But since I'm 'little sister' to you, that means you can't just jump into every situation and be my hero. You don't want to be with me so quit playing the game 'cause you are not only confusing me, but more importantly, pissing me off."

It's quiet for so long, I look up to see his face and, oh my God, the look on his handsome face breaks my heart. It looks like I kicked him in the nuts while pulling his hair out with tweezers. His eyes are huge, like he just figured out a puzzle, and that's when it dawns on my dumbass that Avalanche had no idea about my feelings. And I just threw everything at him like a raging bitch on her period. I feel so bad, I don't even realize or comprehend I'm so upset that my eyes are leaking, until he pulls me into his hard body. I know he's trying to comfort me but instead he's killing me. Something he doesn't know about me, because I'm not a good sharer, is I don't have a lot of self-confidence. All I hear in my head is all the nastiness of my past as a child, no matter what I look like or where I am in my adult life. I've been in therapy throughout my life and it's funny, but each therapist tried to hammer into me that what I see in a mirror is not the true view of what I actually am. I've done such an injustice to one of the best men I've ever had the pleasure to know. It hits me that I don't really want Avalanche as a partner for life. I was so intrigued with him and his story. He's kind of like me, which means he's not a sharer. We have spent some time together and both have let out a few personal things about our pasts. Not to mention his whole package caught my eyes. Now as I lean against his body, I can feel he's all muscle. Before I can even start to try to apologize, I hear her bellow first. Then all hell breaks loose, as it does when she's around.

"What in the ever-lovin' fuck have you done now, Big Bird?"

I feel Avalanche tense but she's on a roll now.

"Get your big bear paws off of Rebel, now. What? Now she has someone else interested in her, you decide it's time to make your move? Too late, motherfucker. Don't, Panther, I've tried with him but he's dumber than dumb."

That does it. I can feel my temper raging inside me, so I release Avalanche and turn on our club enforcer and my sister, while blasting her to hell and back, which is my way. Let everything out that can cut someone's heart out before I even take a second to analyze the situation and think before I talk.

"Who the hell do you think you are? Don't you dare ever call Avalanche dumb, you freak from hell. He's been nothing but kind and caring to everyone and you are the biggest arctic bitch to him whenever you get a chance, and I'm sick of it. Like just now, without even knowing the situation, you just assume that he's in the wrong. Well, surprise, Shadow, it wasn't him, it was my dumbass mouth. He didn't have a clue I was crushing on him. The words I spewed his way opened his eyes to where I was at. That and the look on his face broke my heart, and what you walked up on was Avalanche giving me comfort, even though I was in the wrong. So, take your frozen-ass heart out of here and for once in your miserable life, mind your own fucking business. I'm done with you. Avalanche, we need to have a conversation but I gotta go, brother of my heart. Thank you for the best hug I've ever had. You and me, I promise to fix this, but again got to go."

I turn and go to walk past Shadow, but she is in the way and isn't moving. I pick up speed and when I get close, I pull my hand up and hold it with the other so when I'm just about to run into her, I shift my weight and actually use my shoulder to not only lift her up but move her entire body out of my way and into Panther. I can hear her gasp, but all I do is flip her off as I'm walking down the corridor. When I hit the main room, I'm shocked to see about half of my club sisters waiting. Tink, Glory, Squirt, and Raven are on one side; while Taz, Vixen, Dottie, Dani, Heartbreaker, and Wildcat are on the other. When Taz sees me, she rushes toward me with little Mickie strapped to her chest. I know if she touches me, I'll lose it so I put a hand up.

"Raquel, please don't. I know you mean well, but something is up with Konstantin and I need to get to the high school. I'm going to need you though, can I come to the house later? Think I just fucked up one of the best people I have in my life."

I watch as her eyes move behind me at whoever is walking out. By the sounds of their heavy footsteps, I know it's Avalanche, Panther, and probably her bringing up the rear. I can't take Shadow right now, so I blow a kiss toward both Taz and Mickie. Then without a word to anyone else, I move toward the door. When I go to open it, someone grabs it, which shocks me so I turn and see red hair. Heartbreaker, with the most serious look on her face, stares me in the eyes and says two words.

"Let's go."

For some reason knowing she's coming with gives me comfort, which is strange 'cause my go-to is always Taz, but I say nothing and run to my cage. Not a word is said as I drive to the high school which, thank God, isn't that far. We both jump out and run to the doors, pulling them open. As we enter, I realize we both have our kuttes on and that's a huge no-no with the principal, Catherine Knolls. She's been a total bitch and pain in the ass since before time, if what I've heard is true. Since I didn't grow up in Montana, it's all hearsay.

We head straight to the office area. The receptionist, Natalie, who we know very well—as she's one of our survivors—gets up, walks around her desk, and comes toward us. She hugs Heartbreaker first then me. Since she moved into town from the club's ranch, we've not seen a lot of her. Seeing her doing so well, I'm proud of the work we do, as it shows it does help those we try to and manage somehow to save.

"Hey, didn't know you were coming in. Is there a problem or is the Devil's Handmaidens club looking to get in on our upcoming potluck dinner and auction? It's for a good cause, one of the kids here needs a kidney transplant."

Her hands cover her mouth immediately and her eyes go huge.

"Please don't tell Principal Knolls I divulged that information. She hates me because of my history with the club and is looking for any reason to get rid of me."

That's pissing me off because Natalie has worked so hard and come so far. As I go to tell her that, the door swings open and out walks the bitch who happens to be the principal. Principal Knolls looks around, sees the two of us with Natalie, and puts the ugliest smirk I've ever seen on a person's face. Then the tiny hairs on the back of my neck stand up when her eyes shift to Natalie.

"Natalie, why wasn't I informed that these two are here, and why are you away from your desk? What have I told you about that? When you are working, you stay at your desk and do whatever you're told. In this school you are an employee, not one of those biker chicks. Don't make me have to write you up."

Natalie goes to run, yeah run, to her desk. I'm holding myself back but Heartbreaker, not so much. She grabs Natalie's arm and pulls her to a stop. Then she lives up to the red hair theory as she makes her way to Principal Knolls. Then she gets up on her tippy-toes and gets in her face.

"What is your problem, lady? That woman has been to hell and back. You should know how lucky you are to have her working here at the high school. Instead, you're a bully and a hater. Just a reminder for you not to bite the hand that's feeding you. Who's been helping the school out with all the expansions, repairs, and building that fieldhouse you cried to Tink about? Yeah, the biker chick club. So, get off your high and mighty horse and come back down to earth. Oh, almost forgot, we aren't biker chicks, though nothing wrong with that. We are grown women who decided to take on the degenerates of this world so we could try to protect women and children from their sick asses. If you'd attend any of our monthly seminars detailing what we do, you'd know that. We are also a club of businesswomen as we own quite a few of the businesses in town. Finally, our president, Tink, helps the ranchers and farmers out when life is too hard and their businesses fail to keep them afloat. So just a suggestion, Principal Knolls, don't judge a book by its cover. Now, Rebel and I are here for Konstantin Giannopoulos. What's going on and why did he need to put a call out for help?"

She's looking a bit humbled but when Heartbreaker mentioned Konstantin's name, she gets that ugly, hateful look back on her face.

"Of course it would be one of you two redheads who would snag Dr. Giannopoulos's attention. Us normal women don't stand a chance with all of you around. Which one, let me guess? You could be sisters, though Rebel is a bit more conservative than you are, Heartbreaker. Both of you have mouths like truck drivers. Knowing the doctor like I do, have to go with you, Heartbreaker. What's the old saying men want a lady on their arm and a slu—Ugh."

One minute her mouth is moving, the next I've pushed the mouthy bitch up against the wall by her door. She's gasping and crying but I don't let go. I've had enough of her bullshit so if she can dish it, she better be able to take it.

"You hateful bitch from hell. Don't ever let me hear you talk to Heartbreaker like that ever again. No, let me clarify, don't speak to any of my club sisters so disrespectfully. I can't help it if Atlas has no interest in you, he probably can see right through you. People talk, Catherine, and it's gotten around how you're like a bitch dog in heat whenever a single man is close to you or glances your way. Not being a good mentor or role model for the young women in the school. Not to mention the young men see you acting so desperate, throwing yourself at men, they might alter their impression of women seeing you being so easy. Now, who's the slut? I'm gonna let you go, we're going into your office, and you'll explain what is going on with Konstantin. Oh, forgot to tell you, it's not Heartbreaker, it's me Atlas is interested in. I'd be a fool to let that man go and, lady, I ain't never been called a fool. Let's go."

I remove my arms and she rocks back and forth, rubbing her neck. Then to both of our shock, she turns and goes to walk in the door but Konstantin is standing in it, white as a ghost. I'm moving before he says a word, thank God, because he falls into my arms, out cold.

SIX
'HEARTBREAKER'
DELILAH

Watching Rebel catch Kon, I pull my phone out immediately calling 911.

"911 what's your emergency?"

"Hey, it's Heartbreaker, we need an ambulance at the high school in Principal Knolls's office. Also, get ahold of Dr. Giannopoulos and tell him it's his son, Kon."

Then I hang up and run over to Rebel and the boy. She's on her ass with him in her lap. Looking at him, I notice he's pale, sweaty, and trembling. I turn toward Principal Knolls and stare.

"You didn't let Kon eat lunch, did you? How long has he been in that office?"

She turns as pale if not paler than the boy and steps back, arms coming up. Then I hear Natalie's voice.

"She purposely pulled him in right before his

lunch period and then when he told her he felt dizzy, she told him a lesson he needed to learn is every action has consequences. He stuck up for some kid she was berating earlier. She was being a big shot at Manuel's expense. Kon recognized that Manuel is like his younger brother, so he told the principal to leave Manuel alone, he didn't do anything wrong. So, when she went to the bathroom I gave him a cup of water, but she doesn't allow me to keep food in my desk and has actually searched it. I'm so sorry, Heartbreaker, I'm going to run and get some juice, be right back."

I don't think I've ever been so pissed off in my entire life. All the women in our club grew up rough. It's made us the women we are, but in my past life I was a whore, literally. Fought tooth and nail for what I wanted and needed. And that bitch was ripping Kon a new asshole because she lost face in front of high school kids. Guess the little I've been around this kid; he's gotten under my skin for some reason.

"You bitch. How the hell did you ever become principal when you don't have a heart at all, especially to deal with kids? I know you were informed that Kon is a type 1 diabetic, so what you did was malicious and purposeful, so you better start praying to whatever you pray to that he'll be okay. Now get me some cool towels or whatever. And some ice. Move your ass, now!"

Before she moves, I head back to Rebel, who's loosened Kon's top two buttons. Without thinking, I reach over and rip his shirt open then lift his torso up so I can get it off of him. His T-shirt is soaked and his face is now flushed. I move down to his shoes, removing them, along with his socks. Lastly, I loosen then pull his belt completely off. By this time Natalie is back with apple, grape, and orange juice in little bottles. I scream for her to give me the one with the most sugar. She quickly looks at them all and then tosses me the apple juice, which I break open and hand to Rebel.

"Dribble a little over his lips and put some on your finger to rub on his gums. If he takes it, keep dribbling it on his lips."

Rebel immediately does as I tell her. Hearing footsteps, Catherine returns with a grocery store plastic bag of ice and some wet paper towels. Grabbing the towels, I place a few on his forehead and then wipe up and down on his arms and toss it to Natalie to pass on the bottoms of his feet. Then I grab a few ice cubes and try to place them on his wrist, but they keep falling off.

"Shit. Rebel, sister, don't know what else to do. Does he have an insulin pump? See if you can get a read off of it. Natalie, did he bring a book bag with him, if so, check for a meter. Catherine, didn't you tell the nurse what's going on? For fuck's sake, call her and get her ass down here now."

I lean down and gently shake Kon's shoulders, calling his name. Nothing. Then I switch it up and called him stud muffin, which Rebel sadly grins at. Back and forth Rebel and I call his name, then the nickname, and after about four or five times he moans. Rebel starts screaming his name, telling him to wake up. That's when I hear the sirens. Finally, the real medics are here. Hearing boots to the floor not even a few minutes later, along with wheels, I turn just as they hit the door. Two guys rush in and start assessing him. Rebel is giving them as much information as possible. Principal Knolls is standing off to the side wringing her hands. Natalie comes up next to me, eyes wet, which no way I can take.

"Sister, knock that shit off. The kid is going to be fine now that the EMTs arrived. Thanks for the help, Natalie. You did real good."

She turns and hugs me so tightly I can barely breathe, but I don't say a word. Instead, I reach over and hug her back. Then I hear Rebel scream the kid's name and tell him never to scare her like that ever again. We turn to see Kon's eyes are open and he's looking around, confused. We both move closer, just as the one EMT tells Rebel they gave him a shot of glucagon, which is used in severe cases. That's when I hear the desperate, loud male screams coming down the hall and feet hitting the floor. Turning, I see Atlas almost fall into the doorway, and immediately I'm moving because I see his knees buckle when his eyes take in Konstantin. I barely make it before his legs totally give out. I try but he's so not a lightweight, and we both go crashing to the floor. All you hear are our moans and groans until we hear a weak laugh.

"Damn, Dad, I'm the one who should get that girl. Go figure, I pass out and you land a hottie on top of you. Well, Rebel, what do you say? I am his son. I've been told I look like a younger him."

Then I hear Rebel's laughter ringing out loudly and I finally take a breath, just as my body feels like it's underwater. Then suddenly I can't catch my breath and I'm dizzy. Someone is hitting my cheeks, telling me to stay awake, but the darkness already has a hold on me and I'm gone.

* * *

What the hell is going on and why do I feel high? Oh shit, please God, don't tell me I fell off the wagon yet again. I go to raise my hands to my head then I hear a voice I've feared, hated, and started to trust all at once in my ear.

"Heartbreaker, don't you dare pull that fuckin' IV out again. You're okay, sister, relax. Someone call a nurse. Hey, all's good. Nurse will be here in a minute or two. Want a drink of water?"

I nod and hear noise, then a straw as it's placed on my bottom lip. When I open my mouth, my eyelids raise, and to my surprise it's none other than Shadow holding the cup with ice water in it. Damn, it feels great on my throat. *How did I end up in here?* I think to myself as my eyes take in the room. It's packed with Shadow and her man, Panther, Tink and Noodles, Glory and Yoggie. Pushed off in the corner are Squirt and Presley. Well, shit, was I about to die or something? Half these men I've barely said a word or two to. When I catch Squirt's eyes, she makes a fish face at me with her huge green eyes sparkling. With Presley by her side, she's blossomed. The door opens up and a young woman comes in with an iPad.

"So, a little birdie told me my patient is awake. Oh, there she is, look at those beautiful eyes. Hello, gorgeous, I'm Maria, your nighttime nurse. I'm gonna ask everyone to step out for a, holy son of a biscuit."

Her eyes get big and when I shift it makes total sense, as her eyes are glued to Shadow. Everyone waits for it but, damn, Nurse Maria shocks everyone.

"I gotta tell you, that is fucking awesome, pardon my French. Would it be okay to take a closer look? Don't want to invade your private space."

Shadow looks confused for a second or two then grins huge.

"Sure, Maria, look all you want."

Maria walks toward Shadow then starts leaning to the right then the left, back and forth, inspecting the full tattoo on our enforcer's face. When she stands back, she looks ecstatic.

"Where did you get that work done? I've been wanting one, but didn't really know anyone in the area. My nephew does it out West but that's not going to happen. I love that tattoo and it fits you somehow, and I don't even know you. Like I shared, I'm Maria. You are?"

As Shadow introduces herself, the room relaxes. I close my eyes and just listen to the conversations start back up, along with the laughter. These people dropped everything to be here for me. Oh shit, my eyes pop open and I ask loudly.

"How's Kon?"

The room instantly goes so quiet, I swear if someone dropped a pin, I'd hear it. I'm watching their faces for some kind of reaction when Panther makes his way to my bedside.

"Heartbreaker, thanks to your quick thinking, he's in the hospital but is going to be fine. They are checking his pump because Konstantin told his dad and his endocrinologist that he didn't receive any warnings from the pump. So they are not taking any chances. I know Rebel is with them so maybe once you're checked out by Maria, we can get you up to see him. That kid is something else, even stood up for that principal lady, after all the woman did today. Told his dad he shouldn't have gotten involved and maybe he could have spoken to the principal in her office. She's been suspended until an investigation can be done. Atlas has to be a proud dad. I hear his other two boys are just as great."

"Thanks, Panther, takes a load off my mind. I was worried I did something wrong and messed Kon up.

And if they allow it, I'd love to go up there and see with my own eyes he's okay. Again, appreciate the peace of mind."

Maria walks around Panther and announces everyone out. Then she does her work, and damn, is she good. Stats, questions about how I feel, and what exactly happened. Told me she'll report to the physician on duty and they will decide if I stay or go. I let her know I'd rather go home and she said she'd tell them that too. She saved the best for last and it made my evening.

"I heard Shadow's husband telling you about that young man. Dr. Giannopoulos is one of our favorite physicians on staff. I'll get a wheelchair so you can go up there and make sure young Giannopoulos is okay. I'll give you no more than forty-five minutes though. And no exerting yourself. Do I make myself clear?"

Nodding, I reach for her hand and squeeze it.

"Thank you so much, Maria, it means the world to me. I'm beyond worried about the kid, so seeing him will help to put my mind at ease. Can I go now?"

She laughs, gives my hand a squeeze, then stands up and walks out the door. Everyone starts to pour back in immediately. Before I can answer the hundred questions thrown my way, she's back with the wheelchair. She claps her hands to get everyone's attention.

"Okay, this is how this is going to work. I can't say they will let all of you up there but that's their decision, not mine. This young lady needs to be back in no more than forty-five minutes. If she's not, I'm calling security about a gang of troublemakers. Got it?"

As everyone chuckles, I'm already swinging my legs over the bed. I wait as the IV is moved to the smaller pole on the wheelchair, then Maria helps me up and into the chair. Squirt steps up and giggles.

"I'll push your wheelchair there, grandma, just hang on tightly."

With that, she takes off like a bat out of hell. The force has my hair slightly blowing back and it actually feels good on my skin. I've hated hospitals since my last overdose when I flatlined. I do everything and anything I can to stay the hell out of these places. Though this is a nice hospital and Maria is great, still don't like them. We're waiting for the elevator to arrive, when I hear Noodles challenge the other men to see who could make it to the floor first using the stairs. Like a group of boys, they all take off for the stairs when a nurse walking by tells them this is a hospital not a school gym. They immediately shut up but continue to the stairs. At that moment the doors slide open and all of us women and Presley, who stayed back with Squirt, get in. I'm feeling anxious and not sure if it's from Kon's situation, that bitch of a principal, passing out and being brought to the hospital, or that slight need I'm having for something I swore I'd never do again because if I do, my club will take my kutte and my ink then kick me to the curb. I can't lose these women; they are my lifeline. So deep in thought my head jerks up as Squirt takes off toward the room we were told we'd find my answers in. Arriving at a door that's shut, I lean forward and softly knock. I hear a muffled, "come on in," and Presley pushes the door open. As Squirt wheels me in, I see the rest of the prospects Dani, Dottie, and Kitty, along with Wildcat and Dr. Malcolm, and finally Rebel. When she sees me, she jumps off the bed and rushes toward me, bending down and hugging me. When I look up, I see Taz and Enforcer in the corner before my eyes stop on Kon. His eyes are on me and it hits me, he looks beyond exhausted. The poor kid. When he spreads his arms open wide, I immediately stand up, grab the IV bag, and walk toward the bed. I lean over and he closes his arms, holding me tightly. I can feel his body trembling so I tell him to hush and not upset himself. That makes him even more emotional, so I lean back and put my hand to his cheek. His eyes go wide at my touch and that's when I understand his feelings. Probably besides family, he and his brothers don't have many women in their lives. Boys need a mom or mom figure around them. Damn his mother to the bottoms of hell. I wipe a tear then another away, as I notice my club sisters start to move toward the door. That's when this kid breaks my heart and my heart falls in love. The love of a mom and son, even though he's not mine and never will be.

"Heartbreaker, I've been waiting. Are you okay? 'Cause everyone kept telling me all was good. I fought falling asleep because shit, Rebel, come here too, please."

He waits until Rebel goes on his other side, sitting on the bed—which doesn't have a lot of room—so I pull the chair up close, never letting his hand go. Rebel grabs his other one, which cause more tears to fall down.

"I wanted to thank both of you from the bottom of my heart. Besides my yia-yia, or as you say here in the States, grandma, aunts, and a few close family friends, I've never had a woman who really don't know me go to the lengths both of you have. Being a kid with type 1 diabetes, I've gotten used to hospitals and doctors and have seen the worst of people. I'm grateful to see the best in two people I don't know. Don't take what I said as I'm saying my dad ain't great because the three of us are beyond blessed with him as our parent. One day, I'll tell you about the bitch who gave birth to us. I'll never forget what you ladies did for me, and maybe one day I can be there for you."

With that, he drops his head. I look at Rebel and she nods, so the two of us lean over as close as we can get and hug on Kon. Not sure who's crying harder when I hear three voices at the same time. Atlas and two young men.

"Dad, is Konstantin okay?"

"Why are those two women hugging on him?"

"What the hell is going on in here? Rebel, hey feisty, is my boy okay?"

With that I hear Kon chuckling at first then he lets out a kind of a hoot.

"Look, Dad, in less than an hour I have two of the hottest biker chicks, not only in my bed but hanging on tightly to me. Better wake up, father of mine, or this redhead on my left is going to find someone who is willing to do the work. This redhead on my right will need my permission before she lets anyone catch her. She deserves only the very best man out there. Since you're hanging your star on Rebel and I'm just too damn young for her, I'll take on the job and make sure I vet and approve all her male suitors. That's what you old folks call it, right? Looking at her, shouldn't take too long before some muscle-bound moron wins her heart, which will surely break mine."

That has every single person let out a relieved chuckle or giggle. With that right there, my anxiety disappears and my heart has a new person to love. Well, actually three because got to include Kon's two younger brothers.

SEVEN
'REBEL'
MYA

Today has been one of the longest days of my life. Jesus Christ, when Heartbreaker went down and with Konstantin messed up, for the first time since I became a Devil's Handmaiden, I didn't know what to do. I panicked and then started to have an anxiety attack. When Atlas got there and stood at the door, for a millisecond the look on his face said it all. Devastation, worry, panic, and love were all visible. He didn't hide his emotions like most men do, or maybe it was his emotions for the boys. With Konstantin still in my lap, Atlas stared at me with a look I didn't understand. It was like relief and anger mixed together. I didn't give a flying whatever if that look was truly directed at me because either way, his son needed someone and he called me. As I went to move, I watched as Heartbreaker ran toward Atlas just as his knees buckled. Holy shit, my sister tried her damnedest to keep him upright, but the man is a Greek god so they both tumbled to the ground hard.

What happened next confused the hell out of me at first. Hearing Atlas screaming at Heartbreaker while gently slapping her cheeks, he then started yelling orders at the EMTs who split up, with one staying with Konstantin and the other moving to Heartbreaker. That's when it dawned on me that my friend, no my sister, passed out. Gently, I moved Konstantin's head off my lap and got to my knees, humping it to Heartbreaker. When I was holding her hand, I whispered to Atlas I had this and he should go to his son. He nodded and as I did, Atlas kneed it to Konstantin. What a total clusterfuck, and I felt so bad for the EMTs. Natalie called 911 for another ambulance to come as we had two patients. After seeing how competent Natalie truly is I'm going to talk to Tink and Glory, maybe we can find her somewhere to work where she'll be appreciated. Then I realized we needed an assistant manager at our trucking company. I put that thought in the back of my mind for a discussion later.

After both patients were loaded into waiting ambulances, Atlas checked and Konstantin told him he was fine. Atlas wanted to go get his other two sons so they all could be at the hospital. By that time, school was about to dismiss so when I felt a warm hand at my elbow, I looked up to see Atlas staring down with that same look in his eyes. He led me outside and then right to my cage.

"How the hell did you end up here, Rebel? I was doing a procedure, which means I didn't have my phone on me. Not sure why Konstantin didn't call my parents. Shit, I'm messing this up, as usual. Thank you from the bottom of my heart for taking care of my son. He's such a good kid carrying a heavy load. I can't figure it out, he's so on top of the management of his diabetes. He's the one who plans our meals so we can all eat the same thing and he's not left out. We all shop and cook together; this doesn't make any sense. I'll talk with him about it, but please know I owe you more than all I have, my feisty Rebel."

I can tell he's still flustered, so I step closer and wrap my arms around his middle. He leans down as he puts his arms around me, and I feel surrounded by all that is Atlas. And God what a feeling it is. I can feel the adrenaline dropping and when I softly start to sob, he comforts me. Knowing I must look a mess, without thinking I wipe my face on his shirt. Oh shit, what was I thinking? Leaning back, I see one section of his tailored shirt is wet with some—no, please God—snot on it. He lifts my chin with his long fingers and starts to wipe my face off. I pull back, so embarrassed.

"Don't worry about it, Rebel. It can be cleaned. Your body is finally realizing that this panic situation is over and the 'adrenaline rush' you experienced during Kon's episode is done, so now your body is trying to catch up. Let it happen, it's perfectly normal. Come on, let's get you in your car so you can sit awhile. I'll wait with you to make sure you'll be okay. Give me your keys."

The dominant and alpha traits are front and center with Atlas. This man hides nothing and what you see is what you get, which is perfect for me because I'm exactly the same. Never thought I'd let a man boss me around, but something about this particular man is different. I reach into my crossbody bag and pull my keys out, handing them to him. He leans down, kisses my nose, and in a deep gruff voice tells me, "You're a good girl, Rebel." *How in all that is holy does he do that?* I think to myself as my clitoris swells and seems to shiver down there in my girlie garden. He opens the SUV then helps me into the driver's seat before closing the door. I'm stunned as I watch his long body pass in front of my vehicle, and before I know it he's sitting next to me, adjusting the heat. He grabs my hand and seems to be taking my pulse, so I sit quietly.

"It's a little high but to be expected. How do you feel? Good, drink some of that vitamin water, it will help. Damn it, wish we were in my car. I have all kinds of snacks and shit in there."

His phone starts to buzz and ring at the same time. He pulls it out of his coat pocket and looks at it. When he answers, I know it's the hospital by the way he's talking. That is until whoever says something that pisses Atlas totally off. He starts giving orders and tells the person on the line to call the police and no one is allowed near his son. That has my ears opening as I lean closer to try and hear what's going on. When he hangs up, he looks to me with those sapphire eyes that look torn. I grab his hand and squeeze.

"Go to the hospital. If you want, I can go get Stefanos and Thanos for you. All you need to do is call their school. They do go to the same school, correct? No worries, I've got this."

He does that, staring at me for a few seconds, then he shocks the ever-lovin' fuck out of me when he explains the phone call.

"That was the hospital. Apparently, my ex-wife with her drug-dealing boyfriend showed up in the emergency room asking about 'her son' Konstantin. How she knew he was even there or having a problem I don't have a damn clue. Everyone at that campus knows what happened between us, so the charge nurse put a call out to me. You heard my response, but I'd feel better if I was there. First, you sure you're okay with getting my boys? And if so, is it too much to ask the woman I've not even had a date with yet to do me another favor regarding my boys? But I don't have a choice, Mya, so if you don't mind, can you please pick the boys up and bring them up to the hospital? I promise to make all of this up to you, cross my heart."

Halfway through I close my eyes because his voice

is pure sex, and he has me so excited I imagine those thick football thighs naked with my hands on them, then my tongue tasting and nipping as I make my way to the junction between them. Again, my breasts are aching and my girlie garden feels like the sun is shining down there. When I open my eyes, all I see are dark sapphire-blue eyes right in front of me. Watching as if it's in slow motion, Atlas slowly bends down and plants a short but hot kiss on my lips before pulling back. He takes his phone, scrolls, then pushes call. It's so quiet in my car that when the line is answered, I jump a little bit. He explains the situation and when I hear them ask my name, I whisper to him to tell them Rebel from the Devil's Handmaidens. The woman on the line says she knows me, so sure, just stop by the office and show some ID. He disconnects and places his phone back in his pocket. Then again he leans over and kisses my nose first then my lips, with the sweetest ever kiss I've ever gotten in my entire life. Then he jumps out of my car and runs to his. Before I can even process that he's not in here anymore, I watch his vehicle drive away like a maniac. I think to myself *that bitch better stay away from Konstantin if she knows what's good for her.* That's one of my last thoughts before I pull away myself, in the opposite direction, to pick up Atlas's two younger children.

* * *

What a zoo. When the two younger boys and I arrive, two older folks are waiting in the foyer. Thanos runs to them and Stefanos turns to tell me they are their grandparents. After introducing myself and meeting Apollo and Athena Giannopoulos, I have to promise to come to dinner when all the drama is over. With that promise, they let me go and swear they'll keep their eyes on both boys. Thanos hugs me before I leave, while Stefanos waves at me.

Between all the employees who know Atlas checking in on Konstantin, so are the Devil's Handmaidens. He is so enthralled with my club sisters and their club names. When one walks in, he wants to know her name, rank, and her marital status. This kid is cracking me up. It's so easy to see his type, which is he doesn't have one, he's all over the damn board. When Squirt walks in his eyes nearly pop out of his head. And she's oblivious to how gorgeous she is. Konstantin almost growls when Presley shows up a few minutes later, putting his arm around his ol' lady. When they leave to check on Heartbreaker, he asks me who Presley is and how they met. Cutting this off at the knees, I tell him she's too old for him and they are committed to each other. He pouts until the next club sister walks in which, of course, would be my bestie, Taz, with Enforcer. This time Konstantin has no questions which shocks me. I take a minute and see how intimidated he is by Enforcer, who can be an asshole sometimes.

"Hey, Enforcer, knock it off. If you're so afraid a high school kid can steal your Que then you have more issues than I ever thought you did."

Enforcer doesn't say a word but flips me the bird. Konstantin sits up in the bed and growls.

"Hey, don't disrespect Rebel like that. Just 'cause you're a big muscular dude, have some respect. If my dad was here, he'd kick your ass for that. Especially you being rude to Rebel."

"Konstantin, calm down. Enforcer and I have a hate/love relationship. Don't worry, he doesn't bother me, and I have to put up with him because he's with my BFF."

That brings a smile to his face. I ask who's watching the kiddos and Taz said Momma Diane and Tank. When Konstantin turns to look at me with a puzzled look on his face, I explain.

"Our club is made up of a bunch of misfits who came together. All of us grew up rough, that's why we try to protect the innocent, abused, and taken. Tink, our prez, and Shadow, our enforcer, started the club a few years ago. Since then we've grown and have had good and bad times. Tink's parents are Momma Diane and Tank. You probably have seen Tank around, he's an older guy, huge with tons of tats. He's the prez of the Intruders."

His eyes get big and his head jerks toward Enforcer, who is in his Intruders kutte. The kid turns white then green like he's gonna vomit. Taz grabs the garbage can and passes it to me. I go to give it to Konstantin but he pushes it away and swallows big.

"Hey, I owe you an apology. Didn't mean to be an ignorant pain in the ass kid. Didn't know you were part of that club. I've seen some of your, what do you call them... brothers... around in town. Should have kept my mouth shut. My dad is always telling me that."

Enforcer is staring at the kid with no emotion, that is until Taz plants her elbow right into his ribs, which brings an "umph" out of him. Then he looks down and smiles at her. That right there is why I put up with that asshole. He looks my way again, flips me off, then gives it to Konstantin.

"Kid, don't worry about it. I wasn't. That you would try to protect Rebel is admirable. Just remember, once you let those kinds of words out, you better be able to back them up. I'd think twice about being a cocky bastard when lying in a hospital bed. Just sayin'. We ain't got a problem as long as this badass dad of yours doesn't try to kick my ass 'cause gonna tell ya, kid, I won't hold back."

Enforcer doesn't realize as he is speaking that Atlas has quietly walked in and is standing in the doorway. When Konstantin sees his dad, the first emotion that runs across his face of course is love, but then I see his worry when he realizes his dad must have heard Enforcer. Seeing the young man staring behind him, Enforcer turns and I wait for it as their first meeting wasn't all that great. Both are very dominant alphas, so this could go in so many directions. Both Konstantin and I never expect it to go like it does.

Enforcer moves toward Atlas and I can feel Konstantin tense up. Then all hell breaks loose. In a good way.

"Atlas, how the fuck are ya, man? Wait, is this your kid? Shit, with all that went on that day, I don't think I ever saw your boys. Actually, didn't see much besides this one next to me. Well shit, small world ain't it, brother?"

In shock, I watch as the two grown men catch up on life that's happened since Mickie was born. I've gone with Taz to her post-birth visit when she had an issue with her girlie garden. I stayed in the waiting room when she went in to see Dr. Giannopoulos, or as I'm getting to know him better as, my Greek god, Atlas. That thought stops me immediately. When the hell did I start thinking of him as mine? Before I can process any of this, I feel lips on my cheek and a hand on my waist. A very warm male hand on my hip that sends such an electrical jolt, I jump. I hear Taz and Konstantin chuckle and more tempting is the slight growl I hear coming from Atlas.

I'm so in trouble. As I stare at my bestie, knowing I'll never get one ounce of help from her. She is grinning like the Cheshire cat.

EIGHT
'ATLAS'

I'm so fuckin' pissed off and want to punch something right now, but I can't let it loose with all my boys here. Goddamn it, why can't she stay away or, better yet, just drop dead. Never have I made that wish before but after what I just went through, it would be a blessing. Thank God my parents showed up, thanks to Stefanos. The kid might have some problems relating to people and other issues, but somehow he can sense when trouble or danger is near. He saved his brothers and his own life the last time they ever saw their disaster of a mother. She was drunk and high, wanting the boys to go with her to the store, if I remember the story straight. Kon told her straight out "no way" and Thanos just hung out with his older brother. Stefanos is my emotional one. He hates when people fight, but he knew he couldn't get in a car with her in that condition so he called his papou, which is granddad in English.

That one little action by my middle son started the process of the breakup and dissolution of my marriage. He saw what she, to this day, refuses to see. When I got here, she and her drug-dealing boyfriend were already in security for causing a scene. I guess Mindy insisted that she was Konstantin's mother and demanded to see him. The charge nurse knew our history and told her take a seat, as Konstantin was having some tests done. She didn't want to hear anything and started to actually bully her way in. That's when Brenda, our charge nurse—who's been a nurse for over thirty years—put Mindy in her place and called security. That's when the drug dealer, Scott, tried to step up. In seconds it was over. As the security guards were leading the two to their office, Brenda walked over to Mindy and told her she'd never see any of my three boys as long as she was breathing and working at this hospital. Mindy shot back in public, with witnesses, that an easy fix was to make sure Brenda stopped breathing. When I arrived, Brenda was filling out a complaint that was going to land my ex-wife in jail, yet again. I don't have any feelings either way, as long as she stays away from the boys.

When I walk into this entire fucking mess and I enter the guards' office, Scott, the drug dealer, tries to get up and approach me, but Jamie, the guard, told him not to move, sit his ass down, and shut up. Mindy glares at me the entire time but doesn't say a word until I turn to leave.

"Think you're so almighty, don't you, Atlas? Well, this isn't over, and when the day comes that you realize the boys are lost to you forever, then you'll remember how you've treated me over the years. You're a one-hundred-percent Greek jagoff with a tiny dick. I should know, lived with that puny shit for years. Have you ever wondered why I left? Well, now you know."

Laughing, I turn to face her but first give a look toward the guards, who hit a button. I'm going to be pushing her buttons, so here goes, she opened the door.

"Wait, Mindy, do you mean the 'tiny dick' that gagged you every time, or the 'puny shit' that you couldn't take without K-Y Jelly? Come on, grow up. We tried and it didn't work. Let it go, because I'm sure you're so happy with Scott and his huge junk. Makes me wonder why you are even here. You have no rights over the boys, so take a minute and try to make the last two brain cells work. You signed away your rights over two and a half years ago. Now I have to check on my son. Enjoy jail, both of you."

I walk out to both of them screaming and cussing, until the one guard slams the door. Then it is muffled the farther I walk from that office. By the time I find the room my son is in and open the door, I'm shocked to see the crowd in there. Enforcer is going on for some reason about taking me down. Right, I know he runs with a badass one-percent club but, damn, I'm no bookworm. Then when he turns, I'm glad I didn't take what I heard as negative because he greets me like an old friend. Behind him is his woman, Taz, and finally, on Konstantin's bed, is my feisty woman. *Well, what the fuck is that thought?* I think before I push it down. I'm here first and foremost for my son. I make my way to the bed as Enforcer and two other women say they'll be back and walk out the door, leaving just the four of us here. I lean over, giving Rebel a kiss on the cheek and a squeeze on her hip. When she jolts and Taz, along with Konstantin, laughs, I feel the pressure suddenly leave my body. I plop into the chair next to the bed and then do the twenty-something questions to my son. I'm so confused as to why his pump never alerted him. Thank God it turned out the way it did.

"Hey, where are Stefanos and Thanos? You did pick them up, right, Rebel?"

She looks at me for a moment then at Taz and back at me. I can see her friend is trying not to laugh out loud.

"Uh, duh, Atlas, yeah, I picked up your boys. I think Stefanos called your parents because they were waiting for us when we arrived. Nice people, by the way. They are in the lobby with the boys and said to tell you when it's good to make their way up, let them know. Taz and I can go now that you are here."

When Rebel goes to get up, Konstantin grabs her arm, keeping her next to him.

"Do you have to go, Rebel? Could you stay for a little bit longer? Taz, if you have to go, I totally get it with the kids and all. I appreciate you even coming to see me, though I know it was to see her."

Taz looks at me on the bed, Konstantin still holding my arm, then to Atlas. When she smiles hugely, I know trouble is coming. Then she reaches in her pocket, pulling out a crystal. *Oh, not now, come on, Raquel,* I think to myself. She steps closer to the bed, pulling Konstantin's other hand out, placing the stone in his hand. He's looking at it, trying to figure out what it is. Taz fills him in, as usual.

"Konstantin, that is a clear crystal. They call this the 'master crystal' and it's known to help with healing. Keep it on you at all times or if not on your person, in your presence. It might seem weird, but I truly believe in crystal healing. And I'm not just here for Rebel, I was worried about you too. Get used to it, you're family now, kiddo, and have plenty more aunts and uncles. You've only met maybe one third of our club. Now, I'll leave you three to be, and I'm going to find my ol' man. Need to make sure he's not getting into any trouble. I'll be seeing you, Kon. Do you mind Kon?"

Looking to be in some kind of shock, Konstantin

just shakes his head. Taz leans down and places a kiss on his cheek, which has him blushing. She places her hand on his cheek, giving it a squeeze, then turns and walks away.

When she's gone, I'm still sitting behind Rebel so I lean in, putting my elbows on her thighs to get closer to my son.

"Son, you okay? I know today has sucked big time, but you're okay and safe. Now talk to me."

"Dad, why do you say today sucked? I don't think so at all. Yeah, we gotta figure out why this stupid pump isn't working right. Besides that, not including you, Papou, and Yia-yia, no one has ever gone the extra mile for me. If Rebel hadn't shown up with Heartbreaker, I think this would have ended a lot different. Not to mention all those women from the motorcycle club, who dropped everything to check on me. Well, me and Heartbreaker. I'm just overwhelmed with emotions, Dad, and don't know how to process them."

Then he bursts into tears. I go to move but Rebel stands and we literally come together. Placing her back on the bed, I sit directly in front of her, grabbing my son in my arms and rocking him slightly. Poor Kon, he's overwhelmed and his body is trying to come back from his sugars being so low. To top it off, my son's filled with unknown emotions that his tired, stressed-out brain won't let him process them. Rebel leans into me, I'm guessing to give Kon a squeeze. I reach a hand behind my back and grab her calf. The three of us are connected when my son lifts his head and tells me, "Love you."

I look into his eyes that look like I'm looking in a mirror and mouth back, "Love you too, Son."

* * *

It's late, everyone is beyond exhausted. The club's cook had sent over boxes of food earlier for everyone and apologized for not being able to come up to visit. She included an entire sugar-free pie just for Rebel and the boys. That got Kon's eyes sparkling and, swear to God, seeing him excited for a piece of pie has my heart shatter. Now it's after visiting hours are over and my parents took Thanos and Stefanos home with them. Rebel's club sisters have all left as well, and Heartbreaker was released just a bit ago to go home, from what Enforcer told me. Taz told us both that if we need anything to give her a call. Rebel told her some shit about calling a busy person. I could tell Rebel felt something when Enforcer was saying his goodbyes and told both Kon and me, when everything calms the fuck down, that we should get together for breakfast. Both of us agreed.

Now it's like déjà vu as we finally say our goodbyes to Kon and I'm walking her out. The hospital is eerily quiet, but I know we're safe. When I told Rebel what my ex-wife and drug-dealing boyfriend did, she called Tink and asked for a favor. So there are two guards outside of my son's room. Not what I expected when I saw them, but along with Rebel, I say goodnight to Yoggie—who I find out is also a sheriff's deputy—and Presley, the two men I recently met. I thank Rebel for reaching out to her prez and for the solution she came up with. The hug I give her takes both my breath and heart away.

Knowing she's not paying attention until she looks up, we are not at her car but mine. I look down to her and lay it all out.

"Jumping the gun for sure but, fuck, Mya, I don't want to be alone tonight. We don't have to do anything, just want to keep you close. Just going to say, I don't beg… ever, but tonight I will. Please come with me? The thought of getting home to it being empty, I'll never sleep. Probably spend hours in the gym, then clean up and check on Kon, before I go to my parents' to pick up the boys. Come on, Feisty, what is the worst thing that could happen?"

Knowing I had her at "I don't beg" then I did just that. This woman is breaking down walls I never thought would come down, and with such little effort. I grin then nod, which brings a massive smile to her face. I can see how extremely exhausted she is, physically and emotionally. I could never imagine how much today affected her. I'm sure she's had shit come up in the past, but not being a parent, I'm not sure she truly gets the uncontrollable fear. Though if I remember correctly, her bestie, Taz, and her boy, Teddy, along with another of the women in the club's little girl had shit go down in the grocery store, so she's been close to others who totally go manic when something goes wrong with their children.

"Let's go home, Rebel."

Oh shit, didn't mean to say it like that. Damn, she's gonna think I'm a control freak. But nope, not Rebel, she grabs my hand, swinging it up and down like a teenage girl who's crushing on a boy. I get her settled into the passenger seat of my car and then walk around to the driver's side and get in. Thank God my house isn't that far, just under what I'd say is nine or ten minutes. When we get there, I pull into the garage, turning I tell her to stay. I can tell she's fighting on telling me to go to hell, but again, this is Rebel, who's never what you think. When we walk into the house, I see her shock. Because I promised myself the boys deserved only the best home possible, I made sure it's homey with an open floorplan. Yeah, I see kid shit here and there that the boys haven't put away, but it's not only clean but tidy too. Hey, four bachelors live here, so not too shabby,

"Close that mouth, Rebel, or I'll take that as an invitation, which I know it's not. What shocked you?"

"Well, and you're right, not an invitation. The place is so warm and welcoming. And, yeah, I'm shocked at how tidy and organized it is. You must be a great dad, Atlas, the boys are lucky to have you."

I stalk toward her, never taking my eyes from hers. Instead of kissing her, I lean down and lift her up. She immediately wraps those long legs of hers around my waist, which has me kissing her 'cause I have the urge to taste her again. And, damn, can this woman kiss. Don't think there's another woman I've wanted to worship like I do her. To be frank and honest, I'm usually not a fan of French kissing. My trips to Billings usually have none of the niceties, just get down to business. But shit, to my surprise, I can't get enough of Rebel's unique taste. It mesmerizes me every time I try to pull away. In a fantasy world, I could kiss this woman all day and night.

I move into my bedroom, instead of going to the bed I made just this morning, which I know surprises her when I pass it to enter the master bathroom. I hear her soft moan when she says quietly, "Oh my God, I've died and gone to Heaven." That brings a smirk to my face as I gently place her on the counter and turn to start the tub. Reaching over, I pull a few jars and ask her lavender, rose, or musk. She tells me to put the rose and musk in and that brings a smile to my face.

"What's that smile for?" Rebel asks me shyly.

"You're perfect, Rebel. I want you to relax. I'm going to go downstairs and make some chamomile tea and some scrambled eggs. Don't argue, we need to get back to our normal routine. We'll eat then go to bed to sleep. Don't give me that look, sweetheart, we're both exhausted, and for our first time it's not gonna be a quick fuck. We'll do those too, I promise the hard and fast, but I want to take my time with you, taste you, and indulge both of our fantasies. Can't do that being so spent with the emotional overload we've both experienced today. I'll talk to my folks and once Kon is home and feeling his normal self, the boys can spend a weekend with their grandparents. You good with that, sweetheart?"

She's staring at me like she's in a trance so I wait. Fuck, it's been so damn long since I've had any interest in a singular woman. I'm in awe of this woman for some reason. When she softly says, "Yes." I tell her she's my good girl, which I see causes the flush on her face. She likes that so I put that in the folder in my head. I help her down and then kiss her button nose first, then her full as fuck lips. Not hot and heavy but just as good. Before I make a fool out of myself, I turn to walk out but swing around, intently watching her. My God, she's so stunning, even exhausted, she takes my breath away.

"Rebel, get used to this. We aren't going to play games. This is the two of us agreeing to see if this can work. You and I are adults who are entertaining a relationship. Take your time and come down when you're done."

Then I turn and walk out, closing the door. She needs time to digest what I've been trying to put out there. Now I need to make us some eggs, then get

Rebel into my bed before jumping in the shower. There I can take care of this beast between my legs 'cause I'll never be able to sleep next to her smokin' body with this problem swinging between my thighs. Yeah, for some reason I've reverted into a horny teenager with his first girl. What the fuck am I doing? *Only time will tell if it's a good or bad thing,* is my last thought before I put on the kettle and start cracking some eggs.

NINE
'REBEL'

MYA

Watching the door close after Atlas walked out, I'm stunned and kind of out of it as I remove my clothes, step into the bath, and as soon as I take a whiff, I get why he smiled. The rose smells like me, but the musk is definitely all Atlas. Together the scent is the mixture of both of us together. A thought pops into my head. *I don't know why she left, but his ex-wife is fucking crazy to let this man and those boys go. Her loss is definitely my gain. And I'm not crazy or stupid.* Then I lay my head back and let the water and scents do their job of relaxing me, when it suddenly hits me. Besides Taz and my club sisters, no one, and I mean no one, has ever taken care of me like he's doing. My God, it should be him in this tub trying to wash off this day. But nope, Atlas is one of those men who will always put those he cares about first. Not saying he's madly in love but it's pretty obvious something is starting between the two of us. One thing we have to keep at the forefront is it's not only the two of us, there are three boys who are also involved. I promise myself at this moment, in his tub, no matter how much I want this—and I do—if it starts to hurt any of the boys, I'll walk. No matter how much it kills.

With my head back, I close my eyes and do what my bestie is always preaching. I try to do, shit, can't remember what Taz calls them, but I try to relax and take deep breaths. I feel my body start to decompress and I kind of drift into a very comfortable zone between wakefulness and sleep. I don't hear the soft knocking on the door or see the door opening with Atlas sticking his head in. The next thing I know, I'm smelling something fruity, like apples, with an outdoor scent like fresh-cut grass. Slowly opening my eyes, I see a steaming mug in front of me. I continue my venture, tilting my head and, yeah, there is Atlas with a cup of what smells like chamomile tea for me. I softly smile, leaning forward. I reach for the mug and take a drink. Aww.

"Wow, this is perfect, Atlas. Thank you."

"My mom gets it from one of those New Age places, but I have to agree with you, it's perfect. Okay, take another sip then let's get you out of this tub, the water's cooling off. Don't want ya to get sick."

I giggle, for Christ's sake, he's a doctor. That's an old wives' tale. He grabs my mug and holds out a huge towel. Oh no, not happening. I've not shaved or groomed my "girlie garden" in quite a while, as there was no need. Not how I want him to see all of me the first time.

"Nope, not happening. Put the towel on that stool thingy and get out. I'll be down in a minute or two. Scoot."

He tilts his head in that way he does when he's, I'm guessing, analyzing the situation. I've seen him do the exact thing with the boys, so I wait. In this aspect we are different, and I don't want to change that about him. He nods, places the towel down, and walks out, closing the door behind him. I waste no time getting to my knees then standing up awkwardly. Reaching for the towel, I wrap myself up and step out of the tub. Going to the sink, I grab the toothpaste and put a little on my finger to freshen up my mouth. I had put my hair in a messy bun so I leave it and open the door, walking into Atlas's bedroom. Man, for a guy, it's so nice and clean. I wonder if he has a cleaning lady. Looking around, I see on the corner of the made bed is a sweatshirt and shorts. I grab the top first and pull it on. I can't believe how big it is because I'm not a tiny girl by any means. His shorts actually almost fit. I mean, he has that V-shape with huge shoulders narrowing down to that tight waist and hips. Love the smell of his clothes, they smell so fresh.

Going back in the bathroom, I rinse his tub, put the towel on the hook, and grab my chamomile tea and head down. When I turn toward where I think the kitchen would be, my nose picks up on some tantalizing scents. So the doctor can cook too. I wonder what he can't do. Making my way into the kitchen, I see two plates on the counter filled with eggs, fruit, and toast, with a few different kinds of jelly in front of the plates, and finally a huge container of ketchup. That makes me want to fall in love with him. My club sisters give me so much shit for putting ketchup on my scrambled eggs.

"Hey, if you don't use ketchup, no worries. All my boys do and I've even come to like it, to my surprise. Sit down. Let me get some more hot tea. Hand me your cup."

As I watch him, it hits me how comfortable he is in the kitchen. Guess that happens with raising three kids on his own. When he picks up a mini strainer and pours the tea through it, I laugh. Of course, why would Atlas use a simple tea bag.

"Come on, cut me some slack, sweetheart. You know it tastes so much better than the crap you buy at the grocery store. Now let's eat before it gets cold."

And that is exactly what we do. I devour my food like I've been starved for a week. It's so good and crap, it's only eggs, fruit, and some toast with jelly. What totally blows me away is, at my age, he's the first man to cook me breakfast or dinner or anything. The few men I've been with since turning twenty-one have been losers, each and every one. Taz is right, I shoot for that level of men because that's what I think I deserve. Atlas is tilting my center, along with my way of thinking, and for some reason I like it. Again, with him, I feel a safety that never in my life have I felt. I reach for his hand and give it a squeeze.

"Thank you, Atlas. You have no idea how much this means to me. This is our first date and I'll cherish it forever."

"Aww, Rebel, sweetheart, you have no idea what's coming your way. Now eat up, don't know about you, but I'm dead on my feet."

The conversation flows with an ease I can't believe. When we finish, I tell Atlas to go take his shower and I'll clean up. I can see he doesn't like it but he concedes this time. He's so tidy and organized that really all I have to do is put some things in the refrigerator and wipe the plates and dump them in the dishwasher. I wipe down the counters and turn the lights off. By the time I make it back to his bedroom, he's already in bed asleep. My poor baby. My head snaps back, then I let the feeling of knowing, if I want, he could be my baby. What's holding me back are the never-ending voices in my head telling me he can do better, that I'm scum, and if he finds out about my past life, he'll leave me at the curb. Actually I've only shared bits and pieces with my club sisters with Taz knowing the most but not the entire history.

As soon as I get into bed, he moves so we are spooning and I can feel he has no pajama pants on.

Oh shit. Then I feel his breath across my ear and cheek.

"Rebel, I'm a grown man who can manage his urges. I promised you our first time will be special, so relax and get some sleep, you have to be exhausted. This is one of those days that feels like it will never end. Night, sweetheart."

With that he leans up on an elbow and kisses my cheek. The last thought I have is *he's like a furnace wrapped up all around me. And I like it so much.* As I'm drifting, I wish his boys were here 'cause that would make this perfect. Maybe one day, if this works, we can be that family I've been searching for my entire life.

A horrific noise brings me out of a very deep sleep. My God, someone or something is screeching like they are being killed. I'm reaching out to see where I am and what the hell is going on so I can help the person. When I feel hands trying to hold me down, my past floods my memory and I pull back and let loose. All I hear is the sound of my fist hitting flesh until whoever is trying to put hands on me disappears. But a second later the hands are back, but this time there's a voice associated with them. I know that voice, but can't place it in my frazzled mind. It's sexy as hell, though sounds to be in some kind of pain. Is that who was screaming? Then it hits me, that's Atlas and I'm at his house. Oh shit, don't tell me one of the boys is hurt. Pushing myself up, that's when I hear a growl before, in a firm, strong male voice, the words finally penetrate my fog.

"STOP. GODDAMN IT, REBEL! Sweetheart, you are safe. Please hear my voice. It's Atlas. Breathe in and out. Come on, just listen to my words. You can do this, in... hold... then out. That's it, let's do this together in—one, two, three, four, five, then out six, seven, eight, nine, and ten. Repeat. That's my girl. Welcome back, beautiful, lie back and relax for a minute or two. I got to grab a towel before I bleed all over you and the bed. Damn, Rebel, you got some right there."

He was fading in and out 'til his last sentence. Oh no, it was Atlas I was fighting. Son of a bitch, why can't I keep my past where it belongs and not keep dragging it with me into every relationship? Not just romantic but every single interaction I have with people. I watch Atlas walk to his bathroom and, just as quickly, he returns holding a washcloth to his face with another one in his other hand. He sits next to me and starts to gently push my hair out of my face and, with a cool cloth, wipes down my face. When he shifts closer and places a gentle kiss to my lips, I lose it. I don't know if I'm crying, giggling, or snorting. What I do know is, this episode must look like I've lost my ever-lovin' mind. Doesn't seem to bother Atlas as he puts both cloths on the edge of the blanket, pulling me up, and holding me carefully like I'm a precious piece of art. When he starts to rock back and forth, my body relaxes and I just let it go. In all of my life no one has ever taken the time to just be with me. Well, that's not true, Taz has but I've never been totally honest with her. I figure if my past ever bursts into my present, she will have deniability. I'm realizing my mistake. Not telling her is leaving her vulnerable to outside sources. I can't let that happen, not with Teddy and now Mickie. Even Enforcer, they are Taz's heart. She'll break if anything happens to them.

"Sweetheart, come back to me. Hey, doubt either of us is going to be able to fall back asleep. Let's go downstairs and maybe have some tea or coffee. I've got that fancy as shit coffee maker down there; we can try to make one of those frou-frou coffee drinks. You up to it, Rebel?"

I reach for one of the cloths and wipe my eyes, face, and finally the snot from my nose. Damn it, this man is always seeing me at my worst. So why the hell is he working so hard to make this work between us? Being me, I just come out and ask the question.

"Atlas, why work so hard for this? Can't you see I'm fucked up and damaged way beyond being fixed? You and your boys deserve only the best, and that's for sure not me. Maybe we should just cut our losses and go our separate ways. Best for all of us."

I drop my head because, honestly, this is my first real attempt to let others into my life and, more importantly, my heart. Konstantin already took a small part, along with Thanos. Stefanos is a harder nut to crack, but I'm not one to quit so have been trying to come up with something to chip away at him. And then there's Atlas who, if I'm honest, is every woman's dream guy. I mean, the prospects read all those books and even went to that Texas signing, so yeah, they've drawn me in too. They aren't all the stupid boy meets girl and, snap, they live happily ever after. Some stories are truly life inspiring. Those authors are truly phenomenal in their craft. Even the one author, D.M. Earl, who happens to be writing about our club, though none of us knows who the person behind those books is. And their stories are so close to our lives it's eerily scary. I feel for whomever it is because Shadow is going to tear them apart, limb by limb.

"Hey, Rebel, not so fast, sweetheart. We all are 'fucked' up in one way or another. Not sure what happened in your life to traumatize you to this extent and, believe me, as much as I want to know, not going to push you. When and if you're ready, you'll tell me. I will say you're worth fighting for. My God, look what you've done for my boys in the little bit you've known them. Their own bitch of a mother hasn't done a tenth of what you have. I mean, seriously, she signed her rights away. Who the hell does that, and what's wrong with me? I not only dated her, I married and had kids with her. My radar's batteries not only died but leaked out that white shit too. We all have damage, sweetheart, it's how you move forward that truly matters. Now, come on, Fiesty Rebel, let's go fuck up that coffee maker my mom said, 'I just had to have.'"

I throw the washcloth to the side and grab his face, planting my lips on his in a hard, closed-mouth kiss. He holds on to me but gives me control, which I know to the depths of my soul is extremely hard for him. We kiss for who knows how long but no tongue or sexy shit. I'd probably even call it desperation kissing because at this moment, Atlas is my lifeline. A line I don't want to lose or let my baggage mess with. When he gently nibbles my bottom lip and places a kiss on the tip of my nose, I smile. For such a masculine, alpha guy, he's so gentle and caring too.

"All right, Atlas, let's go downstairs. When we break that machine, do not tell your mother it was me. I have to make a good impression on both of your parents if I'm planning on sticking around."

He jerks back for a second or two, his eyes taking in all that is me, then he snags me close, hanging on for dear life. Guess we both have those luggage bags full of past trauma. With my fingers crossed, I hope we can help each other carry them throughout our lives. Otherwise, this man is gonna wreck me.

TEN
'ATLAS'

Since that night when Rebel beat the shit out of me, while also scaring me to death, we've gotten into a rhythm. Kon came home the next day and it was determined his pump was flared, which not only pissed me off but, damn, I thought Rebel was going to lose her mind. She had her club sister, Raven, the one who is computer savvy, get in touch with the manufacturer. The next day two huge boxes arrived at the house, one with a replacement pump and supplies, but weirdly the other with a new gaming console and enough games for all my boys and age appropriate too. When I asked Rebel about it, she put her fingers to her lips because the boys were around. Later she explained that once the Devil's Handmaidens motorcycle club adopts you, then you're part of their family for life. And no one messes with the family or asks questions when gifts arrive.

Which I've gotten to see up close and personal this last week. First, the morning when I opened the door to an older couple. The man was big and the woman looked like that gramma everyone loves. When the lady asked if Rebel was here, I let them in and called her. She squealed then ran to the woman, hugging on her tightly. Then she gave the older man a long hug too. She turned to me and introduced Tank and Momma Diane, who are the parents of Tink, the president of the club. Not sure how, but they are the "parents" of Squirt too, I'm gonna need an explanation for that. Tank turned to open the door and when I looked out, there were, damn, not sure how many bikers in my driveway and out in front. The big man asked if my boys were home and I said yeah. He then shocked the shit out of me when the first two of the bikers carried up trays upon trays of what I'm guessing is food. Oh shit, I hate to do it, but don't want Kon to feel out.

"Hey, wait a second. I know you have the best of intentions, but my one boy is a type 1 diabetic and can't eat a lot of stuff. Don't want to be rude, but maybe you can take that to the hospital to share or something."

Momma Diane steps up, putting a hand on my arm.

"Son, no worries. Rebel told me that, so what's in the trays is a large salad with fixings, some grilled veggies, along with my famous lemon baked chicken.

And Cook sent along a bunch of her sugarless baked goods for your boys to try. She said to let her know which are their favorites so she can keep them on hand."

Just as she finishes, we hear a herd of buffalo coming down the stairs. First is Thanos, then Kon, and finally Stefanos. When they see Tank, Thanos stops and it's like watching the Three Stooges as Kon and Stefanos plow into each other from behind. I chuckle as does Rebel, but the older couple just stands and waits. Shit, where are my manners?

"Konstantin, Stefanos, and Thanos, these are friends of Rebel's. That is Momma Diane and the man next to her is Tank."

Leave it to my mouthy boy to say what's on his mind.

"Wow, Dad, you ain't kidding, he's more than a Tank. Oh, umm, sorry, sir. Didn't mean to be a smart-ass. I mean a smart aleck. Dad always tells me to think before I talk but as you can see, I don't. Nice to meet you both."

Kon is next and he even goes to shake Tank's hand. My oldest is growing into his own body and even with Tank being huge, Kon doesn't seem to be intimidated by him. Lastly, Stefanos just stares and as the minutes go by it starts to get uncomfortable. Then to my surprise, it's Tank, not his wife, who with a quick look my way, walks over, and crouches down to my son's level.

"Hey there, Stefanos, nice to meet you, son. Yeah, I can be scary. All my grandkids looked at me just like you just did, but eventually they figured out I'm a good grandpa. Give it time. A little birdie told me that once stuff settles down, all of you guys are going to my daughter Tink's ranch to watch movies. Maybe you guys would like to see all of her animals too."

That gets Stefanos's attention because he loves animals. I see his eyes get big and Tank doesn't miss it at all, he jumps at the chance to win my quiet son's heart.

"Stefanos, what animals do you like? Now, I mean, besides a dog or cat. Hey, do you have any pets?"

Oh shit, here we go. Just the door I didn't want opened. Stefanos has been fighting me for a while to get both a dog and a cat. Well, a puppy and a kitten because they need to grow up together. He's begged and tried even bribing me, saying he would take care of them. Out of all of my boys, I believe he'd at least try. His room is immaculate and he hates when one or the other of his brothers leaves messes around. Stefanos is the first to volunteer to help clean up the house. I just don't want to put any pressure on those tiny shoulders. Listening to Tank and Stefanos talk, and with Rebel and the other two boys carrying all the food to the kitchen, it leaves me with Momma Diane. When she reaches out her hands, gently putting them on my arms she shocks me.

"Atlas, is Stefanos on the spectrum? No, don't

get your boxers in a bunch, son. It's just all of us have watched Teddy grow up with it and I asked just so everyone will know to not push his boundaries and go gently with your boy. As you can see, my ol' man has that sight with the kids. Teddy loves his grandpa Tank and my husband adores that little boy. And no, there is no blood relationship, but will tell you, sometimes when you pick your family, it lasts forever. Have you met Teddy yet? He's Taz and Enforcer's boy? Well, Taz's son and Enforcer's boy."

I hear the growl before I get a word out and when I lift my eyes, I see Enforcer with baby Mickie on his chest in a baby sling and behind him is Taz holding a young boy's hand, who is grasping on to a young girl's hand. Where are these folks coming from? I hear steps so turn and, fuck, see Stefanos holding Tank's hand, leading him upstairs, which I assume is to show the big man his room. What universe am I in right now?

"Atlas, listen to me, son. We mean no harm. Rebel is one of ours and she seems to really like your boys and you, so take this as a 'hey, welcome to the family.' We all heard what happened to your oldest and it pissed my husband off. The principal is being brought before the board next week for her part in it. Both the Intruders and Devil's Handmaidens clubs donate a ton of money to the school system, so we expect the children to be safe. Now I'm going to help in the kitchen. Guess you're going to have a party here, if you like it or not."

She squeezes my arm then walks past me, following where Rebel and the boys went. I can hear giggling and laughter coming my way from the back of the house. When I turn, Enforcer is in front of me with, holy fuck, a bottle of Macallan whiskey. Damn, I know that shit costs a mint. When I glance up, the smirk on his face makes me chuckle.

"My ol' lady told me your ol' lady saw an almost empty bottle of this in your cabinet, so being the good brother that I am, thought I'd refill your stock. Word to the wise, Doc, don't fuck with Rebel 'cause there isn't anything I won't do for my woman. So if you hurt Rebel that will hurt my Que. You seem like a nice dude, but I've seen others who appeared nice and were the scum of the earth. Not braggin' just speaking the truth. And I'd hate to leave those three boys without any parents. You hear me, Atlas?"

After the initial shock, when I realize where he is going with this, in a way I'm pissed, but on the other hand it just goes to show how much these people care about Rebel, which she deserves. As I go to thank the man, I hear a voice that has Enforcer's face go hard and he grimaces.

"Come on, Enforcer, move your ugly ass outta the way. Want to officially meet the man who's brought our Rebel to her knees."

The sight before me has me wanting to slam the

door, then bolt it and put a chair in front of it to block out these people. Not trying to be a snob, but each one is scarier than the last. The woman squints her eyes my way as a huge, no monstrous, man behind her with long brown hair starts to laugh loudly.

"Shut the fuck up, Big Bird, or you can wait in the truck. Now move, Enforcer."

The man moves, patting me on the shoulder and whispering, "Good luck." Then he walks by. The skull face tattooed woman walks in with the brown-haired man behind her and finally bringing up the rear is a quiet standing man, his black hair braided down his back. It's his intense green eyes that seem to be reading my soul that pulls me toward him. There is an air about him that is not only peaceful but also serene. When he puts his hand out my way, I take it and shake. He doesn't try to overpower me, just shows me that yeah, he's a man. In a deep, raspy soft voice he introduces himself.

"Hello. My name is "chahóółhééł naabaahii t'áá sáhi" or in English, Dark Warrior Walking Alone. Most call me Panther. Nice to meet you, Doc."

It dawns on me I've seen him and the mountain of a man in town, and even in the hospital here and there.

"Hi, Panther, I'm Atlas, it's nice to make your acquaintance. Come on in, make yourself at home."

That's when he hands me a soft basket and when I look inside, I see some sage—I believe—a feather, along with bread, eggs, and wine. Not sure what to do with it, he must see it because he explains.

"In my culture, the sage and feather are to cleanse your home. My woman, Zoey, sorry Shadow, told me you always bring bread and eggs to eat and wine to drink, so that's why it's in there."

Shadow walks back to Panther, leaning into him. Didn't think she could ever look soft, but at the moment she looks like a woman in love. Panther smiles, eyes sparkling, when he leans into her.

"Be careful, nizhoni, you're showing your true colors to the doc here. He sees your soft side."

The softness immediately is gone and replaced by, I swear, the devil reincarnated. When those arctic, icy-blue eyes look my way, a shiver goes down my spine. Then she gives me a mocking smirk.

"Atlas, right? I'll say this once, don't fuck with Rebel. She's my sister and with that she has my protection from anything and everything. Treat her right or your loved ones will never find you, not even a piece of hair. Got me?"

"Stop it already, Shadow. For Christ's sake, don't scare the man away before I get my claws into him."

Turning, I see Rebel, but it's the looks on my boys' faces that have me worried. Thanos is hanging on to Kon, whose face is white, which is hard because we are olive skinned. It's when I look back to Rebel to see her face pasty that I follow her glance to the mountain man whose eyes are soft on her. Oh, fuck to the no. I walk over to her, pulling her tight to my side, arm around her waist, my fingers spread out—half going to her hip—the top two under her full breast. He flinches but I don't give a flying fuck. She's mine. If he let her go, that's his fault.

Panther and Shadow outright laugh. Walking past us, it leaves my two boys, Rebel, and the guy. As I try to think on how to approach him, I hear the fear in the scream from my youngest, Stefanos. Turning, he's hiding behind Tank staring at Shadow, who's grimacing. Taz's young son comes running from the kitchen, jumping toward Shadow, who catches him.

"Auntie Zoey, you're here. Wait 'til you meet Auntie Rebel's new boyfriend, he seems nice. He's got three sons. I might get a new friend. Olivia is helping Mom in the kitchen with Momma Diane."

Stefanos is watching Teddy intently and, to my surprise, he pushes his little shoulders back and steps around Tank. Now for as far back as I can remember, my boy is definitely not a people person. Besides his brothers, I can't think of anyone he calls a friend. When he walks down the stairs, I can actually see his little shoulders trembling and his hands are in his pockets. At the bottom I see Shadow slightly shift, whispering in Teddy's ear. The boy turns and sees Stefanos. He looks to his aunt, I guess he called her, and Shadow places him down. The room goes eerily quiet as every adult watches the two boys approach each other. By the time they are facing each other,

Stefanos's bottom lip is twitching. They face off about two or so feet apart.

Not knowing what's going on, Rebel comes barreling in and jerks to a stop when she sees what's in front of her eyes, which shoot to me immediately. I raise my shoulders just as Teddy raises his little hand toward Stefanos.

"Uh, hi, I'm Teddy."

When I take my eyes off my son, it hits me that Teddy isn't looking to shake hands but has a fist ready for a bump. When Stefanos sees it, he immediately grins and bumps Teddy's fist. Something transpires between them because, after the fist bump, they start chattering like they've been best friends forever. I hear Teddy talking about his new sister. To every adult's surprise, Stefanos tells his newfound friend that if his dad doesn't screw stuff up with Rebel, he might have a chance at a baby sister because he sure doesn't want any more brothers 'cause they are so sloppy. Teddy agrees and we all laugh. *Disaster adverted*, I think as Rebel makes her way to me, until her eyes catch something behind me. I turn to see the mountain of a man right behind me, his eyes on Rebel. Well, fuck it, I might as well climb that hill now. Hand out, I figure what the hell.

"Hey, don't remember meeting ya before, man. I'm Atlas Giannopoulos, you are?"

I see Panther step closer to him as Shadow moves to take his other side. What the fuck? Who is the guy and why do those two feel they have to take his back? When Rebel sidles up to me and entwines our hands together, that guy's eyes watch the two of us closely, even tilting his head. When he turns to Panther, I see the very slight shake of his head. Shadow's hand is on the guy's forearm when she leans into him. He jerks, looking down at her shocked. Then she smiles and I hear the gasps and "holy shits" around the room and out the open door. He drops his head, takes a breath, then looks up at me, face lacking any emotions.

"My name is nitsaa yikah tsintah, which means Big Walking Trees. To make it easy, everyone calls me Avalanche."

When he takes my hand, I assume he'll break it, but instead he shakes it firmly and also politely. Then he lets it go as everyone lets out a breath. Well, fuck me, guess there is more to the woman at my side than I ever assumed. We are going to have a conversation because I can't let my boys get even more attached to her if there's no chance for me. When Rebel gives Avalanche a brief hug, both look uncomfortable.

Yeah, we are definitely talking sooner rather than later.

ELEVEN
'REBEL'
MYA

Pulling my jeans up, I rub my temples because I have a headache coming on. Life has been crazy between my work with the club and also with the center. We have about fifteen new survivors in the large building from a recent circuit we busted up. It was comprised of, to our horror, a lot of younger children, like grade school age. Now that I'm part of Atlas's three boys' lives, it really hits home. If anyone ever put their filthy hands on any one of the boys, if anyone thinks Shadow is a merciless, cold-blooded killer; she will look like a kid in the park when I get done with the assholes who touch my boys. I stop, putting my bra down and sit on my bed. Wow, need to think about this because they aren't mine. They have a mother, though she's a piece of shit. Mindy and her drug-dealing boyfriend, Scott, have both been released on bail, pending their court date. When Atlas found out, Shadow went to her dad, who is Sheriff George, and he said both were let go because they have no room or, more importantly, staff for the jail. That sucks but he promised to try and keep an eye on the two of them. When Tank found out, he put two prospects on their asses. First though, he put a shout out to Atlas to make sure he was good with it, which he was. Atlas told Tank he'd do anything to protect his three boys from their biological mother. I think Tank asked some questions because Atlas shared how Mindy signed her rights away. I could hear Tank's pissed-off voice, so I walked away to give them some privacy.

Tonight is finally here. It's Friday night and Atlas is not on call, and his two sons Konstantin and Thanos are going to their grandparents. To everyone's utter shock, Stefanos quietly asked to spend the night at Teddy's. We all went out to Taz and Enforcer's house so Stefanos could be familiar with their home before the sleepover. Between the dogs and Mickie, Atlas's middle son was in Heaven. It also showed Atlas how much his son wants a dog. Stefanos was so cute with Mickie. When he hesitantly asked if he could hold her, I laughed out loud when Teddy got up, lifted Mickie from Enforcer's arms, and plopped her in Stefanos's arms. Teddy showed him how to protect her head and neck, then he sat next to Stefanos as the two boys fawned over the little girl. I literally had to reach over and close Atlas's mouth. Konstantin and Enforcer hit it off and Thanos hung with Stefanos, Teddy, and Olivia, once she got there. Glory and Yoggie were also there, which I know was my bestie's way to make Atlas comfortable.

Enforcer and I watch Atlas looking around at all of Taz's crystals and stuff, so no one says a word until Taz walks into the kitchen. Enforcer leans over to Atlas and tries to whisper, which is a joke with him.

"Atlas, I feel ya, man. I allow all the rocks everywhere because it makes Que, sorry, Taz feel good. Remember at Mickie's birth we had to lay all that shit everywhere? If you think this is a lot, you should see the rest of the house. Only place they don't go is in my garage and workshop."

Atlas gets up, moving to one of the many handmade shelving units holding Taz's collection. He picks up a huge yellow piece that I've always loved. He turns and flips it around until we hear a gasp.

"Oh no. Please, Atlas, be careful. That's a very expensive piece that I'm so proud of because it took me a long period of time to be able to afford it. Citrine is a crystal known to promote spiritual growth. It can also clean the aura by absorbing negative energies and transmitting them into a positive vibration. Citrine can also help clear and activate the chakras, if you know what those are, Atlas. The one most associated with it is the solar plexus chakra, which works with personal power and abundance. I mean, look at us, our lives are full. Well, mostly full, since my man over there thinks my rocks are a nuisance and don't mean anything. Maybe if he opened his mind, my ol' man might see the light—as they say—because he knows how much it means to me. Travis, you might like the spare crystal bedroom, it'll give you some time to reflect. Now dinner will be ready in about ten minutes."

With that she turns and I giggle. I saw her standing there and figured Enforcer would put his foot in his mouth, and he did. Seeing Atlas looking around, I bump into him.

"What's wrong?"

He looks around one more time before glancing at me.

"I'm confused, Taz is with Enforcer, right? Then who the hell is Travis?"

Beside me Enforcer, Glory, and Yoggie start to chuckle. Atlas watches them to make sure no one is laughing at him. Enforcer walks up to Atlas.

"Welcome, brother. In this family circle, everyone has at least two names. One is their given or government name, and then their club's name. I'm Travis and seems like I'm in the doghouse. Again. How long was she listening, Rebel, and why didn't you give me a sign? Thought we had a truce."

Atlas's head jerks down to me, and I know my eyes are sparkling.

"Paybacks are a bitch, Enforcer. Remember that time we were moving that one shelving unit in y'all's bedroom and that one crystal tower fell off and broke. I was able to glue it back together, and you promised not to tell Taz. We even shook on it. Well, to my surprise, three weeks later she comes into Chapel, flames shooting from her eyes with that crystal tower wrapped in a towel. She went to clean the shelf and saw a small little bit of glue. When she asked you if you broke it, what did you do, brother? Yeah, she told me how fast you threw me under that bus. So what goes around comes around."

I'm laughing and then snort. Everyone loses it, including Enforcer. The three younger kids come back in, looking from one of us to the other. Teddy then leans into Stefanos, whisper-screaming.

"Get used to this, brother. They are either screaming, laughing, or in my case, my mom and dad are kissing all the time. It's disgusting. Let's go back to my room."

From the kitchen, Taz yells for everyone to clean up and get their butts into the dining room. Teddy looks to Enforcer, who shakes his head no. The little guy's head drops, then he lifts up and tells Stefanos, Olivia, and Thanos they all need to wash their hands. Konstantin is actually in the kitchen helping Taz, so all the adults stand up and head into the dining room to continue our discussion. The night turns out to be one of the best we've had as a couple. I'm hoping tonight turns out even better. The plan is Atlas is cooking at his house then we're going to take it as it goes.

This is huge for me since I can't remember the last time, you know, I've gotten me some. Between partnering with Raven at the Handmaidens Fitness & Holistic Center and being a member of the Devil's Handmaidens club and taking on the responsibilities of S-a-A, life is busy. I've been trying when I can to help Atlas with the boys, which gives me the opportunity to get to know them individually and as a group. We've been eating quite a bit at The Wooden Spirits because Cook loves the boys, especially Konstantin. She's working on an alternate menu now so between the two of them, Cook and Konstantin, they are trying to come up with tasty meals. To add to that, I've been helping Taz with Mickie, who's not sleeping too well. Sometimes I don't know why Atlas is sticking around because between his shifts at the hospital and the volunteer time he puts in at the clinic, our time together is like the last thing on our lists. Thank God, we seem to fit though. Even his parents, Apollo and Athena, seem pleased we're giving whatever this is a chance. So now, once I'm dressed, after putting a quick call to Taz to see how things are with Mickie, I'm heading over to Atlas's for a sleepover. Or that's what smart-ass Konstantin is calling it. An adult sleepover. As much as I love that kid, he's a pain in my ass at times.

Thirty minutes later, again in my cage, I'm heading back into town and with all the excitement I'm nervous as shit. It took me quite a while to not only shave my arms, legs, under my arms, then damn, my girlie garden had gone totally wild. Could have used some electric clippers. Though, got to say, as I shift my legs and my panties rub against the garden, I can feel how smooth it is. Personally, I hate hair so I'm surprised I left it for so long. Never again. Been thinking of getting waxed, though some of my younger club sisters have had it done and it's split down the middle if it's worth it or not. I choked when Squirt told her story. She went with Heartbreaker, who goes regularly. Squirt barely made it through the pelvic area and below, but when the esthetician told her to get on all fours and spread her cheeks, Squirt started screaming so loud for Heartbreaker she caused a scene. They both got kicked out and told never to come back, which for Heartbreaker sucked since her esthetician just started to wax her bikini line. Between Dottie, Dani, Kitty, and Squirt they managed to get the wax off, but Heartbreaker was raw for a week. We all laughed like idiots, which Squirt didn't think was funny. When Heartbreaker explained the esthetician would have put some Vaseline over her back star, the look on Squirt's face was priceless.

As I'm driving, I could swear someone is following me but who and why, don't know. We broke up that one circuit a few weeks ago but the whole operation went smoothly. We got the tip from one of the girls who works at the Wooden Spirits Bar and Grill. Her sister went missing and the town was going crazy with worry. Jeanie told Heartbreaker that her sister met some guy on one of those dating apps. Raven tracked it down and found where the phone was pinging because the dumbass didn't shut his phone off, and the rest was history. Unfortunately, not before those assholes did some massive damage to Jeanie's younger sister, Alexandria. After Tink and Taz talked to her parents, she is spending some time at the ranch, talking with the therapist. Her wounds are about healed and the bruises are fading, though that's not what we worry about; it's her depressed state. So between the prospects, with Peanut and Kiwi, they are keeping a very close eye on her. The one thing the club was able to give to Alexandria was that none of those men would ever hurt another girl again. Shadow and Spirit took care of that.

When I make my way to Atlas's block, my anxiety kicks in. I've been wondering for days if I should tell Atlas about my past. I talked to Taz about it and she seemed surprised. She asked why I'm worried since I've spent nights at his house before. I explained that, yeah, we've spent a few nights together, but the boys were there and we didn't have sex. In fact, besides some very heavy petting and groping, we've done nothing. Watching her mouth drop surprised me. She asked how I managed to keep my hands off that

Greek god of mine, and I almost choked. Her hands covered her mouth as her cheeks turned bright red.

"Ummm, bestie, got something to tell me? You fantasizing about Atlas? Do I need to have a conversation with Enforcer?"

She smirks but the cat seems to have her tongue. She tells me to pull over and check my texts. Well, fuck me blue.

"What the hell is this... You've got to be fucking kidding me. You biotches have a pool to see who can guess when Atlas and I—ugh, you know—do the deed. You are all crazy."

"Know that Rebel. And don't you mean when you and Atlas... *make hot, sweaty love.* Come on, just spit it out, it won't bite you, sister."

Ignoring her, I'm trying to see who picked what. Well damn, most of my club sisters must think I'm an easy slut. A third of them think Atlas and I have already done the deed. Looking for Taz's date, I almost choke. She picked today. How the hell did she know? Right after her are Squirt, Dottie, and of course, Shadow. Tink picked a week from now and Glory gives me another two weeks. Raven shocks me; she picked a month from now. Well, I can't tell if I'm pissed or just surprised. Who I don't see are Wildcat, Heartbreaker, and Dutchess. She must be reading my mind over my cell phone.

"The three saints said they weren't playing because it's none of their business. Whatever, it's all in fun. Now get your fine ass over there and have fun, so pleased do the deed before midnight or I lose."

My bestie keeps rattling on when I see something that has me telling Taz to call Sheriff George and get deputies to Atlas's now. Then I hang up and reach under my passenger seat, pulling out my travel gun box. I put my finger on the biometric fingerprint sensor and open it, grabbing my Sig Sauer P365-XMACRO. I also grab two extra magazines and quietly get out of my car. So much for the hair and makeup thing. Damn, it's looking like Atlas and I will never be able to take our relationship to the next step.

Making my way around the front to the backyard of Atlas's, I see Scott with a can of gasoline under his arm and a bag of shit in the other. He's not even paying attention to what he's doing. *Dumbass,* I think to myself as I hear the siren a second before he does. By the time he turns around, my arms are out, I've taken a stance, and scream out for him to drop to the ground. He drops the gasoline can and the bag and turns to run, not realizing Atlas is right behind him. I watch in amazement as Atlas pulls back, and when he connects with Scott's face, the punch literally lifts Scott off the ground and then he lands on his back, out cold. When my eyes make their way up Atlas's shirtless body, I'm shocked as always at how ripped he is. I mean, no disrespect. *He's a physician of the girlie gardens. And a father of three, when does he work out?* I'm thinking to myself as he stalks, yeah, stalks toward me.

"What do you think you're doing, sweetheart? Why didn't you call and tell me this jagbag was up to something. You put yourself into unnecessary danger. Damn it, Rebel, fuck, what if he hurt you? Don't you get it, you're part of me and my boys' lives? We can't have anything happen to you. You'll learn tonight, I'm gonna paddle that fine ass."

I take a step then another backward, plowing into someone who lets out a grunt.

"Well shit, Rebel, could warn a man. Damn, woman, you've got some muscle on you, don't ya? Anyway, tell me what we got."

Turning, I see Yoggie and another deputy standing, their guns out. I put mine in the back of my jeans and start to explain what happened as Scott starts to come to. The other deputy walks past us, flips him over, and slaps the cuffs on him. Atlas walks over, throwing an arm around my shoulders, eyes roaming all over my face. He likes what he sees as he snarls my way. I watch Yoggie lift his head, look at me then Atlas, and he screams at his partner.

"Theo, get his ass in the squad, let's go. These folks have plans, don't need our asses here. Need you both to come into the station tomorrow to give a statement. Enjoy your evening."

Then he slowly smiles and I finally get what Glory loves about this man. Damn, yeah, he's younger but with that smile, who cares? When Atlas's hand squeezes my shoulder, I look up to see his eyes squinting at me then Yoggie.

"Rule two has absolutely no wiggle room, sweetheart, you don't fantasize about another man, and especially not in front of me. You'll get five more for that. Let's go."

He literally starts to push me toward his house until I put the brakes on.

"Hey, stop it, Atlas. Hang on a minute, I'm not into that shit. I said stop."

Using all my weight and trying to stop, he moves me like I weigh ten pounds. Oh, no way, I turn and use my training, trying to twist out of his hold, but to my bewilderment, again, it doesn't even make him miss a step. When I resort to the only thing I can think of, biting him, he bends and puts his shoulders in my belly and lifts me up. Son of a bitch. I give up, for now, as some of his neighbors are out. Atlas waves saying hi and that everything is okay, that we caught an intruder. They are all smiling, laughing, and even clapping. Well, fuck me, can't catch a damn break. All I want to do is get out of here and hide at home. How he knows my thoughts, don't know, but then Atlas cracks my ass.

"Knock it off, Rebel, you are home. Better accept it, woman."

I feel myself as I soak my panties and my nipples harden in the cups of my bra. I'm literally panting when he cracks my ass again. Yeah, it burns, but damn does it feel good. What is happening to me? *How is he doing this shit to me?* I think as he walks us into his house.

We are so involved with each other, neither of us sees the person sitting in the car out front, watching our every move.

TWELVE
'REBEL'

MYA

Opening my eyes, it takes seconds before I comprehend that I'm in Atlas's bed. *Last night started out so good,* I think to myself. Problem was, neither of us was truly ready. Even though my girlie garden was singing "Hallelujah," we had shit to talk about, and I went out of my comfort zone when Atlas asked if he could restrain me. Wow, did I see a different side of Dr. Atlas Giannopoulos. He takes alpha to the next level. But he hurt my feelings thinking I'd ever put the boys at risk. It all worked out in the end after we talked. Then me being me when I'm emotional, I eat. So we went downstairs and had some chamomile tea with leftover Greek chicken and roasted potato wedges his mom made for the boys when Atlas was at the hospital delivering triplets, and I was helping out at the ranch. This new bunch of people we took from the last circuit are really in need of lots of help.

The demented shit those assholes did to those poor women and children makes me want to dig them up and kill them again. There's one little kid, a boy about Stefanos's age. He breaks my heart every time I see him. Hasn't said a word but others have told the two therapists who work with the survivors, he was severely abused. One of the older women managed to get the story out before she died from the infection that had been spreading throughout her body. In Mildred's words, she said two of the men especially liked the younger boy. With tears running down her face, she said at night she could hear Bobby's cries of pain and him begging them to stop. We made sure she wasn't alone and it was Kiwi and Dani who were with her when she passed. No one in her family ever looked for her and Glory thinks she might have been sold by them. Even though she was old, there are deviants all over the world. She was supposed to be moved to her new owner, but when she became ill, the people holding her couldn't make the exchange as the new buyer didn't want to infest his existing herd. This was what Mildred said they told her. My stomach aches just thinking about it. I've been trying to manage my time so that each day, or every other one, I can sit with Bobby and try to break through. What surprised me most was that Tink also was spending a ton of time with Bobby. Her and Noodles both. I have a feeling about those two but am waiting to see if I'm right.

Shaking my head, I try to relax lying next to Atlas but, as usual, once my brain wakes up, I'm ready to rock and roll. As I go to get up, two strong arms pull me back down and, before I know it, Atlas is spooning me with that rock-hard body. I feel every muscle and ridge and all his definition. I mean, he works out at the center's gym, as I've seen how all those soccer moms ogle him. Then he goes to the hospital and all the nurses drool as he walks by. Before I can stop it, I ask what's been bugging me.

"Morning, Atlas. Why me?"

I feel his body go stiff before the hand lying on my belly starts to move in circles across my tummy. The rhythmic motion lulls me to relax and just enjoy being in his arms. I'm almost on the verge of falling back to sleep when he answers me.

"I don't know how you women put up with it. Not being vain, sweetheart, I see it when I look in the mirror. Yeah, I've been blessed with I guess you'd call it good looks. Problem is, that's not all I have to offer. I'm smart, funny, and try every day to be a good human being. Though lately, before we got together, I felt like all the women I would meet just wanted a quick hookup with the hot doctor. No, don't laugh, I'm serious. I've had female patients hit on me of all ages. One mother of a patient of mine had been chasing me from the first appointment she brought her daughter to. I delivered her grandbaby, after a very difficult delivery where I managed somehow to save not only the baby but also the mother too. To show her appreciation the older woman offered to "take care of me." Needless to say, I was shocked and played dumb. She had been dropping more and more suggestive hints about her ability to satisfy her younger lover. That's when she said if I wanted, she would like to perform oral on me at the very least. When I asked her what the fuck was wrong with her, she looked stunned. She told me men have been doing it for years, why was it so wrong for a woman to do it? Her daughter heard what she said and apologized to me, saying her mom had been acting strange lately, chasing after any guy who would talk to her. I told her to get her mom checked out. You, on the other hand, Rebel, never once gave any indication that you had the hots for me or were looking for a hookup. In fact, I thought you didn't care for me at all. You made it difficult and an increasingly hard chase, which every man loves, Rebel. Besides being stunningly beautiful, you are a successful business owner, a humanitarian—along with your club sisters—you've got a sharp tongue, and most importantly, you made this, whatever we are calling it, something I wanted so I had to work for it. You ensnared me and, sweetheart, you don't see me trying to get out, now do you?"

When he starts to nibble on my earlobe, it sends shivers down my body as my nipples instantly harden. With his hips pressed close to my ass, I can feel how ready he is to move forward, but everything he's doing is for me. Atlas can feel me relaxing into him so he steps up his actions, one hand moving to my breasts, the other shifting down my belly. My legs are shifting back and forth as I feel the slick wetness in my girlie garden. Last night, I shed my final drape —so to speak—and Atlas not only had me stay but this morning he's making me feel wanted and loved, which is all I ever wanted. Yeah, sex can be good, but if there are no feelings it's just an act. This right here is filled with so many feelings which, in fact, is turning me on so much, I shift, then turn to face Atlas. The look on his face and in his eyes takes my breath away.

"Atlas, make love to me. Please, I need to feel you deep in me. I want you to make me yours. Own me."

Thank God I used the right words, I think to myself as I watch the instant transformation of his face. That alpha dominant takes over and, before I know it, I'm naked, with my hands holding on to the pipe in the headboard, which Atlas told me not to let go of, or he will stop whatever he's doing. And he means it when he is paying homage to my breasts, I tore my hands off to hold his head against the nipple he's sucking and biting, and he instantly stops, looking up, and raising his eyebrow. I immediately return both hands above my head, wrapping them around the pipes. I almost lose my mind as he makes his way down my body, not missing an inch of skin. When he finally gets to my girlie garden, I can't take it and raise up to meet him, which he chuckles at. His warm breath on my bundle of nerves shoots my hips off the bed and right into his face. He never says a single word that I literally shoved my girlie garden in his face. He lapped, licked, and sucked to his heart's content. When he added first one digit then another, my head is shaking from side to side. Then he bent a finger inside me at such an angle that when he pressed down, I flew. Never in my life have I felt like this. My muscles are finally releasing as I continue to orgasm after orgasm. I watch as he pulls his fingers out of me slowly, and deliberately sucks my juices off of his fingers, never taking his eyes from me.

He reaches for the nightstand, removing a condom. Back on his knees, he tears open the wrapper then puts the condom on before he starts to jack himself off, looking at my body from my head to the junction between my legs before meeting my eyes.

"Never take those beautiful eyes from mine. If you do, I will pull out and continue to torture you with my mouth and hands. Do you understand?"

I nod but he scoffs.

"I need your words, sweetheart. Always need to hear those words. Tell me, do you understand?"

Not sure why his assertiveness and demands turn me on so much, but I tell him yes and that's when he totally rocks my world. He enters my girlie garden with steadfast determination. I feel myself stretch almost to my limit, but it's like he can read my mind because he gives me a minute, then continues his forward motion with breaks every couple of pushes. When he's finally seated, I hear the release of his breath, which tells me this is affecting him as much as it is me. Both of us are now glistening with sweat. Atlas is breathing hard and watching me but not moving. I can feel his cock in me as it thickens while pulsing with need. The heat coming from him is burning me alive, inside and out. It has me thinking, *damn, this would be a fantastic way to go.*

"Please move, Atlas."

"It's about time you tell me that, Rebel. Hang on, sweetheart, know I'm not gonna last long. Legs around my waist, put those hands on my back. Give me those lips."

I feel like he's devouring me. His hips are pistoning back and forth while, every once in a while, he shifts his hips while circling. The trunk of his cock is hitting my clit whenever he's pushed in to the max, and I can feel his warmth everywhere. *Why did I wait so long?* I think to myself. I feel it coming and when it finally hits, the noises coming from me sound like a howling wolf. He's whispering dirty little nothings in my ear, continuing to keep these feelings coming and coming. When I feel there is nothing left, he takes my clit between two of his fingers and whispers to me, "Time to fly, Rebel" Then he pinches it to the point of pain. When he releases it and starts to strongly tap it, I feel like I'm having an out-of-body experience.

Vaguely I hear his grunts as he's trying to chase his own orgasm. When he loses his rhythm and plants his hips between my legs and growls, I feel his body tense then let loose. The weight of his body crushes me but I relish it because, without him knowing it, I just gave Atlas everything. I feel my walls come crashing down around me as I lie spent in his arms.

All I can do is hope and pray he doesn't break me because I don't think I'd survive it. He is the one.

THIRTEEN
'REBEL'
MYA

The Handmaidens Fitness & Holistic Center is jumping today. Ever since Taz started her crystal and meditation side of it, people—mainly women—are coming out of the woodwork to attend. Raven is helping Taz set up a website connected to the center that will allow members to gather information and follow some of Taz's crystal information classes, meditations, and manifestations for a small monthly fee.

Looking out on the floor, I see the men's side of the gym, which brings a smile to my face. Atlas, Konstantin, Stefanos, and Thanos are working out together. With them is Enforcer and Yoggie. Since the first meet, my club and the Enforcers have brought Atlas and his boys into the fold. And with Stefanos hanging around with Teddy and Olivia, he's finally opening up. So much so that Atlas's parents have noticed and spoken to us about it. When we had movie night last weekend, between Teddy and Stefanos they have brought Bobby into their group, which I think that young boy needs badly. Whenever we have something going on at the ranch, we try to include the survivors, as it helps them acclimate into society. We leave it up to them if they want to attend or not. Bobby was so excited as he hadn't seen a movie or eaten popcorn in years, he told Kiwi.

When she brought him to the community center, he kind of got shy, but kudos to Teddy—who's come such a long way. He slowly approached Bobby with Olivia at his side and Stefanos bringing up the rear. At first, they sat at a side table sipping juice and eating snacks. Doing the rounds to make sure no one needed anything, I heard Teddy telling Bobby some of his story, which had all the kids staring at Taz's son—who held nothing back—including being shot at. From that moment on, it seemed that Bobby trusted Teddy so the whole day went off without a hitch. Well, except when Atlas, who was on duty, got the call one of his patients was in active labor, dilated to about seven. Knowing that anything can happen when a woman goes into active labor. She could continue to dilate, leading to the birth of their child, or as Atlas has told me, sometimes when women are in labor suddenly for whatever reason it just hits a wall. So not wanting to take any chances after planting a hot kiss on my lips and waving to his boys,

Atlas heads to the hospital, knowing after the movies, hot dogs, and ice cream, I'd take the boys back to his house.

Now hours later, we are at the ranch and after watching two movies, everyone is eating and just hanging around. Kids are waiting to go see all the animals. Glancing around, I see Thanos looking amazed and adoringly at Mickie. Taz is placing her tiny baby daughter into his arms, while Thanos sits in a chair, a folded up blanket on his lap for her to lie on. When she makes a sound, Thanos smiles so innocently and lovingly it makes me think how excited he would be if Atlas and I ever had kids. That has me grabbing the table as I feel dizzy.

"Hey, Rebel, you okay, sister? Too much sugar or not enough?"

Hearing Heartbreaker, I sit in the chair she pushes behind me. My God, that thought startled me. I mean, I truly care about Atlas but having his baby, well, don't think we are there yet.

A loud voice brings me out of my daze and looking around, I see Konstantin with his fists up in one of the teenage survivor's space. Both have red faces and before I know it, I'm up and running to see what's happening. When I'm closer, I hear Konstantin telling the kid to take it back. Not sure what it is, but it's got him really upset. The kid laughs, whispering shit that is going to make Konstantin's head blow off at any second. When I see a little boy zoom past me, it takes me a few seconds to realize it's Thanos. He pushes his older brother aside, makes a fist, and sucker punches the kid right in the nuts. Every man in the room gasps loudly as I push my way to Thanos, pulling him back. With my attention on the young boy, I don't see the other teenager pull back and swing. I see it when it's right in my face when his fist hits my nose. The sensation is like a bomb going off directly in front of you. All hell breaks loose as Thanos looks up, tears in his eyes. Konstantin and, I think his name is, Brian are going at it. I feel myself falling backward and, before I know it, I'm on my ass, blood flowing pretty freely from my nose. Noodles, Malcolm, Ironside, and Ash are trying to pull the teenage boys apart, but from the minute I landed on my ass to now, there are a bunch of kids in the mix, including a friend of Brian's I've seen around and a few young boys who know Teddy and Stefanos.

When I hear that familiar whistle, I've lifted my T-shirt to catch the blood pouring out of my nose. Tink, Shadow, and Glory are storming toward us. All the kids are broken apart and I can see Teddy has a cut on his cheek, Stefanos's lip is split, Konstantin is going to have at least one black eye, while Brian is spitting out a tooth.

"What in the ever-loving fu... Damn it, Goldilocks, whatcha go and smack me for?"

Every club sister smirks because besides our prez

Tink, who Shadow calls Goldilocks, no one would ever consider smacking our enforcer.

"Well, Zoey, there are kids present, no need to use that kind of language."

Leave it to a smart-ass to jump in. And that's exactly what Brian's friend does.

"Let the freak swear, for Christ's sake, like we don't hear it or do it ourselves. And where did you come from, you sweet little thing? Might be older but, damn, lookin' good enough to eat."

The smart-ass is looking at Tink and doesn't see how everyone around him takes a step back, except Noodles. He must feel the tension because when he turns, Noodles is right next to him. Tink's ol' man is a huge ex-military man, actually, he was a Navy SEAL, and usually he's a pretty mellow kind of guy. Except when anyone threatens or disrespects his woman.

"Listen here, you asshole punk, that right there is a lady, in fact, my ol' lady, so watch your damn mouth. Not sure why you're even involved, but I highly suggest next time you mind your own fuckin' business. You got it?"

By the time Noodles is done speaking, the kid is white as a ghost. That's when I see Panther and Avalanche making their way to stand behind Noodles. Oh shit, that's when I see Tank. He moves around Noodles, grabbing the kid by the ear, which has him screaming like a little baby.

"Come on, Tank, it wasn't my fault. They were

fucking with my friend, Brian, so I had to stand beside him. Isn't that what you are always telling me?"

Tank lets his ear go and grabs the kid by the shoulders, shoving the kid toward Tink.

"Colin, this is my daughter, Tink, president of the Devil's Handmaidens who invited you to her home today and you disrespected her. That guy over there, the big dude, is her ol' man. You're lucky this is a family gathering, son, because if not, I don't know what would have happened to you. Now, I told you and that troublemaker, Brian, to try and think before acting like a bunch of morons. I told your dad that since he had to do time, you could stay with the Intruders at the clubhouse. But if this is how you're gonna act, I'll ship your ass back home in the morning and then you'll go into foster care. Now, what's it going to be?"

Watching, I kind of feel bad for Colin, didn't know he was one of Tank's projects. His club has been trying to sponsor young men to show them how to become good men who can contribute to society and, more importantly, our town as it continues to grow. Tears are gathering in the kid's eyes, so everyone turns to give him some privacy. Konstantin walks over, hand out.

"Got no beef with you, Colin, just don't disrespect Rebel ever again. If I hear you do it, I'll break your jaw so it's gotta be wired. Sir, it's both of our faults, sorry to be disrespectful during this get-together. My dad is sure to punish me, but if you want me to make amends, just let me know what I need to do."

Konstantin then walks my way, offering me his two hands. When I place mine in his, he pulls me up, and gently guides me to a chair. Teddy and Thanos both have cups of ice and a towel, I think. Tank watches the interaction with a grin on his face. His eyes meet mine and he winks. I smile back. Yeah, the boys and I are a sort of unit. Atlas is going to be pissed about what happened. I'll try to talk him down from that mountain because the boys, especially Konstantin, were only trying to protect me. I pull him close to my side, which makes him smile. My God, we all look like we are coming home from war. Hearing someone clearing their throat, I glance around Teddy to see Dr. Malcolm and Ironside standing there with Declan and Amelia, Vixen and Ironside's two kids.

"Vixen called me to get my butt here to check out all of ya. Damn, Rebel, who got the jump on you? Never thought I'd see the day. After all that martial arts training, it must have been someone good."

I laugh, explaining to Malcolm what happened. Konstantin squeezes my arm and chin lifts to the left of me. Slightly turning, I see Stefanos staring at Amelia and when I turn, she's staring back with a shy smile. Oh no, too soon, I don't think I can handle this, though it's not my call. I mean, they are just kids, for Christ's sake. As Malcolm checks me out, Ironside takes his two kids along with Stefanos, Teddy, Olivia, and Bobby to see the farm animals. Teddy and Olivia are holding hands, as usual, while Bobby is on Teddy's other side. That leaves Amelia and Stefanos to walk together following them. Watching them go, my heart feels so full. Maybe the boys hanging around me is a good thing as they are making friends.

"You've got to be kidding me. My younger brother is hooking up with a young hottie and I can't even find a girl to get to know. Damn it, Rebel, what's wrong with me?"

Looking at Konstantin, I grin. My poor stud muffin is not feeling the love. As I go to answer him, I see an arm go around him, which shocks Konstantin, then my sister steps in, building up his confidence.

"Look here, Kon, it's not you. These young girls don't see what a catch you are. Let me ask, you sure you don't want a sugar momma? 'Cause to tell ya the truth, I'm half in love with you already. Make my day, gorgeous, and the world will be your oyster."

Konstantin's face is turning a pretty reddish shade as Heartbreaker, on tippy-toes, lands a kiss on his cheek. To both of our shock, Konstantin wraps Heartbreaker up in his arms. She then puts her arms around his waist. She pulls him down, whispering in his ear, which brings a smile to his face. He lets her go and starts to walk to where Enforcer is standing with Noodles and Panther. I turn to my sister, pulling her in for a hug.

"Thanks, Heartbreaker, I didn't know what to say to him. I hope to Christ he finds someone who can see him for all he is. Such a good kid."

"Yeah, maybe we should talk to Taz and she can manifest a nice girl for him. I'm willing to try anything because you're right, he's a good kid. Now let's go grab a drink after that fight, I could use something. Maybe I'll go all out today and get a Diet Dr. Pepper."

Laughing arm in arm, we make our way to where all the drinks are stored in coolers. Taking a second to look around, it finally dawns on me how lucky I am. I thank everything out there that I found the Devil's Handmaidens. They literally not only saved my life; they gave me the direction I needed. I can never repay them, though being a part of the club is a start.

FOURTEEN
'ATLAS'

My back is killing me, as I know this isn't going to turn out the way we all hope for when a baby is being born. This labor and delivery started out like any other normal one, but when Lori dilated to eight, almost nine, and the nurses were getting her ready to deliver her twins, she suddenly started to hemorrhage. They called me as I was in my office, and I immediately went to the delivery floor so I could do an exam and see what was going on. After checking her out, I know without a doubt we need to get her to surgery. Her husband isn't here yet, though I personally think he's trying to avoid it. Looking at Lori, she must see it on my face as she grabs her mom's hand.

"Lori, we need to get you to surgery to save the twins. Don't panic, just try to stay calm."

"Dr. Giannopoulos, if you have to make a choice,

save the babies. Do me a favor, please. I have a restraining order keeping my soon-to-be ex-husband away from the babies. Mom, give that paper to Dr. Giannopoulos. Thank you so much. My mom has medical power of attorney on my behalf. Do what you do best."

I nod to the transport person who, after disconnecting all the wires and monitors, pulls the bed out of the room, moving quickly to the surgical wing. I'm right behind him, hurrying so I can sanitize my hands and get into the surgical area. Lori doesn't have a lot of time and neither do those babies. Her mom is keeping up with me, along with Lori's father. I know her sisters are in the waiting area. When I get to the doors, I turn to her parents and try to leave them with some hope.

Once sanitized and gloved up, I make my way to where Lori is lying back on the bed, drapes all over and around her. Glancing at the anesthesiologist, she gives me a nod, which tells me she's gotten her epidural and that lets me know it's time to start. As I ask for a scalpel, I do what I always do before a surgical procedure. I pray that God gives me the power to save all three lives that are currently in my hands. Then I make the incision to try and get these babies out as quickly and safely as possible.

* * *

Watching as the twins, both in incubators, are taken to the neonatal intensive care unit, or as we call it the NICU, I'm beyond exhausted. Anna, one of the top OB/GYN nurses, is helping clean up the mess I made trying to save Lori. She's also spent but somehow, not sure how, I saved her and both of the babies' lives. All did not end great as I had to perform a bimanual uterine compression and massage, along with the addition of oxytocin. The bleeding finally slowed down, but we are going to need to keep a close eye on Lori. She's going up to ICU, where she can be monitored throughout the rest of the evening.

After placing my orders and making sure my staff is okay, as these types of births can take it out of a person, I clean up and make my way to my office. Opening the door I see an envelope on the floor, so I pick it up and go to my desk. Plopping down, I take a minute or two to decompress then grab my letter opener and slash the envelope open, pulling out a single piece of paper. Unfolding it, my heart stops and I can't breathe. I'm seeing double and can't even read what the cut-out letters actually say. Closing my eyes for a quick second, I then open them and read the letter, already reaching for my phone. Looking for her number, I hit Rebel's contact and wait.

"Hey, Atlas, everything okay?"

Just hearing her voice, I can feel my eyes filling up. Clearing my throat, I try to hold it together.

"Rebel, I need you and your club's help. Just got

out of surgery, came to my office, and found a handmade note telling me that whoever they are took my parents. They demand the only way I can get them back is to switch my boys for my parents. Oh God, what am I supposed to do, sweetheart?"

Not sure, but she must hear the desperation in my voice when she tells me to hang tight, she's on her way. She also told me she is planning on leaving the boys at the ranch, explaining it's the most protected and safe place for them. I agree. She reassures me she's on her way and then hangs up. I place my elbows on my desk, running my hands through my hair just as I hear a ping, informing me of a text. Unlocking my phone, I hit messages and then see the new text from an unknown number. What I see has me putting my fist in my own mouth so I don't scream and cry out loud. It's a picture of my parents. My dad is beat to shit, looks to be barely conscious, but it is my mom that has me wanting to commit murder. She only has her bra and panties on and she's lying on a dirty bed, hands above her head, cuffed to a headboard. Her legs are tied together. Then an unidentified voice tells me to make my choice. Suddenly a picture of my three boys appears on the screen before the video ends. *I'm fuckin' screwed* is the only thought that comes to mind.

Not sure how long I rub my temples. Then unexpectedly I hear boots to the floor running, so I stand, looking for a way to defend myself. I grab the large trophy I got last year for my dedication and contribution to the community center clinic. Shaking my head, I stand ready. The door bursts open and I see bikers in the doorway, down the hall, and I think more after the curve. First in is Rebel, then Heartbreaker. Motherfucker, that's when I see all three of my boys with huge red eyes and desperation across their faces, though Kon looks beyond pissed. Rebel pulls me away from my desk, putting her arms around me, right before all the boys grab onto me too. I can't stop the helplessness that surfaces as I bury my face into Rebel's neck. We stay like this until we hear a voice. Surprised, I look up to see Tink, Glory, Raven, and Shadow standing off to the left of us. Tink is the one waiting to speak.

"Sorry to intrude, Atlas, but we need to figure this crap out. Before you get pissed, Thanos, Stefanos, and Konstantin all insisted they have every right to be here as it's their grandparents in trouble." My head snaps to Rebel, who throws her hands up.

"No, I didn't tell them, Atlas. Thanos overheard and told Konstantin, who then had Wildcat call Malcolm to bring the kids back. Once Stefanos was back, Konstantin told him and all three went directly to my cage and waited for me. Now, we don't have time to argue so let's shove this to the side and get down to business. Boys, you promised, so go over there by the table, sit down and be quiet. I'm treating you like adults, don't disappoint me."

Watching my boys listen to Rebel without any arguments almost makes me smile. I see Raven move around my desk, putting down three laptops and two tablets. Tank and Enforcer push their way past everyone, with Tank pulling me close. The feel of his arms almost brings me to my knees, but got to be strong. Not sure how he knew but Tank whispers in my ear.

"Atlas, time and place, son. You have folks who have your back and nothin' wrong with a man shedding some tears, for Christ's sake. I've done it a time or twenty."

Releasing me, he gives me a small smile which I return. Hearing more noise, I look up to see Noodles, Panther, along with some of Panther's guys, and another huge guy who looks serious. Noodles walks directly to me, stranger at his side.

"Atlas, brother, got no words except we'll get your folks back. Now, this is Ollie, he runs the Blue Sky Sanctuary. He's also ex-military and so are all of the folks at the sanctuary. I see his sister is already at work."

Ollie points to Raven, giving her a nod, which she smiles at before going back to pounding on the keyboard. As Ollie explains that most, if not all, of his people are either in the waiting area, parking lot, or on their way. Then he tells that unlike the Devil's Handmaidens, who have Raven as their own technology person, they don't need such a person. I learn that Tank and the Intruders have their own IT guy too, Freak. As Ollie is talking to me, the guy I met briefly at the ranch this morning before I left storms in —hands full of laptops and cords. He pushes past Ollie with a low "Sorry" before he pushes some of my shit over and puts his computers down. Raven stands, giving Freak a quick hug, then grabs all of my stuff, picking it up and placing it on the floor in the corner. Freak pulls a chair over, asking Raven something and she shakes her head.

"Doc, we need your phone. Gotta put a tracer on it and try to get into the system so we can find the phone those texts came from."

Reaching into my pocket, I pull it out and hand it to Freak. He talks while looking at it. My attention goes back to Ollie, who is explaining what all his people can do. I nod, saying thank you, which draws his eyes to mine. Not sure what he expected but he places a hand on my shoulder, squeezing it tightly, telling me we'll get my folks back no matter what and to keep the faith. My head drops down and instantly I'm surrounded by my boys. I can see my two younger ones have been crying, while Kon looks pissed off. Wait, why does he have…I squint, he's got a black eye. Trying to find Rebel, I see she's sporting two black eyes and a broken nose. I'm afraid to ask, but I do. Kon's eyes shoot to Rebel and fuck me, I can literally see the two of them talking without any words. Rebel walks to me, putting her arms around my waist, looking up at me with those fuck-me caramel eyes of hers.

"Atlas, you have enough on your plate. It's done and I'll explain later. For now, let's concentrate on getting your folks back unharmed. 'Kay?"

Never in my life, outside of my parents, has anyone had my kids' backs. And by the way Kon is standing closely behind Rebel, it's done. Not only do I love this woman in my arms, so do my boys. Fuck, need to find my mom and dad. I nod and place a small kiss on the tip of her crooked nose as her hands squeeze my waist.

"Got something, though probably not gonna help. The texts came from a burner, so can't get a name on whose it is. Do have the ability to locate if the phone is on, which it is. From what Freak was able to figure out, this phone is somewhere near that trailer park outside of Timber-Ghost. I can't get an exact location, but for now that's what we got."

My head feels like it's in a vise. Kon sees it first then Rebel. When she mouths, "What?" I let it out, almost in a scream.

"Motherfucker, that bitch, Mindy, lives in one of those trailers with Scott. I've never been there and neither have the kids. When she was giving me shit, I think last year wanting money, she told me to meet her at the entrance of that place. My God, has she gotten so low she would hurt two older people, for what? Money? That crazy fucking whore."

I shake my head to see everyone staring at me. Well, not Rebel, she's kneeling by Stefanos and Thanos, speaking to them, explaining I'm just overwhelmed, that's why I'm swearing so much. She goes on to tell them never to use those words or else there are consequences. Tank, Tink, Enforcer, and a few people I don't know turn to leave. I grab on to Noodles to tell him I want to go along. He studies me then nods. I tell Rebel and Kon I'll be back. Before I walk out of my office, Rebel is at my side. Turning, she tells Kon he's responsible for his brothers and some of the Blue Sky Sanctuary folks will stay behind to guard and protect them. Then grabbing my hand, we both jog to my vehicle, though Rebel is driving as my hands won't stop shaking. Before we walked out, I let Brenda know what is going on and, not only are my three boys in my office, but some of the people who work at the sanctuary are there. She assures she'll keep an eye out for any trouble. Closing my eyes, I pray that nothing has happened to my mom or dad. I'll never be able to live with myself if either of my parents are beyond help.

FIFTEEN
'REBEL'
MYA

Seeing everyone pulling into an open area, I follow and immediately Atlas is yelling for me to keep going. After I put the car in park, I turn to him, totally understanding what he's feeling. I've felt it for just about every one of my sisters like Tink, Shadow, Vixen, Wildcat, Raven, and especially Taz. Taking a minute, I try to find the words.

"Atlas, I need you to calm down, please. I can't help locate your parents if you are out of control. Remember what the Devil's Handmaidens have dedicated our lives and club to. The Intruders have been on both the right and wrong side of the law. For God's sake, Yoggie is a sheriff's deputy. Ollie and his folks are ex-military, so obviously they know how to work a mission. You, handsome, are the wild card. So it's up to you, how do you want to move forward? I will tell you, as much as you want to be in charge, you don't have the skills. They lie in another direction. Remember this is about your parents not you. Please let us do what we do best."

As he's thinking, I almost shit myself when someone pounds on my window. When I turn, it's Shadow and Squirt with impatient looks on their faces. Well, fuck, can't catch a break. Rolling the window down, I give them a look and Squirt takes a step back though Shadow just stands there, hands on her hips.

"We need a minute or two. Please try to be human today, Shadow, and give me a motherfuckin' minute."

The shock on my club sisters' faces tells me I may have been a bit brutal, but we don't have time for pleasantries. Shadow nods her head then steps back as she and Squirt walk about a half a city block from the vehicle. I turn back to Atlas to see he's watching me with wet eyes. Fuck, I don't have words to make him feel better. Actually, our club usually isn't on this end, having to deal with a victim's anguish before we even start a mission. That happens when we bring back the survivors and search for family members. Grabbing Atlas's hand, pulling it to my lips, I place kisses all over his knuckles. We sit quietly for I don't know how long, while everyone gives us space. When I hear a familiar sound, both Atlas and I look up and see a drone. Knowing it's Freak's, I squeeze his hand.

"Atlas, that drone is Freak's, which means he and Raven must have found something, and he plans to use it to scope out the area. If you don't want all of these people to help you, tell me now so I can stop him from going in. If we aren't going to try and save your parents, I don't want him flying that over the area to give the kidnappers a reason to hurt or do something worse…to your folks. What's it going to be, Atlas?"

He drops his head while his shoulders start to tremble. I don't do a thing as this has to be his decision. When he raises his head, I see the answer in his eyes but wait for him to give me his words.

"Rebel, I want to handle this myself so bad, but I realize my skills aren't for this kind of stuff. Promise me you all will go in with the intention to save my mom and dad. I can't believe I'm going to say this, but I don't care what you have to do, find my parents and bring them home to me and my boys."

Releasing his hand, I lean over and place a kiss on his lips. Then I open the driver's door and get out, moving quickly to Shadow and Squirt. Knowing what I have to do, I clear my throat, getting their attention.

"First, I'm sorry for before."

Shadow puts up a hand, shaking her head. Squirt is mimicking Shadow, moving her head back and forth.

"Rebel, no need to apologize. As I was explaining to Squirt, emotions can get high so we're good. Now what's the plan? Is your ol' man good with us going in?"

As I try to explain Atlas's dilemma, my sisters both listen. When I'm done, Shadow pulls out her phone, hitting a few buttons. I hear her tell whomever she's talking with that it's a go. It's like a colony of ants when I see them all exit their vehicles and start to form groups. Feeling him behind me, I wait for it. When his arms wrap around me, pulling me close, I put my hands on top of his. He leans his head on my shoulder, not saying a word. We watch as Tink, Tank, Ollie, and Enforcer make their way to us. Tink looks at how Atlas is wrapped around me and gives me a sad little smile. Something is up with our prez, she doesn't look like her usual happy person. That thought is gonna have to wait for now.

"Raven found that about a mile or so up are some kind of pop-up buildings. Maybe some kind of hunting cabins or a few small secondary buildings that were placed there recently. From what she found out, there was a home back there but it burned down a few years ago. A few members of the family died in there. Are we flying the drone to get an idea of what we are going to face up there?"

It's Atlas that tells her yes. Tink drops her head for a second then looks at him and gives him some history.

"Atlas, I truly know how hard that decision was for you. Just know it's the right one because if we don't make an attempt to rescue your parents, you might lose them forever. Freak said that mainly those who use those kinds of off-the-grid cabins are either drug addicts, ex-cons who have nowhere else to go, or worse, the Thunder Cloud Knuckle Brotherhood have been known to use the cabins when waiting for a pickup. Before you ask, they have connections and are all over the country. They kidnap and sell people for money to support their cause. Don't go there, with the degenerates out there in the world, some do request older men and women. Don't ask, Atlas, you do not want to know. I promise, we will do everything we can to bring your parents back to you. I have one question for you. When we go up and if your parents are there and we rescue them, what do you want us to do with the kidnappers? I will tell you honestly, when we break up a circuit, generally most are taken care of so they can't ever hurt another person. Saying that, this is your decision, they are your parents so that's why I'm asking you."

I can tell he's shocked because Atlas is a doctor. He's dedicated his life to saving lives, he doesn't take them. Turning, I look up at his face, seeing the devastation. He moves back and I can tell he's not sure what to do. Knowing it's not my decision, I also know he needs some help and clarity.

"Atlas, if you want to wait until we get up there and see the situation, that's okay. That gives you time to try and make the best decision you can live with. Just remember, these people don't deserve a second chance. They've probably had numerous chances and blew each one. Tink, is it okay if Atlas waits and sees what is going on before he makes that decision?"

She nods then turns and walks to Shadow, whispering something to her. I notice that Squirt stepped away so it must have to do with Shadow being our enforcer. Son of a bitch, why can't we catch a break? I was so thankful, since I met Atlas, we've not had the usual drama of a Devil's Handmaiden sister finding love. As everyone starts to gather around us, I wait to see who's in charge. Should have known when Enforcer moves to the middle of the crowd. He looks to Atlas with an intense look on his face. Then without hesitation, Enforcer starts to tell everyone the plans. The main objective is to retrieve Apollo and Athena, first and foremost. Raven has been on the black web and, at the moment, hasn't seen any orders for an older couple or a single older male or female that leans toward retirement age. When Tink tells Enforcer it's a go, I hear Enforcer scream for Freak, who turns and, moving quickly, makes his way to the crowd. Enforcer gives him the green flag, so the Intruders' IT guy literally runs to his drone and gets busy. Enforcer turns and gives everyone the plan.

"Right now we are on pause until Freak or Raven can get more information to us. Once we have confirmation that the senior Giannopoulos's are up there, then we will break into teams and make our approach. At no time do I want anyone to shoot, unless it is a life or death situation. Remember, we are here to get Atlas's parents, first and foremost. Ollie, your snipers need to make sure they are up high enough and can have everyone's backs. They need to be our eyes, as we're walking into this situation blind. Tell them not to shoot unless, like I said before, a situation comes up and they need to save one of our lives or Apollo or Athena's lives. Anyone have any questions? Okay, we now wait until Freak tells us what he's found. Try to relax, we have no idea how long this is going to take."

I turn with the intention to comfort Atlas, but by the time I turn we are surrounded by some of the Devil's Handmaidens, along with the Intruders. Standing around Atlas are Panther, Noodles, Ironside, Malcolm, and finally Avalanche. As I walk closer, I hear Panther saying that Dallas, Chicago, and Jersey are working remotely, looking into anyone who could be responsible. They have already disregarded Atlas's parents being in any kind of trouble. Panther explains to Atlas and me that sometimes people in the dark world see a professional individual and see dollar signs. That is an incentive to try and work a scam to demand money for whatever they have of that person. In Atlas's case, it's his parents. It could have been the boys or maybe even me, Panther states. Or it could be someone who feels like Atlas offended them or let one of their family members die. Now with Atlas being an OB/GYN he speaks up, saying he has the highest survival rate in this part of Montana. Has he lost patients, of course, but they're few and far between. That doesn't help us, it just shows how good Atlas is at what he does. It also gives insight to his limits and what he manages to keep tight and in his corner. I listen as he goes through patients he could focus on that had some kind of problems with the births of their children, or if anyone lost a child and he was their doctor.

When Shadow slowly approaches both Panther and Atlas, I take in a deep breath. I pray she's not going to try and persuade my man to make a decision he's not ready to. She reaches out, very uncomfortably putting her hand on his shoulder, and what she says has everyone within earshot stop dead in their tracks.

"Atlas, this is probably going to be one of the hardest things you ever have to do in your life. First, your boys are safe, those guarding them would die to protect them. Now listen to me very carefully. Our club has gone through quite a few of these kinds of missions and, generally, we know how it's gonna end before we rush in. Look at me, Atlas, I don't lie or talk bullshit so I mean this. You're a healer, so I get why it's so hard for you to even try to comprehend making that final decision of taking others' lives. I'm gonna be honest and if you look at me differently, so be it. I like your boys and you make my sister Rebel happy, so I'm gonna give ya an out. If after we rescue your parents, you see anything that leads you to a decision you can't stomach, reach out to me and give me a look. That's all I need to move forward. Atlas, I don't have a sensitive heart anymore, lost it many years ago. Now I'm trying to make amends by helping my family and sisters. Don't feel bad because those who can do what those kinds of people can do aren't even normal or human. So find me and believe I'll make them suffer like they never have before. By the time I'm done with them, they will be begging me to let them die. And that's exactly what they are going to do, but not until they've experienced immense pain, which I'm very good at providing. That's all I wanted to say. Just trying to give you some peace of mind as you have a healer's soul."

Shadow doesn't look at me, just turns and with Panther grabbing her hand, they start to walk away. I know how hard that was for our club enforcer. Since she got together with Panther, she's been trying really hard to be more than what she's been, a badass, no emotion, soulless enforcer who could and will kill without thought. I've seen how far she's come. When Avalanche reaches out for her, she actually lets him. The two men are her sentinels against everything out in the world that looks down on her. Knowing what I have to do, I give Atlas a squeeze then quickly make my way to her.

Literally pushing under Avalanche's arm, I grab my sister close and squeeze her tight. When I feel her arms hesitantly wrap around my body, without words I let her know how much what she just did means to me. I can feel eyes on us, but thank God for Avalanche and Panther, as they form a barrier around us from prying eyes. We stay close until I hear Freak and Raven screaming they have something.

Shadow lifts her head, looking at me with those arctic-blue eyes and what I see in them is the fine line she walks every single day of her life. I nod and together we make our way to find out what we have to do next.

SIXTEEN
'ATLAS'

Shocked at what just happened, I can feel all the way to my soul Shadow never shows that side of herself. When Rebel let me go and moved to her sister, that confirmed my thoughts. Watching them, it finally dawns on me how much these women are taking on with each "mission" they go on. Lives and death are on the line. No, they might not be like me as far as being a doctor who has sworn to save lives. What they are doing is much more important and their dedication is given without any reservations.

When I hear the screaming, my head moves to the sound. I see Freak with some sort of controller in his hands and Raven with a tablet and laptop on top of a truck gate. Seeing everyone moving quickly in their direction I follow, pushing my way to the front. As I make my way, I feel pats on my back and shoulder, as well as squeezes on my arm. I'm humbled by their support as I barely know these people, When I'm front and center, Enforcer steps to one side and Noodles with Tink on another. As Freak starts explaining what they have found, Raven is passing her tablet to Enforcer, who holds it up for me to see. I'm not sure what I'm supposed to see until Raven comes over, pointing at red blobs, indicating warmer heat imaging all over the said area. I know before Raven even says it that each red area is a human being. My God, I can't even count how many are there. When Enforcer steps forward, I try my damnedest to listen to him at the same time try to send up a prayer to the powers that be to protect my mom and dad. I can't even think about something happening to them and then having to go back and tell my boys their yia-yia and papou have been injured or, oh God, worse. So lost in my thoughts, I miss whatever Enforcer's plan is so I turn to Noodles, who must see it on my face as he slowly goes through what they are planning on doing. No one had any idea so many people would be involved so I see Malcolm and Yoggie grabbing huge black bags out of Yoggie's truck. I thank Noodles and head toward the two. They are looking through the bags, so I wait until they both see me.

"I know that I'm an OB/GYN, but can you use another set of hands?"

Yoggie glances at Malcolm who shrugs his shoulders. It's Yoggie though who gives me an intense stare. What he says almost knocks me to my knees.

"Atlas, we can always use more hands but need ya to think about it. One, if your parents are there, are you going to be able to process whatever we find? Two, have you ever been to war because that's what this is. These ain't normal human beings, they are the bottom feeders who use other humans for profit or worse, other sick reasons. Our world has let those with money feel like they can do whatever they want because of their wealth. I'm not trying to scare you, just want to prepare you for what might be up there. The last circuit the Devil's Handmaidens broke up even made me sick. It was all kids under, I'd say what... Malcolm, maybe fifteen? They all broke my heart, but it was the two I found in a downstairs crawl space that tore my heart in two. They were sisters maybe, I don't know, eight and ten. Anyway, both had been abused physically and their wounds were left untreated. Atlas, I literally wanted to kill those motherfuckers with my own hands. What brought me peace of mind was watching Shadow, Spirit, and don't freak out, Atlas, but Rebel also. The gore is usually Shadow and Spirit, while Dottie helps out. Because this was so big, Rebel did most of the physical beating due to her experiences in the gym and knowing where to hit and how hard. She would prepare them for Shadow or Spirit. What they did and, yeah, I watched without an ounce of pity for those pieces of shit. Little Faith and her sister, Mercy, both had to have a full hysterectomy due to their internal injuries. And to this day, no one has claimed them. They are living in the survivors' quarters out at the ranch. Both are in therapy and from what Glory has told me, are making progress, but fuck, brother, how do you live with seeing that? They were goddamn children, Atlas. So if you start to feel any compassion or sympathy, remember as a doctor you bring life into our world and those types do damage beyond repair to mainly women and children. Do you think ya can handle this shit?"

I barely hear him because after he told me about the two little girls, it dawns on me that I was the one who did their hysterectomies at the clinic. Well, they were transferred to the hospital. The damage was irreparable. I couldn't believe someone would do that to a child. Knowing this, I feel my heart hardening and I look both men in their eyes.

"Yeah, Yoggie, I can do it. Thanks for telling me that, as I was the one who did the hysterectomies on those young girls. Didn't know the whole story, though now I do. I'm good if you two can use me. I won't let you down, you have my word."

Malcolm and Yoggie share a look, but it's Malcolm who comes to me.

"Brother, shit, so sorry, didn't realize you handled Faith's and Mercy's situation. I get it, being a physician, we take an oath to do whatever we can to save lives. I truly believed in that until I came to Montana and my eyes were opened by what the Devil's Handmaidens and Intruders do. There has to be consequences for assholes' actions and, unfortunately, our government's hands are tied. I try to make sense out of it by believing what we do is save others from experiencing the depraved actions of a few. Brother, if you ever need to talk, just reach out."

Hearing Enforcer calling for everyone to gather, he starts splitting everyone into groups of five or six. I'm with Rebel, Heartbreaker, and a few men from the Blue Sky Sanctuary: Phantom, Grey, and a kid named Jeffries. A woman named Josey is pissed she's been told to stay back and be ready to help with any injured. I don't know much about the sanctuary, except they help ex-military find their way back into society, mainly with animal therapy. So they pair a damaged person with an abused or a wild animal that has been injured by humans. From what I've heard from Rebel, it's working quite well, so who am I to judge.

I'm watching as all five are organizing their weapons and to say I'm shocked is beyond words. Rebel is carrying what looks to be a nine millimeter, along with two hunting knives. Also she has two grenades—yeah, can't believe it—that go in a pouch around her waist. Finally, she has a, I think and I'm right, when Phantom asks to see the Steyr AUG SA USA Rifle. No hesitation, Rebel tells him this is the rifle of choice for their club and every vehicle has one in a case, in their trunk. All of the women in the Devil's Handmaidens are trained to shoot with their handgun of choice and that rifle she is holding in her hands. Fuck, how did it not penetrate exactly what their club did? I mean, yeah, I know they rescue people who have been kidnapped and are being sold into human trafficking, but that's where my brain stopped. I was so proud of what she and her sisters were doing. Forgot to think further on how they rescue, as they call them, "survivors," who have no one else trying to get them back home because a lot of the agencies have corrupt cops, agents, congressmen, etc. who are getting paid to turn the other way. When my eyes meet Rebel's, I see the hesitation in them. This is the first time we've come to this kind of an impasse, and I can see she's worried about how I'm going to react. Little does she know that I'm beyond grateful there are people to help me try to find my parents. Walking straight to her, I grab her cheeks, tilt her head, and plunder her mouth, regardless of who sees. My desperation is so apparent and her fear comes to the surface. Together we build each other up. As I get a quick taste of her once I release her lips, I lean down and whisper to her, letting Rebel know how much I love her. Hearing her gasp, she holds on tightly, telling me she loves me too. Together, wrapped in each other's arms, we take a moment or two, knowing the next thirty minutes to an hour could change our lives forever.

* * *

Phantom is in the lead, followed by Heartbreaker with Grey, then Rebel and me with Jeffries bringing up the rear. Phantom instructs us to follow in his footprints and no talking unless necessary. We all have comms in our ears and when I look on both sides of us, there are groups making their way up to the property in the woods. I'm trying to keep my mind clear and to expect the unexpected, as Grey instructed me to do. The man has nerves that never falter. Damn, I'm a doctor and perform surgeries and I can feel my hands and body trembling. He's stellar, well, all of my group are it seems, except me. Keeping to the footprints Phantom is leaving behind, I almost plow into Grey when the man leading puts a hand in the air. Glancing around, the two groups to my left are splitting up and the one on my right is going forward. *Why did we stop,* I think to myself? Grey turns around like I said it out loud and he heard me. Tapping his comm he looks right at me.

"Phantom found a booby trap, which means the area has been wired to blow. He wanted to warn us to stop before he moves forward to check out a path that will be safe. Give him a minute or two, he's a great tracker and has been involved in many missions that had roadside bombs and booby traps."

When he puts his fingers to his mouth, I don't say a thing, though I have a million and one questions. I refuse to risk all of these people's lives, who have decided to help me find my parents. When I look up, I'm shocked to see Rebel following Phantom, gun at the ready. Why the fuck is she going and not Grey or Jeffries? As I go to ask, I see Heartbreaker making her way around Grey to me. She shakes her head then looks around, pulling me toward her. As small as she is, damn, Heartbreaker is strong.

"Atlas, she's trained so let her do what she does best. They'll both be back in a few minutes."

I nod and she doesn't leave my side. Just as I see Rebel's red hair, all hell breaks loose up ahead. All I hear is screaming, yelling, and crying, along with gunfire. I look to Heartbreaker, who sees my face, screams "Shit," and takes my hand, and together we head up to the front line. As we come to the first half-assed put up cabin, I can't believe my eyes. I blink numerous times but the scene is the same. There are bodies all over, I can't tell if they are alive or dead with more running out of each building. Some look fine while others look like dead people walking—clothes ripped to shreds, bruises all over their bodies. Some have bite marks on their skin while others are moving around like dead women and children walking. The kids are tearing my heart out until I hear a voice screaming my name loudly. Heartbreaker, still holding my hand, takes off like a gazelle toward the screaming. We reach an outbuilding off the regular path and when I see both Yoggie and Malcolm, I know it's my parents. Panther comes out motioning for the two men to go in. Avalanche comes directly to me, grabbing my shoulders.

"It ain't good, brother, but they are both breathing. Prepare and if you think you can handle it, get your ass in there and help to try and save them. Go."

With Heartbreaker at my side, I walk through the doorway and stagger, trying to stay standing. Rebel's sister goes to stand behind me to give me some support as I take in the scene before me. My dad is stripped down to his boxers and it looks like someone whipped almost every inch of his body. Both eyes are black and blue, while his lip is split open. His hands both look like his fingers have been broken. When he tries to see me, I say his name and his head falls forward. That's when I make my eyes move to my mom. At that moment, I totally get why Rebel and her sisters do what they do. Looks like Mom is unconscious and I can see Yoggie trying to start an IV as Malcolm is checking her stats. One of them threw a blanket over my mother's naked body, which I'm beyond thankful for. The mattress she is lying on is filthy with what looks to be dried and fresh blood. I can see streaks on her legs and, oh my God, looks to be bite marks on her neck going downward. Moving closer, I take a knee, grabbing her hand.

"Mom, I'm here. Hey, you're going to be okay. Can you hear me, Mom? Squeeze my hand, please. Dad is okay, going to be sore for a while, but seems to be okay."

Nothing for a few seconds then a very weak squeeze. That's when Rebel bursts through the doorway. Without thought, I watch as she moves toward my mom, taking everything in before she's on her knees. Still tongue-tied, my woman immediately starts to talk to my mom.

"Athena, it's Rebel. Hey, come on, we need you to stay with us. Atlas is here too. Listen to my voice. You're okay, and these people will never hurt another soul again, that I can promise. Now I need you to tell me what hurts so these three doctors can help you."

Watching Rebel, even though this situation is dire, seeing the way she is makes me love her even more. She's wiping the hair off my mom's face and I can see the bruises. These sons of bitches, why do this to them? They've never hurt a soul. When I hear my mom's voice, it brings me to my knees. Everyone stops as she tries to talk.

"Rebel, oh my God. I don't want Apollo and Atlas to see me like this. Please, promise me they won't know what happened. I'm so embarrassed."

"Athena, you have nothing to be embarrassed about and your husband and son adore you, like your grandchildren do. Please tell me what's hurting and if you have any allergies. We need to treat you so then you can be moved for transport."

"Rebel, something is wrong with my legs. I can't feel them. I was kicked in my lower back by the men who had boots on. I think my one wrist is broken and I've lost three teeth. My ears are ringing and between my legs hurts badly. I don't know what they used but whatever was shoved inside of me. Also, oh God... they violated me in the back too. I feel so dirty."

That's when I look down and slowly move the blanket up. I can see a pool of blood under my mom so I yell to Malcolm, who shifts so I can't see anything. When he starts to yell for supplies, I grab one of the black bags going through it, throwing items to Malcolm as he calls for them. Mom is very pale, lips looking a bit blue. For some reason I can't think what to do when Shadow walks in, takes one look, and moves to the end of the bed. She tells Yoggie to help her as she moves to open my mom's legs. I can't look when I hear their gasps, but what shocks me is when Shadow starts asking for gauze. Glancing toward her, I see her shoving her sleeves up. When she grabs the gauze, opening it, then layering it; I figure it out that she's going to try and pack my mom. Rebel moves close to her sister and together they start the process to pack my mom to try and staunch the bleeding. I grab Mom's hand and lean in to whisper in her ear, letting her know how good she's doing. My dad is calling for her and Mom smiles at his voice, right before Yoggie screams that she's flatlining. I see Malcolm grab a defibrillator and suddenly the walls start to spin. The thought of losing my mom takes my breath away, and the last thing I hear is a loud roar as the room goes dark.

SEVENTEEN
'YOGGIE'
SEBASTIAN

I can't believe the scene. The cabin we found Atlas's parents in is a disaster. We finally stabilized his dad, but he refuses to move or leave until Athena is with him. When she flatlined, I thought she was gone, but my military training kicked in. Between Malcolm and me, we were able to bring her back after she was hit twice with the defibrillator. She's in really bad shape. Malcolm and I did our best, so all we can do is pray she gets to the hospital in time. Apollo has a better chance to recover as his injuries are all on the surface, though saying that, he's going to be in excruciating pain during his healing. Some of those whip marks are so deep he's going to need both internal and external stitches.

Thank God, Avalanche was walking in when Atlas lost it and passed out. The mountain of a man not only caught him but threw Atlas over his shoulder, taking him outside so he could get some air. Avalanche yelled for help and Dottie came to check on Atlas. What people don't understand about the Devil's Handmaidens is, the ones who were tortured themselves also have knowledge on how to help a person, especially Shadow and Spirit. I've watched them revive people time and time again.

Feeling arms around my waist, I look down to see my Bae looking up at me with smudges of dirt and probably blood all over her face. I bend toward my black medical bag, grabbing some wet wipes, then carefully wipe my ol' lady's face. Her eyes are closed, all her trust in me. When I'm done, I place a soft feather-like kiss on her lips then pull her in for a much-needed hug. If I'd have lost Atlas's mom that would have killed me. It's hard enough when you lose someone and you don't know their family but, shit, Atlas and his family are now a part of ours because Rebel is part of my Bae's family.

"Boo, we got to move. Shadow and Spirit have quite a few assholes they want to take back to the ranch. They refuse to remove them from the earth until they hear it from Atlas that's what he wants. Sheriff George has been kept out of this, so please don't say anything. Tink sent Squirt to grab the huge van for transport. So don't do anything, as we don't know if we are gonna wipe this place off the earth or leave it for the deputies to search. The prospects are digging holes though for the dead. We need you and

Malcolm, when you can, to check over the victims. My God, Boo, it's a repeat of the last circuit. The victims are mainly young kids under the age of like fifteen, maybe sixteen. Atlas's parents, with a handful of women, are among the few adults."

I listen to my Bae as she lets out all of the emotions she has to, because this kind of shit will definitely fuck with your head if you let it. I mean, to this day, I still have occasional nightmares from when I was in the service. My Bae or as she is known by her club sisters, Glory, her daughter, and granddaughter have changed my life, all for the better. As we walk toward where the doors are open with victims all over. My eyes can't believe what I'm seeing. She wasn't lying, as it is almost all children with a few teenagers. The damage done to them is visible and heartbreaking. Wait a fuckin' minute, I know that kid. He's been beat to shit, trying to sit but has to lean to one side or another. I walk directly to him and when his two swollen black and bruised eyes look up, I see the utter devastation. I scrunch down, slowly putting my hand on his arm. That breaks him as he starts to cry. Taking a seat next to him, I pull him close and can tell he's pretty severely injured. Up close I can see the damage right in front of my eyes.

"Colin, brother, what happened? How did you get involved with this shit? Come on, let it out."

Before he can even start, I see Avalanche coming our way. I shake my head and mouth for him to get

Tank. He nods, turns, and goes to look for my brother and the man I respect wholly. As I wait, I just sit next to the kid and give him time to figure out what he wants to share.

"Yoggie, it was Brian. Oh my God, how was I so wrong about him? Tank was right. I disrespected not only him but his daughter and Konstantin's dad's girlfriend. I don't know what to do 'cause Tank will toss my ass into the street now, and I have no one or nowhere to go. My dad is in prison so I'm on my own as you know that's why Tank is helping me. Son of a bitch, I'm such a fuckin' idiot."

Trying to console Colin, he starts to have a panic attack so I help him to catch his breath. I breathe with him until he's calm again. Then he starts to share his story and I'm shocked. I can't believe it after everything I've seen and done,

"After that barbecue where Brian and I were called out in front of everyone, he was beyond pissed, Yoggie. He was saying all kinds of bullshit and I just thought he was angry. I think it was like two, no three, days ago, he came by the clubhouse, telling me he needed my help. I told him I needed to let Tank know first. He called me a pussy and other shit. So without telling anyone where I was going, I got into a car with him, not knowing what he needed or any information on what I was getting into. Big-ass mistake, Yoggie. He brought me straight here. When I got out, I could feel the energy and it scared me.

When I told Brian that I forgot shit I had to do, he laughed. I could have sworn his face changed as he was chuckling. Two or three dudes came out of that big building and asked if I was their new piece of meat. I started to back away, figuring if I had to try and get away I could just run into the woods and find someone to help me. It was then, I think, it was a van or big SUV came barreling down the road. I saw them drag those two older people out and that's when I knew Brian brought me here for devious means. When that older woman looked at me, fuck, Yoggie, I didn't know what to do. I tried to tell those guys they were innocent but two of them came right to me and started to kick my ass. The older couple told them to leave me alone, and the assholes who brought them up here just kept pushing them into that hut thing over there. I will never forget the sounds coming out of there. Probably about an hour into it, the 'boss' told Brian we needed to get our asses in there, we were up. By this time, I could barely walk, so when my 'supposed friend' grabbed my arm dragging me in there, I didn't say a word as didn't want to get beat on any more.

"When we walked in, I lost my breakfast. The man was beat to shit and whipped. But it was the woman who had my attention. One of the bastards was just getting off of her and when he stood up, he peed on her. She was out of it, thank God. The 'boss,' I think they called him Randy, told Brian he was up to bat then I was next. Brian immediately dropped his jeans, walked up to the woman, and raped her savagely. Then he flipped her and you know. When he was done, he tossed her on her back, pulled his jeans up, and walked to me. 'You're up, Colin. Sorry to say, not as tight as some of those kids but you'll still get off. Come on, don't be shy, we all have the same shit.' I looked him in the eyes and spit at him. Then I cursed him out.

"What the fuck is wrong with you, dude? You raped someone's mother and grandmother. Jesus Christ, Brian, there's no way I'm going to abuse someone like that. What do you think I am? You asshole, I'm not a monster. No, I refuse to do that."

"Yoggie, he looked at me like he was demented. I heard someone step in behind me as the other guys in there started to make their way to me. That's when I knew what the plan was all along. When the guy behind me grabbed me, the others rushed me, getting on the bed next to the woman. They actually pushed her to the edge of the bed like she was a piece of furniture. I could have sworn that a bone cracked when one of them grabbed and shoved her. They each took a turn at me, but it was Brian who went first. I tried so hard not to scream, Yoggie, but—my God—the pain. As one of the last ones was pounding into me, I opened my eyes to see the older woman staring at me, tears on her face. She reached over and grabbed my hand and, from that moment on, I never looked away and never yelled out or screamed in pain. When they were done, all of them left and I lay there. Not sure how, but the woman reached down and grabbed the filthy blanket up and over the two of us. I felt disgusting and I'm sure she did too, but all she kept doing was calling her husband's name: Apollo. As her voice got quieter, I realized she was very pale. Trying not to hurt her, I pulled her as close to me as possible to try and keep her warm. Then I passed out. When I came to, I was here where you found me, with my pants back up. That's all I remember. Dude just let me die, I not only deserve to, it's what I want. I'm not a man any more."

Knowing this is a pinnacle moment in this kid's mental health, I give him what I can to try and ease his mind.

"Colin, dude...fuck, sorry you had to go through that. And no, Tank won't kick your ass out, obviously, you don't know him that well. He won't kick you when you're down. Now that older woman, her name is Athena, and because of you she has a chance. Keeping her warm, letting her lean on you, is one thing that will help pull her through. Now, let me get you some help, you need to get to the hospital. No, kid, don't want to hear it. Good, here comes Tank."

"No, Yoggie, don't tell him. Please don't, he'll think I'm a no good asshole who's weak. I don't want him to know what they did to me."

"Colin, he'll know as soon as he takes a look at ya.

Don't judge him because he's got more heart than anyone I know."

I watch as Tank and Enforcer, along with Avalanche, make their way to us. It's Avalanche who notices first then both Tank and Enforcer. Tank tells the two men to hang back as he walks toward us. He meets my eyes and, swear to Christ, we have a full conversation without saying a word.

"Colin, now that Tank's here, I'm gonna get an EMT or paramedic to help get you down from here so you can be transported to the hospital. Hang tight."

As I walk away, Colin starts to sob and the last thing I hear is Tank telling him he's got him. That has the kid crying even harder.

EIGHTEEN
'ATLAS'

Sitting in the emergency room, waiting on word about my parents, all three boys are attached to me in some way. I know Kon is feeling like it's his fault because at the barbecue he got into a fight with Colin. That was until we saw the poor kid getting wheeled in, looking pasty and beat the hell up. Kon even got up and went to the gurney, telling Colin he's there if he should need anything. I think that's when Colin realized the older couple were Kon's grandparents 'cause he started to sob loudly. I was so proud when my son grabbed this kid's hand, telling him everything was going to be okay. Tank walked in at that moment, putting his arm around Kon and giving him a man hug. He went back with Colin when they took him to the treatment rooms.

When Enforcer walks in, I can see the emotional drain all over his face. He walks toward us, taking a seat across from us. I watch as he runs his hands through his hair. Thanos gets up and goes to the vending machine, returning with a bottle of water he passed off to Enforcer, which has him looking at Thanos. When he quietly says thanks, my son comes back and sits down. I give him a few pats on the back. No one says a word; we just sit quietly as more and more people start to show up. Some of the Intruders are first, then a few of the folks from the sanctuary, who were there where they were keeping my parents. When the Devil's Handmaidens start showing up, I want to ask where Rebel is. However, I'm afraid because that means I have to make a decision on what to do with these assholes, though when I see all the kids being brought in with different levels of trauma, my heart starts to harden against them.

One of the trauma nurses comes out from the back, eyes wet, and tells the emergency room charge nurse, Brenda, she needs some air. Brenda tells her to take as much time as she needs. Letting the boys know I'm going to go talk to Brenda, I make my way to the station she's at. When she looks my way, I'm shocked to see so many emotions going across her face. When she leans in, I don't expect her to say what she does.

"Dr. Giannopoulos, those sick bastards should first be castrated then gutted and left to bleed out. That's not even close to what they deserve. Sorry for my language and unprofessional statement, but there are young girls back there being prepped to have hysterectomies because of the damage done. A couple of the older ones are going in for bowel resection surgery. Oh, I'm so sorry about your parents. Your mom is still in surgery and your dad is being stitched up under anesthesia. Both are critical because of their injuries and their age. Atlas, I'm here if you or the boys need anything. I want you to know that."

Just as I go to thank her, I hear all my boys yelling out at Rebel, who apparently has arrived. When I turn, I think to myself, *Holy Mother of God.* Walking through the automatic doors are Rebel, Tink, Raven, Shadow, and Heartbreaker. Each and every one is covered in blood, dirt, and only Christ knows what else. When Brenda sees them, she moves around the station and heads directly to them unfazed by their appearance. Yeah, guess today is the day of shocks for me, I guess. When Brenda starts talking to them it hits me this isn't the first time they've walked into the hospital like that.

"All right, we have the shower room available for y'all to clean up. Also in the lockers are the spare clothes you left here from the last time. Does anyone need to be seen by a doctor?"

I hear a lot of nos, then Tink turns looking at Shadow, who grimaces. Tink turns looking at Brenda, pointing at Shadow. Our charge nurse walks directly to the Devil's Handmaidens enforcer, asking her what's wrong.

"Brenda, it's nothing. Got poked but I'll survive, we all know I've had worse. I'm gonna shower then have to talk to Atlas. Shit, how are his folks doing?"

Anyone can see that Shadow is trying not to answer Brenda's question. That's when Raven steps up, staring at her friend, daring her to deny anything.

"Brenda, Shadow's got a slash across her upper back from the left shoulder blade to her right one. Probably is going to need stitches if not staples."

Brenda grabs Shadow's arm and starts to drag her down the hallway to a treatment room. All the women either high-five or pat Raven, who just grins. When Rebel sees me, she comes directly to me.

"Atlas, how are Apollo and Athena?"

All of her club sisters make their way to us to hear what I have to say.

"Sweetheart, just don't know. Dad is being put back together with stitches, staples, and glue. They had to put him under due to the level of his pain. They are monitoring his heart since he had a stent put in a few years back. Mom is a totally different story. Rebel, she's critical. They aren't sure if they'll have to take some of her bowels or not. I know the damage, both in the front and back, is substantial. All we can do is wait to see what happens. They just brought in a few of the kids and, holy shit, Rebel, they are in really bad shape."

She's looking up at me with such sorrow in her eyes, and I get it when she starts to explain.

"Atlas, they're the lucky ones. Wildcat and Kiwi found an open hole that had about five or six kids in there. The abuse they took before dying is beyond comprehension."

I pull her to me, filth and everything. She lays her head on my chest and lets out a huge sigh. My eyes move over each and every one of the Devil's Handmaidens present. Don't have the words, but have to try.

"Ladies, not sure how or what to say, but I'm forever in your debt. Without you and all the people you know, we would have never gotten my folks back, I'm sure of it. Not sure why they were taken and probably will never find out, I'm just glad we got them back. I don't possess your skills but if I can ever be of help, please reach out."

As I'm finishing, I hear footsteps to see the boys making their way to us. First Thanos hugs Rebel. Kon literally pulls her out of my arms, smushing her to him. When he releases her, I see Stefanos shyly move close to Rebel. She leans down, whispering he doesn't have to hug her if he doesn't want to, she gets it. That's when my middle boy literally almost jumps into her arms, catching her off guard. As I grab for Rebel, Kon pulls his brother toward him. Brenda has made her way back out and lets everyone know they are already working on Shadow. The boys and I go back and take our seats while the women head to, I'm guessing, the showers. Time keeps moving and when the women are back, the emergency room is quickly filling up. Ollie walks in his arm around Paisley, Grey and Abigale behind them. Coming up last is Squirt, Dani, Kitty, and Momma Diane, all with trays in their hands. When Momma Diane looks to Brenda, our charge nurse nods toward the conference room, which all four women walk to and in. The smells remind me that I've not eaten since early this morning. Squirt walks up to us, giving Thanos a pat on the head and Stefanos a fist bump. Looking at all of us, she tells us to go grab something to eat. When I start to tell her I'm good, my stomach takes that moment to growl loudly. We all laugh, stand, and head to the conference room. Momma Diane immediately comes to me, asking how my folks are. I explain both are being treated. She tells me if they, me, or my boys need anything, she has two motorcycle clubs available, day or night at her fingertips.

* * *

It's after everyone has eaten and some people have left because they have kids or other responsibilities to get back to. Left in the emergency room are, of course, my boys, me, and Rebel at my side, as well as Shadow, Dottie, and Heartbreaker. Tink and Noodles left about an hour ago. Watching Tink, I can tell the process is kicking her ass, going to have to make time to talk to them both. Panther, Avalanche, Dallas, and

Jersey are here, along with Enforcer, Pussy—yeah, that's his club name—Omen, and Malice. Not sure why the guys are sticking around but not going to question it. Everyone is beyond exhausted. Brenda updated me, all the kids have been admitted for observation. Seven of them were still in or almost finished having surgery. They are going to have a long recovery, physically and mentally. I heard Enforcer on the phone with Taz, telling her about each kid and their situations. Guess they will be staying at the ranch to recover. Thanos and Stefanos are leaning on each other, sleeping. Kon is pacing back and forth. I'm sitting with Rebel draped over me, neither of us saying a word. The question I want or need to ask is stuck in my throat. Looking around the room, my eyes come to Shadow, who seems to be watching my every move. I swear, sometimes, she can read my mind because she mouths, "We got them all, no worries." Panther is watching our interaction and I can see the concern on his face. I don't know how he does it. I mean, yeah, Shadow is a nice person at times, but bottom line is, she kills people. Hearing my name, I look up at Panther.

"No, you're wrong, Atlas. She doesn't kill people, my nizhoni rids the world of filth, which is a good thing. Without her, they would continue their hatred and brutality freely. Don't think it doesn't bother her because it does, but she'll never stop until that particular service of hers is no longer needed. She carries the scars to protect the innocent and abused. Remember that. Actually, she has a huge slash that will become her next scar to carry with her on this journey their club is on. Learn my friend not to judge the book by its cover."

My mouth is open because I know I didn't say any of what I was thinking aloud. Some of these people freak me the hell out, and that's saying a lot. Hearing the automatic doors opening, I'm up on my feet immediately, moving toward Dr. Uno, who is taking care of my dad.

"Atlas, looks good. I've gotten most of the open abrasions closed either with internal stitches and staples or using some glue. Your father also has three broken ribs, which you know there's nothing we can do about those injuries, just have to let them heal with some pain medications to help him manage. He's just about bruised from head to toe. We scanned his head and don't see any bleeds, but will be keeping him here for a day or so due to the stent, though no problems so far. He's still pretty out of it, but if you want to check in on him, please do. Probably will be more coherent in a couple of hours. Do you have any questions for me? Oh, I put him on some antibiotics to play it safe. You have my number if something should come up, don't care what time it is."

I thank him, as does Kon. When I turn, everyone's attention is on us. I repeat what Dr. Uno said and take a seat again. One okay, now all prayers go for my mom. I know her case and the outcome will be different than my dad's. A nurse comes by with two blankets, covering up Thanos and Stefanos. Kon thanks her as she walks by. For a second I'm stunned. My God, when did he grow up and become a man? Rebel snuggles closer, looking up at me.

"Konstantin is growing up and is going to be just like you, Atlas. I can see it clearly."

I lean down and place a gentle kiss on her lips. She hasn't told me what happened up there after I left in the ambulance. From what the guys were talking about, it got kind of messy. I won't push her for information, that's up to her if she wants to share. Avalanche walks over with coffee, which shocks me, I didn't even see him leave. Sadly smiling, he tells me —on her way home—Cook dropped them off with some sweets to keep us sugared up. When Kon hears that he sighs, until Avalanche reaches for a bag and hands it to Kon.

"Cook said this is for you and your brothers. It's her sugar-free apple pie."

Thanos's head pops up before he jumps out of his chair, leaving Stefanos to fall down on the chair next to him face-first. With his arms outstretched, Thanos is wiggling his fingers.

"Come on, Kon man, give me a piece. I'm starving."

Kon reaches in and hands a container to Thanos, who even before anyone can hand him a fork uses his fingers and starts to eat his pie. Stefanos is standing now, though still not fully awake. That's when I hear the automatic doors again. Looking that way, I see Dr. Horiss and Dr. Stokes walking out. Rebel stands, putting her hand in mine, pulling me up. I'm afraid to hear what they have to say, but know I have to. Now that the boys are awake, they fall in directly behind us. I can see the strain on both of the doctors' faces, and I say a quick prayer that Mom will recover, eventually. It's Dr. Horiss who steps forward.

"Dr. Giannopoulos, you've had a long day. Sorry for all that your family has been through. Now, about your mother. She made it through surgery, though we lost her twice. Not for long but that's not something we want to happen ever during surgery. She had internal bleeding and problems. First we were able to stop the bleeding in her…"

He looks beyond me to my boys, then his eyes shoot to me. I'm not telling my boys to sit down; this is their yia-yia. I give Dr. Horiss a nod, so he continues.

"We've gotten everything stitched in her well her lady bits."

My head shoots up and I see Dr. Horiss give me a small grin.

"We had to do a bowel resection due to tears and damage. That will require some time to heal. And yes, you know what that means though, fingers crossed, temporary. Her bruises will fade and she'll need to get a few teeth fixed. She doesn't have any broken ribs. Her wrist is severely bruised not broken, but she'll be in a brace to keep it stable. Right now, we have her sedated due to what we assume her pain level. If you want to see her that's fine, but no use sitting in there, she's not waking up anytime soon. If she improves in the next twenty-four hours, we'll start to decrease the amount of pain medication and eventually she'll be moved from intensive care to a step-down unit. Right now, the plan for her is staying here for four to five days, at least."

Nodding, I thank both doctors before they leave. Turning, I see everyone waiting for what, I have no idea.

"I'm going to check in on both of my parents, then take my boys home. I can't thank you enough for all of your support and care. Please go home and get some rest. Again, thank you."

No one moves but they all look at Shadow, who is leaning against Panther with Avalanche on her other side. All of Panther's other guys are right next to them. Shadow leans forward, gets up slowly, her shoulders slumped forward, and makes her way to me. I know what she's going to ask before she opens her mouth.

"Atlas, what do you want me to do? Some of those assholes are hurt, which I couldn't give two shits about. But if you're planning on involving my dad, ya know, Sheriff George, we'll have to have Malcolm or

Yoggie take a look at them, maybe give them some first aid. The longer we wait, if you are going down that road, the easier it is for them to get an attorney and try to get their charges dropped. Right now, they are underground, literally beneath one of our survivor areas. No worries, it's soundproof, and we keep it on the cooler side—ya know—not only to fuck with them but the keeping chilled slows their heart rate and bleeding. Any ideas what you want to do?"

"Kill them all and get rid of the remains."

That's what I hear from behind me and when I turn, it's Kon who's said it, though both Thanos and Stefanos are nodding furiously. Fuck, I don't want them involved.

"Boys, go over by Enforcer and wait for me. Please."

The younger ones go muttering under their breaths. Kon doesn't move. I raise an eyebrow. He does it back to me. Son of a bitch, he's so much like me it's eerie.

"Kon, I don't want you involved in this, now please go plop your ass on a chair and wait for me."

Before he can start to argue, Heartbreaker walks to his side, gets up on her tippy-toes, whispering in his ear. His face gets pale and his eyes are bouncing between me and Shadow. Finally, Heartbreaker grabs his hand and walks him to where his brothers are sitting. I look to Rebel, who shrugs her shoulders. Turning to Shadow, I take a deep breath.

"Can you put them on ice until tomorrow, Shadow? I can't think right now and, obviously, don't want my boys to know my decision. If they need medical attention, let me know and I can come out and give Malcolm and Yoggie a hand."

Shadow looks at me then nods, turns, and walks back to Panther, who brings her close. I go to Brenda, ask where my folks are, and then I tell everyone I'm going to see my parents. In the elevator I feel the stress and uncertainty rush through me. As the doors open, my head starts to pound. Walking to the nurses' station, they all know me from my many years on staff. Georgine, one of our older nurses, makes her way to me to give me a hug. Then she starts to walk down the hallway.

"Dr. Giannopoulos, we have one of those extra-large rooms so we put your parents together. I hope you don't mind. After all those years, I'm sure they won't. We hope it will bring some comfort to them. They are both being monitored so we see everything at the station. Your mom has to be up here, your dad could have probably gone to a step-down unit, but Dr. Horiss said keep them together. Now prepare yourself—and, yeah, I know—you're a doctor, but it's different when it's your family. A lot of what you see will disappear eventually. Ready?"

I take a deep breath, let it out, then nod. Georgine pushes the not quite closed door all the way open and walks in quietly. I struggle to take the first step but once I push myself to take one, by the time I realize it, I'm right behind Georgine. My eyes first fall on my dad, who's been placed on his side with wedges, preventing him from lying on his back. He looks ashy under all the bruising to me, but that's normal when you have such severe injuries. I look to the monitor and his blood pressure, oxygen saturation, and pulse all look good. Next my eyes move to my mom, and my God. She doesn't even look like herself. Where Dad is bruised, Mom is swollen. Her eyes are shut but for a slit, her nose looks like it's been reset, and there a fingerprint bruises on her neck. What the fuck did they do to her? I feel like I can't breathe when a bag is placed in front of me. Grabbing it, I start to take slow breaths when I hear Georgine tell whoever gave me the bag that they can't be up here. When that person steps into the light and I see who it is, I thought the nurse would freak, but instead she squeals kind of.

"Shadow, it's been a minute. Where have you been, girl? I told you to make sure and stop by. You can stay. I have to get back, got to check on my other patient. Dr. Giannopoulos, I only have your parents and one other patient, so I'll be in here quite frequently. I'll leave you to visit. Again, so sorry this happened to them. Call me if you want to check up on them anytime."

I watch her leave then my eyes go back to my mom. My God, how is she going to get through this and move forward? And Dad, he'll never be able to live with it.

"They are stronger than you know, Atlas. They've survived the worst and those three boys give them purpose and something to move on for. I think once they are able to leave here, you should think about letting them come out to the ranch for a while. I'll check with Goldilocks, but I'm pretty sure we have open cabins."

Knowing she's talking about Tink, I nod. She's on a roll.

"They will both need therapy, physically, emotionally, and mentally. Your mom will need more than your dad. We have all of that at the ranch, so give it some thought. I'll leave you be."

"Wait. How did you know I needed someone up here? I didn't even ask Rebel to come, and shit, how did you get up here?"

Shadow chuckles softly then squeezes my arm. When I look at her face, her arctic-blue eyes are shining.

"Atlas, you need to realize that I'm better to have as a friend than an enemy. And I've been where you're at with my dad and my sisters in the club. We all were a fuckin' mess when Tank had his heart attack, so yeah, I feel ya. Now, I need my ol' man to get my ass home so I can collapse and process everything that happened today and what I saw done to all those innocents. I'll be back at the ranch tomorrow, probably around noon or so. We can talk then. Take care, Atlas, keep an eye on your boys. They are gonna need you more than ever."

With that, she lets my arm go and walks to the door where, shit, Panther and Avalanche are waiting. They give me chin lifts then all three are gone in a blink of an eye. Shit, I must be tired as one minute they were there, the next, not so much. I turn back to my folks and throw up a prayer that they start the healing process and are back to whatever their new normal will be. I lean down, placing a kiss on Dad's forehead then I go to Mom, where I leave a kiss on her cheek. Then I make my way back downstairs, pick up my boys and Rebel, and we head home.

NINETEEN
'ATLAS'

The drive home turned into a clusterfuck. It was Thanos who lost his shit first, out of nowhere. First, I heard the sniffs, then Kon telling his youngest brother everything was going to be okay. Wrong thing to say because Thanos said that his yia-yia and papou might die and he told Kon to shut up, which was a first. Then he started to weep, which instantly had Stefanos joining him. Before I could do anything, Rebel unbuckled her seat belt and literally jumped from the front to the middle seats, kneeling between the two captain chairs, grabbing both boys the best she could. I couldn't hear what she was saying but whatever it was seemed to be calming them down. When we pulled into the garage and I shut off the car, I heard Rebel tell the boys to go in with me. I didn't get it until I saw Kon in the last row hunched over, shoulders shaking. Fuck!

By the time I get my two youngest boys cleaned up and ready for bed, I know Kon and Rebel are in the family room, both holding bottles of... what the hell? I wipe my eyes and look again. Oh, I should have known they are drinking bottles of root beer. When I glance at Rebel, she's smirking at me.

"How did you know Dad would think you were letting me drink a real beer? Holy Christ, you're good. I was waiting for you, Dad, before I went up to bed. If you hear anything on Yia-yia or Papou, please wake me up? 'Kay, night, guys."

Then to my utter surprise, my oldest walks right into me, hugging me tightly, which I return back. This lasts for quite a bit of time before he pulls back, and yeah, this is going to take some time for each of my sons to process. I do what I need to and let Kon know he isn't alone.

"Konstantin, you have no blame in what happened. No, listen to me, Son. If and when you need to talk about this, or not talk about it, and grab a root beer or beef sandwich with extra peppers or take a drive, I'm your guy. I love you very much, Son."

His eyes get wet and he gives me a quick hug, then almost runs upstairs to his room. Seeing Rebel, I know without her, my parents would have been lost to us all. The Devil's Handmaidens saved our family and I'll never forget it. She's giving me time but I don't need any more.

"Mya 'Rebel' Mikowlowski, I'm in love with you

and need to tell you. Today taught me that tomorrow is never guaranteed, so I'm not waiting any longer."

She's watching me with a small grin on her face. I think she's shocked, which is a first, because usually nothing I say has this reaction. Moving to her, I kneel in front of her, putting my head on her lap. My arms are on either side of her hips, and when she starts to run her fingers through my hair, I finally relax and breathe. Neither of us says anything and before I know it, I can feel it rushing up on me, and the events of the day hit me in the chest. I start to ramble on, my heart racing, thoughts flying through my mind.

"My God, Rebel, how are they going to come back from this? Especially my mom, what they did, I could kill them with my bare hands. She might end up with a bag for the rest of her life. And I know my dad, he's going to feel it's his fault because he couldn't protect her. What happens if this makes them break up because they can't stand to be together any longer? And my boys, this is going to put scars on their souls."

Rebel stops massaging my scalp and softly asks me a very important question.

"What about you, Atlas? Who's going to worry about you, making sure you recover and this doesn't drop you to your knees, no pun intended?"

That's when it starts, I have no control on how quiet or loud I am. Before I know it, I'm being surrounded by all three of my boys. Between them and Rebel, I'm being smothered by their hugs and it's just what I need. I'm on emotion overload so their love settles my heart and soul. I know Mom and Dad are in the best of hands. Not sure how many of the degenerates Shadow and the club have, but those they don't have are dead, which means they will never hurt anyone again. It takes me a while to be able to feel kind of in control. I'm on my ass, leaning against the couch between Rebel's legs, with Kon on one side, Stefanos on the other, with Thanos between my legs. Without words we stay like this for a long time. Then slowly we start to break apart, and the boys say goodnight and head back to bed. Rebel shifts and stands up, putting her hands in front of me so I grab them, and she helps me off the floor. Together we walk up to our bedroom. Yeah, ours, that's what it is. Rebel walks me to the shower, telling me to take as long as I need, she was going to make sure everything is closed up and then she'll set the alarm. When she leaves, I strip, turn the shower on, and walk in. As the water flows down my body, my hands hit the tiled wall, my head drops, and I just stand here. I'm cried out and my body is spent. Guess I'm just taking a minute or five.

I'm so out of it, I literally jump when hands start to wash my back and ass, then go down each leg. When Rebel turns me, she resoaps her hands and starts at my neck, down my chest, past my stomach. Her hands wrap around my cock gently, and she starts to wash my length then my balls before she washes each leg and foot. She rinses her hands and grabs my shampoo, telling me to bend over. When I do, her hands start to wash my hair and massage my scalp. I've never been pampered like this by a woman. Fuck, when I was married it was all about Mindy and my trips to Billings weren't about this, they were about hard fucking and getting off. When Rebel is done, she tells me to rinse off. Once I'm done, she tells me to use the towel she heated in the dryer and to go to bed, she'll be right behind me, she just needs to rinse off the day. I offer to return the favor and wash her, but she tells me that I'm the one who needs special care tonight.

I get out and when I grab the towel, it's still warm. Drying off and then wrapping it around my waist, I make my way into the bedroom to see the bed turned down and a bottle of water on each nightstand. The television is on and the lights are on low. How did I ever survive without Rebel? If this had happened and I didn't have her, I'm afraid I might have not survived, even knowing I should fight at least for my boys. I get into bed, sitting up against the headboard. Grabbing my water, I drink a third of the bottle then put it down, lean my head back, and close my eyes. Next thing I know, Rebel's getting into bed and instantly is snuggling up against my side, her hand on my stomach. Her hair is wet and I don't care. Pulling her as close as possible, we lie in each other's arms. I've never felt like this in my entire life, it's almost like I'm watching myself from above, almost like a mixture between being underwater or in a fog. And even though I've been a doctor for years, I'm lost as to what I should do to get rid of this feeling. Then it dawns on me. I need Rebel. Leaning down, I kiss her, then, with my finger, lift her chin up, placing a kiss on her lips, which she returns.

"Sweetheart, I need you. Need to feel you and your heat surrounding me. I want to make love to you nice and slow so we can both feel every sensation. I just need you, Rebel. I know you're sore, I promise not to hurt you."

Without a word, she lies on her back carefully, then sits up slowly, removing my T-shirt. Then she lies back, looking at me with the most beautiful caramel eyes as she says softly to me, never looking away.

"Atlas, make love to me. I want to feel how hard and soft your cock feels against my skin. I want your mouth on me and your arms around me. I want to love you."

And that is what we do together. We taste, lick, suck, nibble, and touch each other everywhere. There is nowhere we don't touch. When I finally slowly enter Rebel, I can't move for a minute because the feeling is so beyond intense. When Rebel squeezes her internal muscles, I lose it and start to move in and out, first slowly then faster as I hear her moans. When she starts calling my name, I change my pace again until we are both covered in a sheen of sweat. Feeling that sensation moving through my body and knowing I want her to orgasm before me, my hand goes between us and my finger finds her bundle of nerves. I push down on it, then with another finger, I squeeze then pinch. I feel her body tighten for a quick second as she starts to keen, then her muscles relax and she floods my hand, but I don't let up. Plunging deep then pulling out slowly has her orgasm keep going until she finally begs me to remove my fingers. When I do, she lies back with a huge smile on her face as she wraps me up with her arms and legs around me. Now it's about me and that is what my singular goal is. And it takes me a whole one, two, three, and on my fourth thrust I feel everything grow as my balls draw upward. It's like I'm on fire; at the same time it feels like there's a cool storm following close by. As I fill Rebel, my toes curl as my back bows. Letting out a long growl, I drop onto Rebel, who continues to hang on to me, never letting me go. When I'm finally able to breathe, my body is relaxed and my mind seems clear. Placing kisses all over her face, she continues to smile at me. This day was a living hell and somehow she managed to make it okay. No, not okay, but bearable.

"Atlas, hey, look at me. Say it again."

"What?"

"You know, what you told me before. Please say it again."

"I love you, Rebel."

"And I love you back, Atlas Giannopoulos.

We settle together, neither willing to let the other go to clean up. When I think about it, I asked if I hurt her and she says no, not any more than it would hurt if we hadn't made love. Rebel falls asleep and as I hear her breathing, I listen to her, trying to plan the rest of our lives. And somehow my thoughts allow me to fall asleep beside the woman who brought love back to me and my boys.

TWENTY
'REBEL'
MYA

Suddenly waking up, I'm laying in bed with Atlas's heat surrounding me. Then I hear it again and I'm not sure what it is, so I carefully get up, throw on his T-shirt —which fits me like a dress—and then grab my panties. Once I'm decent, I make my way downstairs to see a faint light in the family room. Slowly I walk toward the light and the noise is getting louder. What I see has me quickly moving to Stefanos, getting down and grabbing him without thinking. His forehead is bleeding from banging his head against the wall in the corner. Immediately he starts to fight me, not saying a word. I never knew a kid his size could be so strong. When his fist slams into my bruised ribs, I let out a "Holy shit" and let him go, which has him scrimmaging across the floor. The look on his face is a cross of me being nuts or him wanting to keep pounding on me. I'm trying to find a way to sit here and not feel like my ribs are trying to come out of my side. I'm breathing and gasping, trying to figure out how he could manage to hurt me when hours before Atlas and I made love and I didn't feel this kind of pain, though he was careful. Looking back to where Stefanos was, I see something moving. Looking up, Stefanos is close to me.

"Rebel, did I hurt you?"

Not sure how to answer him, I try to think of anything I might know about the spectrum. When Taz and Teddy first came to us, he was untouchable. It took years for him to get used to all of us. Taking a chance, I look at Stefanos and give him the truth.

"No, buddy, you didn't hurt me, this happened earlier today."

"Was that when you helped to find my yia-yia and papou? If you and your friends didn't help, would they have gotten away? Please don't treat me like a baby and tell me the truth."

"Yeah, the Devil's Handmaidens along with Tank's club, The Intruders, with some others were able to locate where you grandparents were being kept. Finding them, we also found all those kids. And, Stefano, I can't tell you whether they would have gotten out or not. The good thing is, they did and are being treated at the hospital. The best thing you can do for your grandparents is to be there for them because they are going to need you. Help them recover however you can. Now, kiddo, I have a question. Why were you banging your head against the wall? Kiddo, there's nothing you can tell me that will make me not be here for you. I hope you know how much your dad and brothers love you."

Shaking his head, he goes to bang his little hands against the floor, but stops.

"I'm sick and tired of everyone treating me with kid gloves. I'm not a dang kid and I deserve to be treated like what I am almost a preteen for Christ's sake."

Knowing something is eating him up, I just sit and wait. I can see his wheels turning, but after a few he sits completely on the floor, while putting his hands in his lap. His head looks like the bleeding is slowing, so I wait. I don't rush him or ask a million and one questions. As time goes by, I start to get tired but refuse to give in. I've gotten Thanos and Konstantin to let me in. Stefanos is my only holdout. I've tried not to pressure him, maybe I was wrong. I think he's gotten the wrong impression, so need to make my intentions clear.

"Hey, kiddo, look at me. Come on, give me your attention. I know it's late but we need to talk. I think I made a mistake and I owe you an apology. Trying to give you time to get used to me might not have been the right thing to do because I was already bonding with both of your brothers. I'm so sorry, Stefanos. Can you forgive me for not thinking this through? Can you cut me some slack? Remember, I don't have any kids and I'm new at all of this."

To my utter shock, Stefanos gets up on his feet and just when I think he's walking away and going back to bed, instead he walks toward me. He sits down next to me. I barely breathe, let alone move, not sure what to do. That's when it feels like the earth tilts, as slowly he moves closer until he's almost leaning into me. I say fuck it, and wrap an arm around him, pulling him close. Before I know it, he's turned toward me and has both arms around me. When I hug him back, I hear his gasp, right before his arms tighten and his head goes to my chest. After about, I don't know, five or ten minutes, I go to shift and, in a whisper, Stefanos asks quietly, "Please don't stop hugging me, it feels good." My arms lift him onto my lap and I cradle him to me, no matter how bad my ribs hurt. The house is quiet except for when the furnace turns on. The noise is luring me to sleep when I hear small snores coming from Stefanos. Just as my eyes start to droop, I hear a floorboard and immediately my eyes fly open to see an amazed Atlas looking dazed while watching us. He moves our way, scrunching down in front of me, his eyes taking both of us in. I shake my head, putting my fingers to my lips, not wanting to disturb Stefanos sleeping. Atlas reaches over, picking his son up and giving me a hand up. Together we take Stefanos back to his room and

Atlas places him on the bed, then I cover him up. Leaving his door slightly open, we go back to our bedroom. That thought stops me in my tracks until Atlas grabs my hand, pulling me into the bedroom. After he shuts the door, he roughly brings me to his chest, holding on tightly. I feel wet on my forehead and when I look up, Atlas has tears on his cheeks.

"You okay, baby?"

Shaking his head, he starts to rub his hands up and down my back.

"How did you do that, Rebel? I can't remember the last time I was able to hug on my boy. What were you doing up?"

I explain how I woke up hearing noises and the rest is history. As we talk about Stefanos and what he said or did, it's like a light bulb goes off. Stefanos needs to be in therapy at least singularly, I'm thinking maybe one for him being on the spectrum, but also for the entire family. I tell Atlas how he doesn't want to feel left out and he definitely needs interaction, physically and emotionally. He can't stop apologizing, which after the first ten times I tell him to stop. Back in bed, we cuddle, just enjoying each other's company. My mind is spinning because these boys have been exposed to shit they didn't have to, and then their grandparents, if they make it out of the hospital, are going to need a lot of help. They will all need therapy, got to speak to Atlas about this tomorrow. Right before I fall asleep, I hear him softly whisper in my ear that he's falling in love with me more and more each day.

TWENTY-ONE
'SHADOW'
ZOEY

It's been a long fuckin' night of sitting on my hands. Well, that's not exactly true, when we finally got home from the hospital—after I tried to talk to Atlas—I told my ol' man that instead of putting all of this on Atlas's head, I was going to go and take care of the problems we currently have at the ranch. He told me I wasn't and that started World War Twenty-Three. One thing I can't stand, and Panther knows it, is to be told I can't do something. When I tried to just go, out of nowhere Avalanche was guarding the door. Jersey and Chicago had the back door and the basement entrance. Dallas was following me. Usually, if anyone else was doing what these assholes were, I'd drop them in a second. I don't because I know none of these men would hurt me, but there is no way in hell I'd be able to drop any of them.

Watching those boys in the hospital, I can't get their

faces out of my mind. The anguish and hurt is bothering me. I want to make the motherfuckers pay and make it painful. But I can't because I promised the Doc that I'd wait to see what he wants to do. So here I sit at six thirty in the morning, waiting another five and a half hours before I get an answer. To make it worse, none of the guys went to bed either. They are all sitting around in our great room. Someone turned the television on, I guess for noise since no one is talking. Dallas, Jersey, and George are playing cards while Chicago is reading a book. Panther is right beside me just sitting here. Avalanche is on the floor, looks to be meditating. I'm the only one losing her mind as the clock is taking its time moving. Not able to take it any longer, I get up and go to the kitchen to make some coffee. And, of course, my guards follow behind me. Avalanche opens the refrigerator, pulling out eggs and bacon. Chicago grabs the juice while Jersey and Dallas start setting the table.

I watch these grown men trying their best to not only protect me but take care of my crabby ass. I'm not good with my words and usually do my best to never have to talk to a lot of people at the same time. But I owe my ol' man and his brothers thanks because not many others, well, besides my sisters, would give two shits what I do or don't do. Clearing my throat, no one looks my way, so I whistle to get their attention.

"I owe you all an apology, yeah, I can admit that

my bitchiness is at an all-time high. I want to try and explain why this means so much to me. First, Atlas is a good guy, who has spent his life making sure babies are born healthy. Then there's his kids, who he's raising because his ex-wife is a total whore. I mean that literally.

"You throw in his parents, not to mention all those women and children up at that camp. Who knows how many people didn't make it. We had no clue they were up there, this close to our town. Something is telling me to get rid of them and fast, and if you ask Panther, I'm a firm believer in trusting my gut. But again, I must be getting soft because I left the decision up to Atlas, a man who took an oath to save lives. So probably should just call my dad and tell him what's going on."

Panther walks my way, throwing a big arm around my shoulders.

"Nizhoni, have some faith. You are forgetting what Atlas has seen with his own eyes over the last twenty-four hours. Not to mention the brutality done to his mother and father. Lastly, his boys have been affected. The man is not dumb and must know letting them off or calling Sheriff George, there are no guarantees that they will be found guilty and sentenced. We have no clue if they were involved in this, or how wide The Thunder Cloud Knuckle Brotherhood is. They have connections everywhere, it seems. Something to remember and tell Atlas about. Keep an open mind, Zoey."

Panther gives me a kiss then walks back toward the stove and starts cooking. While I have a free minute, I make my way to the master bathroom, drop my clothes, and take a quick shower, washing my hair too. When I'm finished, I get dressed then dry my hair. Once done, I grab my kutte and go back down to get some breakfast. We are halfway through when not only my phone but both Panther's and Avalanche's ring also. Instantly grabbing my phone, I say hi and hear Atlas's voice telling me they are on their way to the hospital first, then they are going to the ranch. I tell him to let his folks know I'm—no—we're thinking about them, wishing them well. I can't tell anything by his voice, so I'm guessing Atlas is a good poker player. When I end the call I see Panther staring at me, while Avalanche is pacing back and forth. George and Dallas have taken over cooking. Both Panther and Avalanche walk me to the great room, sitting down with me. I wait, sure I'm not going to like what I hear. My ol' man is first and I'm right. Hate this.

"Zoey, that was your dad. He's trying to get into the ranch and both the Intruders and Devil's Handmaidens are blocking his entrance. Since he doesn't have a search warrant, he has no legal right to enter. From what I've been told, Noodles and Tink are on their way down."

Avalanche then moves closer to me, capturing my eyes with his.

"That was Yoggie. Your dad suspended him because he won't talk, so your dad is assuming he knows something and isn't sharing. George told Yoggie he has to choose between being a sheriff's deputy or being a member of the Intruders. From what I'm getting from Yoggie, he told your dad there is no contest. Even though he respects George as a man and sheriff, no one will ever have his loyalty like Tank. That didn't go over too well, and now Yoggie is on an unpaid two-week suspension. Just as your dad said this, Tank was driving up and the two older men got into a screaming match. Yoggie thinks you should get to the ranch before one or the other does something they won't be able to take back. He's worried because Tank and Sheriff George have been friends for so long. Sorry to add this shit on your shoulders, sister."

When he hugs me, that does it. And as usual, when emotions overwhelm me, I get mean. *Poor Big Bird*, I think as I start punching, pinching, and stomping him. To his credit, he takes it all, letting me beat it out. He grabs my hands though as I go to scratch his face.

"Come on, skull anii', don't damage the goods. You were about to break women's hearts all over Timber-Ghost. Now don't be a hater, you got your one and only, give me a chance."

Looking at his twinkling eyes and the smirk on his face, I can't help it, I chuckle and then start—yeah, me, Shadow, enforcer of the Devil's Handmaidens—to giggle. Fuck, he always knows how to bring me off the ledge. He lets me go, leans down, and puts a soft kiss on my head.

"My work here is done. Let's scarf down our breakfast and get on our way to the ranch before those two kill each other. That would be not only a horrible mess, but would affect everyone we know. Come on, Dallas, George, move it along."

As we eat our breakfast standing up around the island, my mind is split. I get my dad, Sheriff George, having a job, but he knows what we all do and always seemed okay with it. And for my "other" dad, Tank, why is he rocking the boat? When he gets in a mood, usually all hell breaks out and the only one who can bring him down is Momma Diane. Once done, we all clean up quickly then make our way to Panther's huge garage. Dallas, George, Avalanche, Panther, and myself pile into the huge SUV Big Bird just bought. Why he needs this monster with the enormous truck he bought months ago, who knows. Jersey and Chicago will be on their way in a bit, as they are taking care of the animals. The guys' wolves need to be fed, along with the studs in the barn. Panther surprised me a week ago with four mini donkeys and three mini cows. I'm in love and it's pissing me off I can't take care of them. After much discussion everyone agreed, except me, to give them the far southern stalls so they are away from the crazy as fuck Arabian horse. Don't understand why but they are nuts. The palomino and Appaloosa are so docile and kind. One of the hands got a finger bit off because, I guess, the Arabian stud was having a bad day. With my little herd on the other side of the barn, Avalanche hopes the horses will stay calm so when they are in breeding season the Arabian isn't stressed. Yeah, not stressed, both Avalanche and Panther have wolves that are their pets, for Christ's sake. I'm sure when the wolves are walking through that section of the barn the horses feel so safe. Shaking my head, I take a seat in the second row and buckle in, knowing that Avalanche drives just like me if not worse. I feel a headache coming on and am dreading this day, as I can't think of a happy ending. Panther turns to face me from the passenger seat, making sure I'm okay.

"Nizhoni, breathe, it's going to work out however it's supposed to. We can't change fate. Now sit back and try to meditate. No, don't give me that look, Zoey, you know it works. We'll get there when we can, Avalanche can only go so fast."

I glare at my ol' man for a few minutes then push my head back and close my eyes with the intention to meditate. Instead, with the deep breathing, I relax and fall asleep.

* * *

We approach the ranch through the back road that leads through the woods and comes out by the cabins behind Tink and Noodles's house. When I tell Avalanche to go straight to the survivors' area, the mood in the car changes immediately. As we approach, I see Dani, Kitty, Malachi, Squirt, Presley, and Omen to one side. Across from them are Heartbreaker, Vixen, Ironside, Wildcat, and Malcolm. Each are heavily armed. When I get out of the car, all my club sisters approach me. Vixen is the closest to me so it seems she's been elected to update me.

"Shadow, we lost two of the jagbags overnight. One must have been bleeding internally and the other, we think, might have had some kind of existing condition. Doc Malcolm, along with Yoggie, tried for at least twenty minutes to revive him, but no go. The rest have been given water with a little bit of pain medication, but no food as of yet. We've been waiting to see what the plan is. Any ideas on what we're going to do with them?"

I look down on one of our more petite sisters, who could probably—if needed—kick anyone's ass. Then I catch Malcolm's eyes and when he shakes his head that tells me most hidden in our safe rooms are in pretty bad shape. I assumed that because they are giving out pain medication, which I never allow. It's okay though, no matter what happens, Atlas will feel better knowing that they weren't in constant pain throughout the night. That's the caretaker in him.

Hearing a vehicle come racing up the road, we all turn to see Atlas and Rebel making their way to us. Behind them is Taz and Enforcer. Great, a show, just what I don't want. What really starts to upset me is when I see the sheriff's car with my dad driving with Tank next to him. Yoggie is with Glory in her vehicle. Finally, bringing up the rear, is Tink and Noodles. Great, the beginnings of a shitshow. This is exactly what I didn't want. Usually, it's at my discretion who is around during this time of our missions. My go-tos are Dottie, Raven, Rebel, Heartbreaker, Glory, and Wildcat, though my right hand has become Spirit, who I don't see. Before I can ask, it's like she can read my mind, the door opens up and she walks out covered from head to toe in blood and guts. Fuck, did no one tell her it was hands off until Atlas gave us his decision?

"What the ever-lovin' fuck, Spirit, we haven't gotten word yet. Why are you bathing in blood and guts?"

She turns those dead violet eyes my way before looking down to the ground. Oh shit.

"Shadow, I've spent the better part of the night making sure that the bodies of the two dead assholes can never be traced back to your club or the sanctuary."

That's when it dawns on me that she has always been the cleaner. Making sure nothing identifying remains for the law to find. And I can't believe I'm thinking it, but she's extremely good at what she does.

I hear doors opening and can feel bodies surrounding me. When I hear Atlas whisper, "What the fuck?" I turn to face him. He looks like total shit, which is to be expected. This part of our lives will weigh you down eventually. For me, I'll never stop being the Devil's Handmaidens Enforcer until I'm either voted out or die. It's part of what keeps me alive, that and that Panther is able to accept what I am and do. I walk toward Atlas and Rebel, trying to figure out where he's leaning but, damn, this man can keep his emotions hidden.

"Atlas, before you lose your shit, Spirit was taking care of the remains of two who died overnight, not at our hands, but from injuries sustained during our rescue. Have you made a decision?"

"Shadow, all I've done is think about this and try to come up with an answer that would appease everyone involved. When we got here, Tank pulled me over, telling me no matter what, he wanted someone named Brian. Then Tink told me she needed to make sure the men who that touched the two young girls in the hospital needed to stop breathing. I need the ones who beat and whipped my dad, and especially the ones who raped my mother to pay. Sheriff George told me that for some reason he hasn't divulged to me, he'll not fight my decision. So before I tell you, Shadow, I need to go in and see them. All of the men and try to make sense to a senseless situation. Rebel understands, I hope everyone here can try and see why I need to do what needs to be done."

Nodding, I make my way to Spirit and together we walk through the door and follow the hallway to where the hidden floor door is already open. Spirit and I go down first, then Atlas and Rebel. Tank, Tink, and Noodles bring up the rear. Why my dad is going along with this, I have no idea, but I'm leaning toward Tank winning the battle. Spirit unlocks the outer door and you can start to hear screaming and moaning. Behind me I hear Atlas asking Rebel, "What the hell?" Well, Doc is in for a big surprise, I'm guessing. By the time we reach the main door, I use the keypad and unlock the area. What meets my eyes makes me smile. Yeah, I have a black heart. Who the fuck cares, these aren't good people. Like I always tell Goldilocks, what goes around, comes around.

We have chains attached to the walls all the way around the huge-ass space. Men are cuffed to the chains, sitting on their asses, or standing, each with different levels of injuries. In the center are tables, pulleys, and other instruments of torture. I see Spirit was very busy as by the door, off to the one side on one of the larger tables, are two body parts sitting on it. On one side is a head and directly across is the other man's head, both faces showing the fear they were experiencing right before they died. Atlas gasps loudly, and when I turn he's bent over trying to breathe, while running his hands up and down his legs. Rebel is next to him, not touching him, just there within reach.

"Atlas, these two are some of the original men who started this group in our town. We had no idea they were near, which they took advantage of. Both of them begged for their lives when we brought them in. No one laid hands on them, they died eventually from their injuries. Spirit only did that to protect not only our club but also the survivors. Not one is in the shape to withstand a court case or get up on the stand reliving the tortures they've been through. Now, follow me as I point out some of their crimes. These two are the ones who beat and whipped your father. That one pissed on him and laughed while doing it. He forced your dad to watch the men who raped and sodomized your mother. Those four are some of them. The younger dude, I'm sure you recognize. He's the one who was fighting with Kon at the barbecue a few weeks ago. He not only brutally abused your mom; he raped Colin because he refused to hurt your mom. Those two in the far corner are the ones who repeatedly raped the two little girls. The damage done to them you already know about. I will tell you no one who was at their 'camp' will come out of this unharmed, and I don't mean physically. They will carry scars for the rest of their lives, while fighting the urge to commit suicide, or just giving up, hoping for death to take them. We've already started to clear one of the buildings so when the victims are ready, they will come here to recover. One of the larger cabins is being made ready for both your mom and dad. Raven's brother, Ollie, has alerted the therapists at the Blue Sky Sanctuary that their services will be needed. The ranch will take care of everything, including their living expenses, medical and therapy bills. Everything will be made available to them, but we can't force them to accept it. That's their decision, as you have a decision to make. Atlas, what's it going to be?"

Watching Atlas's eyes take in every single man in the room, everyone waits patiently. When he approaches the kid, Brian, my heart bleeds for him because that asshole doesn't have a soul. My eyes catch Rebel's and I give her a look, so she follows him. When he's close to Brian, the bastard hocks up something and tries to spit it at Atlas. Rebel pushes him out of the way and, with her fist tight, goes right up to him and punches him right in the nose. We all hear the cartilage give and I laugh out loud when she tells him that was from Konstantin. When Brian snorts saying that Kon is a pussy, Rebel pulls her leg back and sends her foot right into his dick and balls. Then she leans really close as tears roll down his face.

"Who's the fuckin' pussy now, asshole? Might want to enjoy these last minutes because you're on the fast track to hell. When your rotting, Konstantin will be living his life to the fullest. No one probably ever told you, but good always prevails over evil, dumb asshole."

With that she turns and goes right to Atlas, who pulls her close. I know what he's going to say before he does. I can only imagine how hard it is for him. The pain is in his eyes.

"Shadow, get rid of them all. Make it hurt. Let Tank and Tink have who they want and anyone else. Do me a favor please? The ones who savagely put hands on my mom, after you're done doing whatever it is you plan on, cut their dicks and balls off and let them bleed out. I owe you, Shadow, and no, I can't be here. This decision will weigh on my soul the rest of my life, but I have my parents, three boys, and this woman at my side to protect. If any of them are released, I'd be looking over my shoulder until I die."

He walks up to me, giving me a side hug, then walks straight past everyone and out the door to the outside. Rebel comes to me, touching my face, which generally I don't allow or want. She stands on tippy-toes and kisses my other cheek.

"I know you think of yourself as a monster. To me you're an avenging angel for those who can't fight for themselves. That includes Atlas because, yeah, he's tough, but his heart would die slowly if he tried to do what you are about to do. I'm forever in your debt. Make sure that asshole Brian hears Konstantin's name right before he dies. That's for me. No matter what never forget, Shadow, that I'll always love you."

When they are gone, I remove my kutte and take my boots and socks off. Then I braid my hair while every single degenerate watches me. When Spirit comes next to me with a thick rubber apron, I put it on, thanking her. Tank and Tink are off to one side, waiting for me to give them what they want. First, though, I have some playing to do. I put the deadliest grin on my face and with my icy eyes look each and every one in their eyes. The fear on their faces feeds the hole in my soul.

"So are y'all ready to have some fun? I know I am so let's get this party started."

They all start to scream, cry, piss, and shit themselves. Ignoring all of their pitiful sounds, I look to the table at what's on it. Grabbing some wire cutters, I hear the door close and see Dottie and Raven waiting, their kuttes and boots off too. Smiling at them, I move to the first dickless piece of shit, and without a single thought of mercy, start cutting off his fingers one by one. Today is gonna be a great day, as these bastards will never hurt another innocent again. I plan on making sure on this day they each take their last rotten breaths.

TWENTY-TWO
'ATLAS'

The last week and a half has been terrible. First, the decision I made is eating me alive. I've second-guessed that moment in my life every minute of every day. I know they were the scum of the earth but me signing their death sentence, what does that make me? Then in one way or another each one of my boys is suffering from the actions of that day. My little guy is the worst. Taz offered for him to stay over this weekend and after Rebel and I talked about it, we figured it would be a good idea. Teddy seems to be an empath. Taz and Enforcer spoke to him to keep an eye on Thanos, which he promised he would. Stefanos won't leave our sides. Well, that is Rebel's. Since that night when they bonded, they are inseparable, which has Kon feeling like the third wheel as he's always been Rebel's shadow.

The Devil's Handmaidens are in the process of

doing the research on who those assholes were. Raven, with the help of Freak, has found a money trail leading to The Thunder Cloud Knuckle Brotherhood. We don't know who their contact was because everything is encrypted. I don't have a lot of knowledge with this kind of stuff, as I don't break up human trafficking circuits. Rebel has been such a lifeline in this aspect for me. Also, she's there when I wake in the middle of the night with night terrors. Rebel talked me into starting therapy, which I'm doing weekly at the Blue Sky Sanctuary, and am beginning to see the tiniest shimmer of light, though it's so far in the tunnel I can barely see it.

Dad got out of the hospital first and we welcomed him into our home without any hesitation. He said that neither he nor my mom will ever enter their home again. That saddens me but I totally get it. He's also in therapy because of what he witnessed when taken. He has so much guilt, he's a ghost of the man he was. I swear he's aged a good twenty years overnight. When Mom finally woke she didn't want to see him, which I think broke his heart. Everyone got why she was acting that way, except her. It took visits from Tink, Taz, Vixen, Wildcat, Heartbreaker, and finally Shadow. They each spent time with my mom, telling her their stories, which every single one was raped at one period in their lives. I thought Mom would relate to Tink or Taz but, to my utter surprise, her new best friend—God help us all—is Shadow. She managed somehow to get my mom to let Dad come in one afternoon and since then they haven't been separated from each other, except when she was in the hospital, they let Dad stay a few days but not every night.

Once they told Mom she was getting released, her stress got so bad that Shadow and Tink rushed to her room with options. Shadow offered my parents space at Panther's stud ranch, while Tink offered them one of the cabins. Mom wanted to go with Shadow, while Dad picked Tink's ranch. His reasoning won Mom over because it was closer to me and the boys. Mom does go about once every week and a half or so to spend time with Shadow and their animals. She's in love with Panther's two wolves Ma'iitsoh (Wolf) and Zhį'ii (Raven). Yeah, and they are real wolves. I almost shit myself the first time I saw my mother on a lawn chair with the bigger one up on his hind legs, his upper torso on my mother, while—as she puts it— he gave her kisses. The female was lying at Mom's feet. I screamed, jumping out of the car, running toward her until I was faced with two snarling wolves right in front of me. Thank God Avalanche was outside with his two wolves, coming back from the stables. Before he could say anything, I was facing off with four really pissed-off wolves. In a split second, he said something in his native language and they stopped snarling and approached me slowly. He told me to drop my arms down, hands open, which I did, and each one of the wolves sniffed me then moved on. When I looked at my mom, for the first time since all of this happened she was smiling hugely. Avalanche whistled and all four wolves walked to where he was. He raised his hand and said one word "guard" and they all went by Mom and laid down. Mouth open, I was shocked as he walked toward me.

"Never thought I'd say this to a person not Native, but maybe you should think about getting your mom some kind of hybrid wolf. She seems to have a connection with them. They have done so much for her spirit as she heals, brother."

We walked back to Mom, who was taking turns scratching behind each of the wolves' ears. I spent the day out there and was totally surprised at the size of their business. It just isn't a stud ranch, they also rescue horses and donkeys from the slaughterhouses around here and as far as the Dakotas, Idaho, Wyoming, and even on occasion, Oregon and Utah. They added multiple barns and stables since Panther purchased it. As Avalanche showed me around, I was amazed at the amount of work and dedication it takes to run a business like this. If I remember correctly what Rebel told me, Tink talked Panther to taking his rescue business and making it a 501c3. It helped because both Panther and Avalanche are registered members of the Navajo tribe in New Mexico, and they are also veterans with military backgrounds. I asked Avalanche if it would be okay, if the boys wanted to, they could donate some time and help out around there. The big man enthusiastically said, "Hell yes." Even as a man, I can see how my Rebel would lean toward this man. His gentleness, honesty, and softspoken ways draw you to him. I'm just glad he didn't feel the same way. Rebel and I spoke about it and she said she was drawn to him because he was comfortable. And that she's not the first sister to crush on Avalanche. Now I'm trying to figure out which one has their eyes on the big man.

So we have gotten into a schedule, sort of. During the week when I'm working, the boys, Rebel, and I stay at the house while my parents stay at their cabin on Tink's ranch. On the weekends, we rotate from the Devil's Handmaidens ranch to Panther's ranch. It's working and everyone is enjoying it, though Stefanos prefers to be at Taz and Enforcer's place. From what Rebel has told me, my son is now Teddy's best man for the wedding of Teddy and Olivia. No one knows when that will be taking place, but neither Taz nor Glory fight it.

Rebel and I are beyond good. I've never had such a deep relationship with any other woman in my life. She fulfills me while giving me what I need. As strong as she is, in our bedroom she gives up her control to me because I need it. And I make sure she never regrets that. She is the best thing to come into my life and I plan on treasuring her forever.

Today I'm in the office taking appointments. Next

up is Tink and Noodles. As I go to walk into their room, I take a breath and open the door. Both turn to me and I walk over, giving Tink a kiss on the cheek and shaking Noodles's hand. We all sit, Noodles and me in chairs while Tink is on the exam table. I turn the computer on and read my notes then turn to two pairs of expectant eyes. Wow, what a choice of words.

"All right, before we go over the results, have you made any decisions on Faith and Mercy? From what Rebel told me, Raven said no one has seen their parents in over four or five months, which makes perfect sense. As you both know, the girls don't know how long they were held captive, though that timeline seems to correlate with the disappearance of their parents."

I watch as Tink looks to Noodles with a very small, gentle smile. I know the answer just from that look. He nods and smiles back at her. Tink looks my way.

"Atlas, thanks for giving us the name of the person working the girls' case. We've thought it through, and are now in the process of becoming foster parents first. Our caseworker, Juan, told us we'd have a better chance to adopt them if they were our foster kids. He said after the courts approve it, to wait maybe three to six months then put in a petition for adoption. So, yeah, we are taking the girls, if they let us."

I'm beyond thrilled to hear that news but now

need to go over the results of the most recent in vitro fertilization procedure (IVF). I know they've kept it close to the vest, so to speak, and part of me gets it, but part of me not so much. Don't think Tink has even shared with Shadow, which seems strange, though not my business.

"Tink, Noodles, as you know this is our fourth IVF attempt. You only had three fertilized eggs remaining and elected to implant all of them. Have you taken a pregnancy test, Tink?"

She shakes her head while Noodles grabs her hand. I can see the results of the stress both have been under. Not sure this is going to help or make it worse.

"Well, as you know, we drew blood to see if you are pregnant. While we waited, I had an ultrasound performed too. The test is back and I'm beyond thrilled to inform you both that you are, in fact, pregnant."

Watching them, it takes some time for it to penetrate. It surprises the shit out of me when Noodles is the one who bursts into tears, grabbing Tink, and putting his face into her neck. From above his head, Tink is watching me with a serene smile on her face. This has been so hard on her, especially since Squirt is actually her biological daughter from a rape when she was a teenager. Long story for a different time. She mouths, "Thank you" and I just nod. Standing, I leave to give them a moment, but Noodles has other ideas. He jumps out of the chair, picks me up, and swings me around. Now, fuck, talk about shock. I'm not a small guy and he lifted me like I'm the size of a child. Tink is laughing and crying, telling him to put me down, for Christ's sake. I will say this appointment and news will always be one of my favorites because I know both of them and because of Tink and her club, my family is safe and recovering. I'm beyond thankful this IVF cycle worked out for them. They so deserve some happiness.

TWENTY-THREE
'REBEL'
MYA

I'm wiped. It was a long-ass day. Today, I went through all of this year's discipline actions I've had to take with our members. Each year I have to collect any unacceptable actions from sisters during meetings, any threats that were made toward our club or a sister specifically, and just keep everything running smoothly. Other clubs consider the S-a-A like the club's enforcer, but in the Devil's Handmaidens our enforcer is Shadow. If she needs help, she'll call on who has the specialty she's looking for during that specific situation. Her usual go-to currently is Spirit from The Blue Sky Sanctuary and Dottie. Raven and I each have our strengths but Shadow rarely calls on us, and I get it. Spirit is like Shadow's twin when it comes to their torture skills.

When I walk into the house I hear arguing, which —damn it—all I want is to get into some comfy lounge clothes then get dinner together and chill. My head is spinning and I'm not feeling the best. Atlas told me earlier he should be home around the regular time, which means we can have a "normal" dinner, whatever the hell that means. Stomping into the family room, Thanos and Stefanos are nose to nose. *What the shit?* I think to myself. Things seem to be a lot better since I convinced Atlas to put all three boys into therapy. It turns out each of them have some issues that pertain to their mom, Mindy. Whistling, both boys turn to look at me then go right back to in each other's faces. When Thanos shoves Stefanos, all hell breaks loose. Trying to separate two growing kids wasn't on my agenda today. I grab Thanos by the shoulders and kinda push and direct him to the sectional, shoving him down on his ass. Turning, Stefanos is directly behind me, so I grab him and get his ass in one of the recliners. Once he's in it, I pull the handle and his feet fly up. Then I give both shit.

"What the shit is going on, and who said it was okay for you two to get physical? If I hadn't walked in at that moment, what were you going for, to try and kick each other's asses? Let's take a few breaths, then someone—I don't really care who—is going to explain what the heck I walked in on. I'm going to get these clothes off. I'll be right back. I'm telling you that neither of you better move out of where I planted your asses. And I'm not joking. Think about what your punishment should be because I'm telling you, something is either getting taken away or more chores will be on you for the next week. Now I'll be back down in less than five minutes."

Turning, I am almost to the stairs when the doorbell rings. What the fuck, why didn't my phone give me a notice? Gonna have either Atlas or Raven look at it. Since I've been spending my time between here and the ranch, Raven took it upon herself to hook Atlas up with the best security system possible. Took some time to get the Giannopoulos men on board, but with Apollo and Athena spending time here, Atlas knew how the security made his parents feel safe. Walking toward the front door, I check the side window and see Sheriff George and Yoggie standing there, I instantly know something is wrong. Flinging the door open, I startle them both but neither says a word. I wait and finally ask them in. Walking toward the kitchen, I see the boys exactly where I told them to stay. I do the only thing I can think of.

"You two, go to your rooms and close your doors. I want you to either sit at your desks or lie on your beds and think about what was going on when I walked in. Now move your butts."

They both get up, running up the stairs. I hear first one then the other bedroom door slam. Turning, I look from Sheriff George to Yoggie and back. Trying to summon my courage, I swallow and just ask.

"Is it Atlas or Konstantin?"

Sheriff George looks to Yoggie then back at me.

"Rebel, it's neither. I'm sorry and I would have waited for Atlas, but we're shorthanded and I know he wouldn't care if we tell you. Earlier today, a rancher called in a body found in one of their secondary pastures. When we went out and after locating said body, it turned out to be, well, ummm, it's Mindy, Rebel."

It feels like he punched me in the chest. Oh my God, the boys' mother. How is that possible, we just ran into her a week or two ago at the grocery store. She looked a little better and she even said hi to the boys. Atlas was just glad she didn't cause a scene. She even asked about the boys' grandparents, which I thought was nice.

"Damn, how is that possible?"

Yoggie moves a bit closer whispering.

"Rebel, it looks to be a drug overdose, though we are waiting on some results from the coroner. Might want to call Atlas, tell him to come home."

That's when I hear the garage door open and a car entering and parking. It's either Atlas or Konstantin. With my fingers crossed, I pray for Atlas. When he walks in, I see the surprise on his face when he sees George and Yoggie in the kitchen. Something crosses his face as he places his stuff on the counter, moving to me. After the pleasantries, he asks why they are here. I hang on as Sheriff George tells him that his ex-wife and mother of his boys is dead. I feel his body jerk before his eyes look toward the stairs. He glances down at me and I nod.

"They are in their rooms on a middle school kid time-out."

As we hear the details, I'm beyond worried on how the kids are going to take the news. After the sheriff and Yoggie answer all of Atlas's questions best as they can, they take their leave. Looking at Atlas, I can see he doesn't know how to deal with this unsettling news. Sitting, I don't say a word just wait, giving him time to process. When the front door opens and Konstantin walks in, Atlas's time is up. Just looking at his dad and me, our boy knows something is wrong. Walking in, he drops his books close to the hall closet, then moves right to us.

"Dad, what is it, Yia-yia and Papou?"

Seeing Atlas unable to answer, I grab Konstantin's hand and look him in the eye.

"Konstantin, no, it's not your grandparents. I'm sorry, honey, it's your mom, Mindy."

Looking between the two of us, he sees something as his shoulders drop. Knowing there is no easy way to say it, I just give it to him.

"Konstantin, I have some really bad news. Earlier today, Sheriff George got a call and when he went to check it out, turns out it was your mom. Honey, she's gone."

His eyes get huge before he drops down, head in my lap, howling, not what I expected. Grabbing him,

I pull him up next to me, telling him to let it out. Hearing a noise, I see both Thanos and Stefanos. I motion them to us and put Stefanos between Atlas and me, while letting Thanos sit next to his dad. Atlas snaps out of it and gently he tells both boys their mom has passed away. We sit together for a long time, no one saying a word. I mean, what can you say?

*** * ***

Turns out someone murdered Mindy, or that's what the sheriff's department thinks. Truly it doesn't matter, except the boys lost their mom. Athena and Apollo came by as soon as the word got to them. So did Tank and Momma Diane, and most of my club sisters either came or stopped by to see that we were okay. Through it all I kept my eyes on Atlas, as he seems to be shrinking right in front of my eyes. Not sure how, but Tank saw something because he starts to tell everyone we need some family time. When it was just him and Momma Diane, he told Atlas that this wasn't his fault. That's when he loses it. No one knows what to do, though Tank gently tells the boys to go into the kitchen and someone will be there in a minute or two. From what we are being told, it was a drug deal gone bad. Or that's the way it was set up, I don't know. Shadow and Spirit went to the crime scene, along with Freak and Yoggie. Looks like either

Mindy or someone overamped her with cocaine. Tank told Atlas he'd take care of the coroner while Momma Diane said she'll handle the arrangements for Atlas, who just nods. Once everyone is gone, he calls the boys back down and tells them what he knows. The five of us sit in the great room just trying to make sense of this. When the two younger ones fall asleep and Atlas goes upstairs to take a shower, Konstantin and I walk into the kitchen.

Without asking him, I start to make hot chocolate until I feel arms around me. I turn and hold him tightly.

"Rebel, why does this shit keep happening? I mean, our grandparents, the whole kidnapping and rescue. We are all already in therapy, what else can we do to get this shit to move on? Now this. She wasn't the best mom out there, but she was ours. How do I help my brothers when I don't even know how to process this?"

I have no answers, so I sit here, my arm around his shoulders, pulling him in tightly. Then he shocks me to my core.

"I remember Dad telling us when she left that any person can either produce or have a child, but it takes a special person to be a parent. You've been more of a mother to the three of us than she ever was. I've wanted to ask you for a while. Why do you call me Konstantin when everyone else calls me Kon?"

I know he's trying to avoid the death of Mindy, and I'm not going to be the one to make him face it. I just give it to him straight.

"Konstantin is such an exceptionally cool-ass name and to me you're very special, so why not use such a cool name for a badass kiddo?"

He face-plants into my chest just as he starts to softly weep. This is how Atlas finds us about fifteen minutes later, with red eyes and wet hair. He pulls Konstantin off of me and helps him to the sectional where the four of them lie together, wrapped around each other. I go upstairs to give them some time and me some quiet time to process what just happened. After I take a shower, partially dry my hair, and put on some clean pajamas, I walk out of the master bathroom to find Atlas and Konstantin sitting on the edge of the bed, I guess waiting on me. It's Konstantin who comes toward me.

"Both Thanos and Stefanos want all of us to sleep together downstairs, so we are here to get you."

I nod 'cause at this moment I'd give them anything if I could. So, the three of us make our way downstairs and with the television in the background playing softly, we sit and the boys ask questions, I guess they never asked before about their mom. And Atlas tries to be as honest as possible without causing more pain to his boys. When Konstantin sits next to me, I put my head on his shoulder, and before I know it, my head is falling forward. Last thing I hear is Atlas's deep, husky voice trying to help his sons through more drama. *He's a great dad,* I think to myself as I fade deeply into sleep.

TWENTY-FOUR
'REBEL'
MYA

Once again, the Devil's Handmaidens and the folks of Timber-Ghost came together to support Atlas and the boys. The plan was to have a simple service at the only funeral home in our town. In fact, it's one of Tank's brothers from the Intruders. Smokey is a quiet member, who does what he's told, no questions asked. His parents own the funeral home and they did a beautiful job for Mindy's service. After, everyone went to the Wooden Spirits Bar and Grill where Cook had prepared a buffet. The grill side of the place is set up so pretty. Simple flower centerpieces with a few large bouquets around. A large photo of Mindy is on an easel. I know Atlas did this for the boys, but I think it's good for him too.

Now, almost two weeks later, and there is still food being delivered and finally the plants stopped coming. I'm worried that none of the boys or Atlas seem to be processing Mindy's death. It's like business as usual, which I know is not good. I'm so concerned, I finally broke down and spoke to Taz about it. She suggested that maybe if everyone agrees, have a "family" therapy session so everyone can talk about their issues together. It took me two days after I spoke to Taz to bring it up one night at dinner. Konstantin agrees immediately so does, to my surprise, Stefanos. Atlas and Thanos, not so much. Once again Konstantin has my back, finally saying that I have never asked them for anything with all that I do for them. Thanos caves first and Atlas agrees when Stefanos tells him he's the minority. That night was not pleasant with Atlas. Well, actually, since Mindy was found he's been very distant. So much so, I decide to give him some time so I'm back to staying at the ranch instead of with them at the Giannopoulos home. Konstantin has reached out a few times, asking me if I was okay. After that, I would go over to Atlas's house, have dinner with the family, then go back to the ranch. It's getting to be too much and I feel drained all the time. And to top it off, Atlas has gone cold to me. He barely kisses me, let alone making time for us to be together. I'm getting the feeling that he's trying to figure out a way to dump me, which I know will devastate me. Not just because I'm in love with the man, but I also love all three of his boys.

One day, as I am helping out with some ranch chores, both Apollo and Athena ask me if I have a minute or two to talk. Of course, I tell them, so we make our way to the conference center and I take us to one of the offices. I grab bottles of water for all of us. When I sit down, I look at both of them and if you judge by appearances, they look really good, though I know the truth. They are also struggling with everything that happened. I see them generally every day but this is the first time they've asked to speak to me, so I'm worried. Athena must see that because she reaches over and squeezes my hand.

"Rebel, honey, don't worry. We don't want to stress you out. Both Apollo and I see that Atlas is struggling, and we wanted to touch base with you to see if we can do anything to help."

Not sure why, but with everything they've been through, they still want to help Atlas and the boys out. That's when Apollo puts it all on the table.

"Like Athena said, we want to help if we can. What she didn't say is that we already consider you like our daughter-in-law, so we want to help you too. Both of us can see how much this is hurting you and after talking to Konstantin, he opened our eyes to his dad's struggles since Mindy passed. Now before we start, honey, please know something must have spooked Atlas because he adores you. He can't say enough about how much he cares for you. So, let's put our heads together to see if we can get his head out of his ass."

His words take me by surprise and I actually

giggle. We are relaxed after that and I explain what I've seen and how Atlas has changed toward me. It isn't Apollo getting pissed, it is Athena. We come to the conclusion that when we meet the therapist tomorrow that they will also be there, but will give us some time before they literally burst in and confront their son. I'm not sure if this plan is a good one, but I'm also not sure what to do to get us back on track. Later that night, Atlas calls to talk for exactly three and a half minutes to catch up on each other's day. He's so shut off that I don't even want to talk to him, which scares me because I love him so much. Fingers crossed; I pray for some positive vibes that tomorrow helps all of us to move forward.

Atlas and the boys drove to the therapist's office and I met them there. When he told me he'd meet me there, that's when I knew this was going to be a waste of time. I tried to get his parents to reconsider, but they both were very upset when I told him about driving separately. Apollo begged me not to give up on his asinine son. So here I am in the waiting room, by myself, because none of the guys have shown up. When the therapist checks yet again to see if they have arrived, I finally know I have to face the fact that Atlas is done with me. I tell her thanks but I have to leave. She gives me her card and says if I need anything to call her.

As I'm walking to my cage, my phone rings and when I see it's Konstantin, I answer it.

"Hey, kiddo, what's up?"

"Rebel, don't leave. I'm driving Stefanos, Thanos, and myself and should be there in less than five minutes."

Then he hangs up with me holding my phone, shocked to hear he's driving. I know he got his license but didn't realize he had a car. That's when I see Konstantin is driving his dad's car. My God, what the fuck is going on? He pulls in next to my car, turns it off, and jumps out.

"I'm so sorry, Rebel, thanks for waiting on us. I'm done with him. Dad's at home, drunk off his ass. We all decided not to just leave you waiting for us, so I took his keys and here we are."

Thanos and Stefanos are now out of the car and both give me hugs. Stefanos looks up at me, tears in his eyes.

"Rebel, can we live with you, please? Dad is being so crazy and now he's been drinking all day. It's like he's turning into our mom, but he's using booze for his fix."

That does it, I reach for my phone and dial Athena. I tell her to come to the parking lot and not even two minutes later, they come around the corner and park next to Atlas's car. When they see the boys, I literally watch as they look around for Atlas. When they get out, the boys explain what happened. Apollo is shaking his head while Athena tells the boys that she'll drive her son's car, but the boys are coming back to the ranch with her. I know what I have to do now. I say goodbye and tell the boys I'll see them later.

Before I can change my mind, I start to drive to Atlas's house. I'm so pissed at him for so many reasons that by the time I get to his block, I'm ready to beat him silly. His boys need him, and here he is drowning his feelings and letting them see him like that. Running up the front stairs, I pound on the door. At first nothing, then I can hear him muttering. When he unlocks and pulls the door open, I push on it so it swings with him holding on, so it takes him off guard. I push past him and once in the house, I put my hands on my hips. He glares at me.

"What the hell, Rebel? Why are you here?"

"Well, to start, Atlas, to tell you what a total fucking asshole you are. While you're drinking your problems away, they couldn't handle it any more so your boys took a chance and Konstantin drove to meet me at the therapy session. I don't know what's going on with you because, just like a man, you're not talking or sharing. I'm so pissed at you because you are acting like an idiot. Those boys love you and you're pushing them away. Why... because your ex-wife who abused drugs was found dead? That's not their fault, but I wonder if you even care. I thought we had something but the first time life kicks us, you just fall flat on your face. Well, have a good life, Atlas. I'm not going to be that woman who keeps reaching out to a man who can't figure out what he wants or how to handle life's bumps in the road. I'm so sorry that happened to Mindy, but for God's sake, Atlas, you were divorced and she didn't even come to see her boys. I don't understand and I'm done waiting for you to explain. The boys are with your parents, so take tonight and figure out what your next steps are for your boys. Try and put them first."

With that I turn and walk out, and he doesn't come after me. I make it to my cage before the tears start to fall. Not sure how I make it to my bestie's house, but so glad I do. When I ring the doorbell, expecting Taz or Enforcer, it's Teddy who flings the door open with Enforcer screaming at him to wait. When he looks up at me and sees I'm crying, he latches on to my legs. That's how Enforcer finds us, me on the front porch, Teddy hanging on to my legs, both of us crying.

"What in the ever-lovin f—"

"Travis, mouth."

That brings a smile to my face as the big badass Enforcer is cut off at the knees by a rainbow-haired woman. When she sees me, she moves quickly, giving baby Mickie to her father, and pulling Teddy and me in.

"Travis, honey, take the kids and give me a minute, please."

Enforcer reaches down and somehow, with little

Mickie in his arms, picks up Teddy too. He leans into me and I brace.

"Just say the word and I swear to Christ, Rebel, I'll rip him apart with my bare hands. If this is how he treats ya, you deserve better, babe."

I go to thank Enforcer but Teddy cuts me off.

"Like Dad said, Auntie Rebel. I'll go with and help Dad rip him apart. One question, who are we ripping apart and why?"

Taz tries so hard not to laugh, well, until she snorts then laughs. Enforcer shakes his head as he walks away, trying to explain to Teddy what he was talking about without telling him the truth. My bestie is watching me, and before I know it, I'm in her arms crying my eyes out. *I'm lucky because Taz always has my back*, I think as she is talking about her crystals and sending negative vibes toward Atlas, but not at his kids. By the time we've gone through two bottles of wine, Enforcer has to help me to their guest room so I can pass out on their spare bed.

* * *

My head is pounding and my bladder is ready to burst. It takes me a moment to realize I'm at Taz's in one of her guest bedrooms. Shit, can't remember much, damn her and her wine. I go into the smaller en suite and pee. Then I throw some water on my face. Back in the room, on the nightstand, there is a bottle of water, saltine crackers, and two, I'm guessing Tylenol. Swallowing the pills down, I drink a few extra sips. Then I grab one saltine and slowly nibble on it. I grab my phone to check the time and see I have fourteen missed calls and squinting my eyes, no way, five voice messages. I put the phone down without listening to any of the messages. I'll get to them when my head isn't pounding. Next time I wake up is to loud voices screaming. I get out of bed, opening the door, just as lil' Mickie starts screaming. Walking down to the master suite, I knock just as Taz flings the door open. Damn, she's a sight, as from the way she looks she's feeling the wine too.

"Well, Rebel, seems like my son called Stefanos to tell him his dad is a big jerk. When asked why, Teddy laid it out—so from what I've heard so far is—Konstantin called his dad to tell him he's a fucking screwup and he was gonna lose you. During this Thanos was so upset he had an anxiety attack. So Atlas thought it was a great idea to drive the car he bought for Konstantin as a surprise out here after he'd been drinking. Knowing he would probably take the chance to drive out to the ranch after they spoke, Atlas told his dad the car was dropped off, Apollo worried not only about Atlas but everyone on the roads. So he put a call to Sheriff George so Atlas got pulled over. Maybe you might do me a favor and go talk to your man."

I nod, she turns, slamming the door closed, so I

move toward the family room where I find Enforcer and Noodles trying to get Atlas's shoes off. The one part of the sectional is made up like a bed. When Enforcer sees me, he shakes his head. This man has been so cool, can't let him try and fix this shit. By the time I get Noodles to leave and Enforcer to bed, Atlas has passed out. Being so tired, I sit down on one of the recliners with one of Taz's blankets she knitted. I must have fallen asleep because I wake up to someone kind of shaking me. Opening my eyes, I see Atlas scrunched down and looking like total shit.

"Son of a bitch, I'm so sorry, sweetheart. Everything hit me at once with my parents, the boys, and where their heads are, and then Mindy, which again brings me to worry about the boys. Honestly, don't know what I'm doing or why. One thing I know is, I can't lose you. Don't think I can make it without you."

I'm listening to him but not sure how we can fix this between us. I need to trust the man in my life to have enough faith in me to tell me when he's drowning or having issues with shit happening in his life. When he reaches for me and I push him out of the way and get up from the recliner, he frowns at me.

"What, you don't want me to touch you, Rebel? Am I too late, because I never meant to hurt you. My boys are pissed and said until I make things right with you, they are going to stay with their grandparents. So tell me what to do to fix this between us."

I take a few minutes to think about the question he just asked. I don't want to lose him or the boys because I love them. I also don't want him to think it's okay to treat me like he did. So I do what I think is the best.

"Atlas, you can't treat me like you did ever again. Besides that, I don't know what to tell you. I'm still drunk so, get some sleep, we'll talk in the morning."

Saying that, I stand on my tippy-toes, kiss his cheek, then I go back to bed. As I'm trying to fall asleep, I know Atlas is it for me. Just need to know he feels the same.

TWENTY-FIVE
'REBEL'

MYA

I've been up most of the night and now I'm just waiting to hear someone else is up, so I can get up and get some much-needed coffee. I know I'm going to forgive Atlas. It hit me last night, everything that has been going on, it all involves him so I just think he's on overload. Stress and anxiety can fuck a person up, I know that. Today is going to suck, trying to function with a hangover, but got to remember stupid actions always come back to haunt you. My feelings for him are real and we just need to be a bit more open with each other and need to talk stuff out.

I'm in the bathroom when I hear the initial pounding. Then the yelling and screaming. Finally my name is being said loudly. Oh shit, I don't need Atlas to wake up either of the kids which, apparently, I'm too late for when lil' Mickie starts to cry. I grab a Devil's Handmaidens sweatshirt to put over my tank and shorts, open the door, and run toward the front of the house. What I see when I turn the corner is Enforcer and Teddy barring Atlas from coming down the hallway toward the spare room, Konstantin, Thanos, Stefanos, and both of Atlas's parents are behind him. My eyes are only on him because he looks like death has taken a permanent residency with him. When he sees me, he immediately stops yelling, which, as Taz walks by me, under her breath she says, "Thank Christ." The only person who looks unfazed is Mickie, who is in her mother's arm, babbling, hand in her mouth, drooling down her face. That's when I hear my bestie tell her ol' man to quit being a moron and let the folks do what they want. The boys run right to me, all hugging on me like they've not seen me in a year. Athena is behind them while it looks like Apollo is holding up his son. Enforcer stays close to Atlas as my protector, Teddy, pushes his way so he's standing kind of in front of me, arms crossed just like his daddy. If this wasn't such a clusterfuck, I'd think he's beyond cute. When Atlas, along with his dad, makes his way to me quietly, he asks to talk to me. As I'm thinking about it, to my utter shock Enforcer tells me to use their office, and that he'll start breakfast. Every boy's head jerks up except Teddy, who when seeing that, laughs.

"What, doesn't your dad cook breakfast? If Dad doesn't have club duties, he's the one who cooks because he's really good at it."

Thanos and Stefanos look at each other then Enforcer. The man in question stops and stares at them. Then he smiles.

"Boys, something to remember. As you grow up, it's no one's responsibility but yours to do things for yourself. Taz and I got together when we were grown, so I had to learn how to cook, clean, and wash my clothes. You know, all the shit that needs to be done. Now, when my ol' lady and I built this house, we talked about it and knew we had to share the workload as we both have jobs and responsibilities. Teddy over there does chores that he gets a weekly allowance for. Don't ya have chores at home?"

The boys shake their heads, which has Enforcer looking at Atlas with a frown.

"My man, you are doing a disservice to your kids but looks like you got bigger issues you need to fix. Now come on, kids, you can all help me make breakfast. Mr. and Mrs. Giannopoulos, please take a seat. We'll get ya both some coffee; how do you take it?"

I turn and make my way to the office with Atlas behind me. Once in and he's closed the door, we look at each other. I know I'm stubborn, but this is his shitshow not mine, so I wait. Finally I move and take a seat on the leather love seat; he follows and sits on the table right in front of me. When he hesitantly reaches for my hands, I remember my first thought when I woke up. I love this man and every relationship has bumps in the road. I let him hold my hands as he struggles to explain.

"Sweetheart, fuck, I don't know what to say except I'm sorry. Something snapped in my head and the more I tried to ignore it, the worse it got. After the shit with my folks and the kids we found, then finding out Mindy was dead, I don't even know how to explain it. My mind started playing tricks on me. I'd have nightmares that instead of Mindy dead it was you in that wooded pasture. I couldn't risk something happening to you, so I started to push not only you but the boys, Mom, and Dad away. Not to mention all the new people in my life. Oh, guess who showed up at my house last night? Of all the people in your life, I opened the door, half blasted off my ass to see a very pissed-off Avalanche. And get in my face, he did. I will tell you, never want to piss that man off ever again."

I'm grinning when Atlas's eyes get all squinty.

"Did you send him to put the fear of God in me, Rebel? Because that's what he did, well, until Panther and Shadow showed up, and that's when I truly thought I was going to die. Not Panther, he's the quiet one. Nope, it was your sister who walked right up to me, looked up into my face, and very softly told me to fix what I fucked up, or she'll make sure I don't upset you ever again. Then she walked away, calling for Big Bird to follow them. I had all night to try and figure out what happened, and it hit me around four this morning. I was so afraid of losing you, either like Mindy, or during one of your club missions breaking up a circuit, unconsciously I figured it was better to push you out of my life, and the boys. Well, they also reamed my ass yesterday, along with my parents. I'm here begging you to forgive my stupidity. Generally I'm not a dumb man. I already called the therapist to apologize and set up another appointment for the family session. Please tell me you'll come with the boys and me? I didn't mean to hurt you, sweetheart. Mindy's death brought a lot of feelings and emotions to the surface, right after my parents' situation, that if I'm honest I wasn't dealing with too well. Tell me, Rebel, do I have a chance or did I blow it?"

Knowing he's punishing himself more than I could ever do, I lean forward and grab his head and drop my lips to his. Right before mine touch his, I whisper while staring into those beautiful sapphire eyes, "I love you Atlas Giannopoulos." Not sure how long we are making out when a knock on the door startles us.

"Is it safe to come in or do you both need a minute to put your clothes back on?"

I can hear the laughter in my bestie's voice. Thank God she always is there for me.

"Come on in, Taz. We're decent."

She walks in with a smirk on her face, taking us in. Then her face gets serious when she looks Atlas's way.

"So, Doc, did you get your head out of your own ass? Because there is a group of people just waiting to see if they're going to have to beat your behind or maybe call for an intervention. Now breakfast is ready, so come on, let's eat. Oh, Rebel, did you hear from Tink yesterday?"

Just like Taz, she's all over the board. I take a second to think but when I checked my phone, I didn't listen to any of the voice messages, so I shake my head no.

"Oh, sister, wait 'til you hear. Nope, not my story to tell. So seriously, are you two good?"

I glance at Atlas, who's looking down at me. I smile at him, grabbing his hand then look at my bestie, sharing the same smile with her.

"I recall a woman a few years back who shared with me that relationships are work, and if you put your best effort into it, the rewards are so worth it. Well, Raquel, you were right. Not only is Atlas worth it, but so are his three boys. Now feed me, sister, I didn't eat last night, was more worried about getting drunk with your crazy ass."

When the three of us walk out and everyone sees us holding hands, they all start to clap. Leave it to the children to know what's best for the adults in their lives.

* * *

It's been a long as fuck day. I skipped work, well, with Glory's blessing. After breakfast the kids played for a bit with Teddy's two dogs, while Enforcer showed Atlas and Apollo his new car project. A 1967 GTO. I don't know who was drooling more, father or son. We finally left, me following Atlas to his house. Konstantin drove my car and he did a great job. It took a bit for us to straighten up the mess Atlas left and the boys gave him smack throughout the cleaning process. We decided to make today a movie lounge day, so I go upstairs to find some comfortable clothes and when I come back, all four of the Giannopoulos guys are waiting on me. The boys are sitting on the sectional, while Atlas is on the ottoman. He pulls me on his lap then looks to the boys who nod vigorously.

"Rebel, we've come to a decision and need your thoughts. Stefanos brought it up, while Thanos and I agree wholeheartedly. Kon said it's totally up to you, but he's on board. Mya, will you do us the honor of moving in with us? No, not asking you to marry me yet, though just a heads-up, I will one day. Today though, as a family, we all realized that without you this house is definitely not a home. It's a place to eat and sleep. Each of the boys has fallen in love with you, as I have. Why keep your place at the ranch when you're here most of the time? And this way you'll be closer to the clubhouse and your office. What do you say?"

My mind is doing a fast spin through my life and

there is nowhere else I'd rather be. So with a huge smile, I tell them a most definite yes. As we celebrate, I've never felt so happy and secure. That's what they give me and I hope I return that back to them. After a long day of junk food and movies, I excuse myself to go to the office and check my messages. There were quite a few so when I get to Tink's, I'm thinking she's going to tell me something about the club or one of our sisters. She surprises me twice. Once when she tells me she and Noodles are going to foster Mercy and Faith with the intention of eventually adopting both girls. I'm beyond thrilled for the two of them as they've wanted to start a family for a long time. I'm already trying to think of some things to buy the girls who have lost so much. What my prez says next stops me dead-on. Tink tells me that she and Noodles have been trying IVF and after four tries, it finally took and they are expecting a baby. She goes into detail saying she's high-risk and will be watched closely by her OB/GYN. She tells me they are slowly letting the "family" know. I finally can accept that all those years ago, when I came up to Montana, what I was looking for was right here in Timber-Ghost. I'm so glad I took that opportunity and gave the Devil's Handmaidens a chance.

As I'm reminiscing, something Tink said has my head throb. Son of a bitch, he knew and didn't tell me. I stomp back to the family room, hands on my hips, glaring at Atlas. That's when the boys all get up and go to their rooms and my man stands and walks toward me.

"What has you ready to kill me this time, sweetheart?"

"Forget to share something with me, Atlas?"

I watch him try to think about what it could be and I can't wait, I put him out of his misery.

"Tink and Noodles's news?"

"Rebel, come on, you know I can't talk about my patients. Don't go there because, sweetheart, there are some boundaries I can't cross, even for you. Now are we fighting or celebrating their phenomenal news?"

Laughing, I jump into his arms, knowing that life in the club is definitely changing, that's for sure. And when the boys walk in a little bit later, we tell them the news and they are super excited. Then we do what I guess "normal" families do to relax, eat dinner and then go to bed. And I wouldn't change it for the world because I'm sure in the near future we will be dealing with degenerates who want to destroy what a family means. *We won't let them*, I think as I cuddle with my ol' man in, I guess, what is now "our" home.

Want more Mya and Atlas?
Click here to download a bonus chapter.

Scroll for a preview of Heartbreaker, Book 8

***

HEARTBREAKER
Chapter One

There are times in my life I truly believe my purpose in life is to always struggle or face diversity, no matter how hard I try to stay on the right path. Rebel had a talk with me today because she saw me in town without my kutte, which is a violation of one of the rules. She was cool about it and, yeah, I forgot because I was running late to my "meeting" that night. Since the whole episode with Rebel and Atlas when I passed out during Kon's shit, that old familiar craving is back. I woke in the hospital with the angel and devil on their respective shoulders. On the good side, I was beyond thrilled that one of my club sisters told them about my addiction though, on the bad side, that devil was dancing on a pole waiting for some of the "good stuff."

Since then it feels like bugs are crawling all over my skin. I'm scratching myself raw. Even with everything I know, it's getting worse instead of better. One of the only things keeping me from taking that dark road is if I fall off the wagon one more time, I'll lose my place in the Devil's Handmaidens club. They'll take my kutte and blacken my club ink. Then they'll send me on my way. I have no place or no one to go to without them. Not only will I lose the club and my sisters, but that will also include Momma Diane and Tank, and all of the guys who work with Panther and Avalanche. Also all those people at the Blue Sky Sanctuary. So it would mean my whole "family" would be lost to me. Then I'll lose my job at the Wooden Spirits Bar and Grill, which I've come to love. And finally, I'll lose the work I do with all the survivors who we bring to the ranch after we break up the circuits and those who remain with us. My part in their recovery is very important not only to them, but also to me. I can't let them down as they are fighting their own demons. Too many people depend on me to stay on the right road. Tonight though, it seems so hard for some reason. I can almost feel the needle entering a vein and that immediate rush of pleasure before everything goes numb, especially my brain. It shuts off everything from the memories to the voices who hardly ever shut up. That's the only time it's quiet. Well, except after a meeting, but I checked and there isn't one tonight. My sponsor—well, my old one—moved away and it's been well over a month that I've not had one. Stupid mistake on my part. Thank God I still go to the therapist at the sanctuary or when she's at the ranch. Without her, I'd either be on the streets selling my ass again for a fix, or dead.

So instead of staying at the ranch I'm in my cage, heading to the Wooden Spirits to get my other fix, which is Cook's desserts. If I can't get high I'll eat my cravings away. I'm being stupid, I know, because all I'd have to do is pick up my phone and call one of my club sisters. Every single one of them would drop whatever they are doing and come to me in an instant. I'm sick of being that "sister" though. Since all that shit went down with Tink and Hannah, I swore to my prez "never again," and I've kept that promise. Well, had a few slips in the beginning but now I've been clean for almost a couple of years and counting. And no, it doesn't get easier with time, don't care what anyone says.

I pull around to the back to park and get out of my cage. The parking lot doesn't seem too full so maybe I'll get lucky. Once inside, I slam the door closed and lock it. Turning, I'm surprise that I don't hear much noise. Usually, you can kind of hear the music from the bar side but, nope, can't make out anything. Not sure why but I reach for my gun in the holster under my kutte. As Shadow jokes, we should never leave home without our weapons.

I just about make it to the kitchen when I hear a familiar voice shouting for everyone to just stay sitting and get their wallets out and put them on the tables. Slowly I pass the opening to the kitchen to see Cook trying to get off the floor, blood pouring from somewhere under her hand on the back of her head. When she sees me, she shakes her head. I mouth call, "911." She nods and I pray the alarm is setting off alerts and Raven is catching it. When I see motion, it's

Cook on her feet, grabbing her cast-iron skillet. No use telling her no, that woman ain't gonna listen to me. So I take it slow, leaning against the wall. Looking up I see the mirror Peanut wanted up so when the waitresses were walking, they can look up to see the front of the building. Thank God 'cause right now I see one—no—two guys, guns in their hands, swinging them back and forth. Not too many people in the grill side, and that's when I see a third guy ordering those in front of him to move their asses. Shit, those folks must be from the bar side. I turn to Cook, holding up three fingers. She pulls her phone out and I guess starts to text one of the Devil's Handmaidens. I take a second, trying to assess, but the guy from the bar is being a total asshole. When he swings that gun of his and hits an elderly man at one of the tables because he's too slow getting his wallet, I can't wait.

Even though it's stupid with just me and Cook, before I move I switch my Glock 18 to full-automatic mode. I rush out through the small hallway and take a stance at the end, at the corner of the doorway. Leaning forward, I see the three assholes have herded all the people into the far corner. Every table has at least one wallet on it, along with jewelry. As I squint to make the three guys out, it hits me square in the chest. Son of a fuckin' bitch. Of course, should have known. Two of the assholes are dealers who also use their own stuff. I've bought from them in my past life.

Last I heard, they were in prison, not sure how or why they are out. The third guy, don't have a clue, but it's obvious he's the one in charge. Cook taps on my shoulder so I turn to her. She holds her phone up and I see a text from Tink, telling us to observe but wait for backup. Help is on the way. I'm good with holding as long as no one goes off the deep end.

"Motherfucker, told you all jewelry on the tables. Think your special, you old whore? Give me the ring now, or I'll blow his brains all over your pretty blouse?"

Leaning again, it's the third guy and I see it now. He's tweaking bad because the gun he's got pinned on the man is shaking all over the place. Shit, shit, shit. *Give him the ring, lady*, I think to myself but of course not.

"Please, it's not worth much money but to me it's priceless. Vincent gave this to me on our fiftieth wedding anniversary. It's an infinity ring with the four small diamonds, one for each of our children. I can't let it go."

When he lifts his gun a little and then pulls the trigger by the man's face, I can almost guarantee the gunman popped the poor old man's eardrum because blood is starting to run down his neck. Oh God, I can't wait much longer. Just as I go to walk out, someone taps me again on the shoulder. When I turn, it's not Cook or one of my club sisters. He has eyes that look like a burst of color staring at me. Looking down, he has a bulletproof vest on and a badge clipped to the top of his jeans. He puts his finger to his mouth then motions for me to move behind him. I look and, yeah, there is Cook behind the second dude, also with a vest and a badge. Not sure who the hell they are, but okay, the cavalry has arrived.

Just as I go to move behind this mystery man, we hear the crazy dude scream again to give him the ring. The woman, who I recognize as Mrs. Thronston, starts to cry, begging him to please let her keep it. When I look, I see the crazy in his eyes, maybe from the drugs, or maybe he's just crazy. Without thinking, I move forward and with my gun out in front of me scream, "Asshole." When he turns, I throw myself to the ground and that's when all hell breaks loose. I hear a gun fire once and then the screaming of Mrs. Thronston. Heavy footsteps move past me as I go to maneuver my way up to standing. Just as I get my footing, someone grabs me from behind, putting an arm round my neck and something sharp hits my skin.

"Motherfuckers, drop those guns now. Don't pull any funny shit or little Delilah here will pay."

My skin crawls when I hear him say my name. Son of a bitch, I knew it was Donny. Yeah, talk about your past coming full circle. Here I was craving a fix and, apparently, my devil won 'cause my ex-dealer is right here and, just guessing, holding a syringe filled with who knows what. I lift my head and my eyes lock on those eyes that look like they are filled with fire. He's a big guy, almost as tall and wide as Avalanche. Hair is on the longer side and I see some ink. Great, I'm in a serious situation and I'm checking out a man. No one ever said I was the smartest sister in the club, that's for sure. Something behind the guy catches my attention and that's when I see Kon sitting at a table with a couple of his guy friends. Oh shit, no, that kid has been through enough. Our eyes meet and I barely shake my head but I know he sees it because he blinks then nods. Donny is very impatient though and starts to scream again.

"I told, you assholes, to put the weapons down. I'm not afraid to die if that's what you're holding out for. Got nothin' to live for so gonna take out as many as I can."

The other two guys look at Donny shocked. Oh well, guess he didn't fill them in on his suicide by cop idea. Both of them move back at the same time and drop to the ground, pushing their guns away. I watch the other cop nope when he turns around I see DEA on his vest as he slowly put his gun down, but not my mystery man. He stands tall, just watching. Donny is flustered I can tell, but is also a major bastard.

"What's the matter, dude? Don't tell me you haven't had a taste of our girl Delilah here? I mean, if you have the money, she has no problem spreading these tender thighs of hers. What's you're going rate, D? I mean back when I knew you it was a quick fuck for a fix, but now you're one of those badass biker chicks so I'm sure you're gettin' a pretty dollar. Once a whore, always a whore though right?"

He moves the syringe down, away from my neck, but now the needle is pressing into my upper arm. I don't even think he realizes he moved it, he's tweaking so badly. Then I see Kon looking at the guy on the floor but I know he's thinking about reaching for the gun. No, Kon, don't please don't thinking to myself. I couldn't live with myself if something happened to that kid. I truly care about him and his brothers. When he slowly goes to get off his chair, I do the only thing I can think of, which of course is so wrong.

"Kon, no, stay down. Don't do it, kiddo. NO."

It all happens so quickly, Kon goes down on his knees, reaching for the gun, grabbing it. Before he can get up, I see Dottie coming through the bar area and, in a second, she glances around, sees Kon, and runs his way. Mystery Man doesn't move but his partner does, which freaks Donny out. Instead of pulling his arm back, the dickwad pushes the needle into my arm. I'm screaming, "No-no-no-no-no!" when he starts laughing like the devil himself and pushes the plunger on the syringe down. It like a flood of going down my arm and I can feel whatever he injected making its way through my body. My legs give out and that's when I hear shouting and yelling, though I don't hit the ground. I land on something hard but soft and that makes no sense. One voice stands out, it's Shadow and it's getting closer.

"Motherfucker, let her go. Someone call 911 she's a recovering addict. Heartbreaker, stay with me. Come on, don't close those eyes. Sister, goddamn it, don't you hear me? Don't you dare die on me. Son of a bitch, I think we're losing her. Where the hell are the paramedics? Yoggie, thank God, not sure what he shot her up with. You got Narcan? Well, motherfucker, come on, give it to her…"

Then I hear a deep raspy voice demand, "Fight, Crimson, fight." Then whatever drug Donny injected into me takes over and I go on a wild ride into the darkness, not knowing my mystery man never lets me go.

ABOUT THE AUTHOR

USA Today Bestselling author, D. M. Earl creates authentic and genuine characters while spinning stories that feel so real and relatable that the readers plunge deep within the plot, begging for more. Complete with drama, angst, romance, and passion, the stories jump off the page.

When Earl, an avid reader since childhood, isn't at her keyboard pouring her heart into her work, you'll find her in Northwest Indiana snuggling up to her husband, the love of her life, with her seven fur babies nearby. Her other passions include gardening and shockingly cruising around town on the back of her 2004 Harley. She's a woman of many talents and interests. Earl appreciates each and every reader who has ever given her a chance--and hopes to connect on social media with all of her readers.

Contact D.M at DM@DMEARL.COM
Website: http://www.dmearl.com/

- facebook.com/DMEarlAuthorIndie
- x.com/dmearl
- instagram.com/dmearl14
- amazon.com/D-M-Earl/e/B00M2HB12U
- bookbub.com/authors/d-m-earl
- goodreads.com/dmearl
- pinterest.com/dauthor

ALSO BY D.M. EARL

BLUE SKY SANCTUARY

Ollie's Recovery

Grey's Rescue

DEVIL'S HANDMAIDENS MC SPINOFF

Running Wild

Running Alone

Running Free

DEVIL'S HANDMAIDENS MC: TIMBER-GHOST, MONTANA CHAPTER

Tink (Book #1)

Shadow (Book #2)

Taz (Book #3)

Vixen (Book #4)

Glory (Book #5)

Raven (Book #6)

Wildcat (Book #7)

Rebel (Book #8)

SUSAN STOKER'S OPERATION ALPHA (POLICE & FIRE)

Claire's Guardian

Lourde's Sentinel

GRIMM WOLVES MC SERIES

Behemoth (Book 1)

Bottom of the Chains-Prospect (Book 2)

Santa...Nope The Grimm Wolves (Book 3)

Keeping Secrets-Prospect (Book 4)

A Tormented Man's Soul: Part One (Book 5)

Triad Resumption: Part Two (Book 6)

Fractured Hearts - Prospect (Book 7)

WHEELS & HOGS SERIES

Connelly's Horde (Book 1)

Cadence Reflection (Book 2)

Gabriel's Treasure (Book 3)

Holidays with the Horde (Book 4)

My Sugar (Book 5)

Daisy's Darkness (Book 6)

THE JOURNALS TRILOGY

Anguish (Book 1)

Vengeance (Book 2)

Awakening (Book 3)

Printed in Great Britain
by Amazon